THE SLEEP ROOM

F. R. TALLIS is a writer and clinical psychologist. He has written self-help manuals, non-fiction for the general reader, academic text books, over thirty academic papers in international journals and several novels. Between 1999 and 2012 he received or was shortlisted for numerous awards, including the New London Writers' Award, the Ellis Peters Historical Dagger, the *Elle* Prix de Letrice, and two Edgars. His critically acclaimed Liebermann series (written as Frank Tallis) has been translated into fourteen languages and optioned for TV adaptation. *The Forbidden*, his ninth novel, is a horror story set in nineteenth-century Paris and this, *The Sleep Room*, is his tenth.

For more on Frank Tallis, visit his website
www.franktallis.com
or follow him on Twitter @FrankTallis

By F. R. Tallis

The Forbidden
The Sleep Room

Writing as Frank Tallis

FICTION

Killing Time
Sensing Others
Mortal Mischief
Vienna Blood
Fatal Lies
Darkness Rising
Deadly Communion
Death and the Maiden

NON-FICTION

Changing Minds
Hidden Minds
Love Sick

THE SLEEP ROOM

A NOVEL

F. R. TALLIS

PEGASUS CRIME
NEW YORK LONDON

THE SLEEP ROOM

Pegasus Books LLC
80 Broad Street, 5th Floor
New York, NY 10004

Copyright © F. R. Tallis

First Pegasus Books edition 2013

Library of Congress Cataloging-in-Publication Data is available.

ISBN: 978-1-60598-476-6

10 9 8 7 6 5 4 3 2 1

Printed in the United States of America
Distributed by W. W. Norton & Company

THE SLEEP ROOM

1

I was nervous that morning: the morning of the interview. It was, as I recall, late August, and one of the last warm days of what had been an exceptional summer. The sky over Trafalgar Square was unblemished and the fountains looked like sculpted glass. In my pocket was an envelope containing Hugh Maitland's reply to my application, written on thick cream laid paper. 'I wonder if we could meet at my club? That would be most convenient as I have another appointment there at half past nine.'

When I was a student, I used to listen to Maitland on the Home Service. He was a frequent contributor to discussion programmes that were invariably preceded by the strains of a string quartet, often something modern and forward-looking – like Bartok. I would lie on my bed, with the lights off, hanging on his every word. An educated voice, pleasant, well modulated, avuncular, but capable of dropping (when it suited him) to a lower register that conveyed absolute authority. Looking back now, I can see that he was an example of a particular type, a member of that emerging, professional elite who came to dominate public life during the post-war years, all of whom possessed unshakeable self-belief and a profound conviction that it was their destiny to shape a better future.

Maitland was head of the department of psychological medicine at Saint Thomas's; however, he had also managed to retain consultancies at three other hospitals: the Maudsley, the Belmont and the West End Hospital for Nervous Diseases. His scientific papers appeared regularly in the *British Journal of Psychiatry*, and his influential textbook (I still remember the pale-blue dust jacket) had just come out in its second edition.

The Braxton Club was situated on the south side of Carlton House Terrace, overlooking Saint James's Park. Inside, everything was as I had expected: oak panelling, antique prints, and the smell of wood polish and tobacco. The doorman took my coat and directed me to a reception area, where I sat in a leather chair and listened to a particularly resonant grandfather clock. Several daily newspapers had been laid out on a nearby table, neatly folded and without a single crease. The mastheads were so smooth, I strongly suspected that they had been ironed. I was too anxious to read any of them. After five minutes or so, I was taken upstairs and ushered into a library.

I have noticed that some tall men have a tendency to

stoop, but in rising from his chair, Maitland exploited his height to the full, standing erect with his chin elevated. He was wearing a pin-striped suit, the cut of which was so perfect, one immediately thought of Savile Row. An insignia on his tie suggested some collegiate affiliation. His eyes were brown, sunken slightly, and his hair was slicked back with what I judged to be a little too much pomade. The teeth of his comb had left deep furrows which recorded the direction of each stroke. He was, I suppose, someone who would be described as handsome, although the manly effect of his rugged features was compromised by an accumulation of flesh beneath his chin and the horizontal lines that divided his forehead.

'Dr Richardson,' said Maitland, extending his hand. I recognized the voice immediately. His grip was firm and I was inclined to tighten my own in response. 'Thank you so much for coming.'

At that time, I was a locum at the Royal Free, where there had been an outbreak of an unusual and as yet unidentified disease. Symptoms included muscle pain, apathy and depression. Over two hundred people had been affected, including a large number of hospital staff. Maitland asked me if I had come across any of these cases and encouraged me to speculate with respect to diagnosis and possible causes. 'The overall clinical picture,' I ventured, 'suggests encephalomyelitis – most probably viral in origin and spread by personal contact.'

Maitland nodded approvingly, before spreading my application and references out on the table in front of him. We talked a little about my student days, and in particular, my sporting achievements. He noted that I was a rugby blue.

'Why did you stop playing?' Maitland asked.

'A leg injury.'

'Bad luck,' he said, with sincerity. I later learned that – due to a nasty bout of tuberculosis – he had also been obliged to bring a promising rugby career to a premature end.

We discussed my stint at Saint George's with Sir Paul Mallinson, the research I had conducted at the sleep laboratory in Edinburgh, and my two articles (only just submitted to the *British Medical Journal*).

Maitland collected my papers together and tapped the edges so that all the sheets were aligned. Then, leaning forward, he said, 'Tell me, Dr Richardson. Why does this position appeal to you? The pay is adequate for a man with your credentials – but you could probably do better elsewhere. Sir Paul has written a glowing reference.'

'I have a long-standing interest in your work. I view this appointment as a great opportunity.'

Maitland could not resist flattery and the corners of his mouth curled upwards, but his satisfied expression was not sustained. His smile faded and was quickly replaced by a frown. 'Have you considered our location?' I didn't understand what he was getting at, and seeing my puzzlement, he added: 'Wyldehope is somewhat off the beaten track. Rural Suffolk.'

'There are trains, I take it?'

'Yes, yes of course. And local buses.'

'Then I don't think that will be a problem. I don't have a car. But if there are trains and buses . . .'

Maitland repositioned himself in his chair and the horizontal lines on his forehead contracted together. 'The previous registrar – Palmer . . . I don't think he gave the matter enough thought. It was my impression that he felt rather isolated. I try to get up to Wyldehope at least once a week, but most of the time you would be working on your own.'

I shrugged. 'Providing I am given clear instruction.'

Maitland smiled again. 'Forgive me. Palmer's resignation was somewhat unexpected. My fault – of course. I misjudged him. Let me tell you about the hospital. It's all very exciting.' He took a slim silver case from his jacket and offered me a cigarette. He lit mine, then his own, and pushed a chrome ashtray towards me. 'Wyldehope was originally a hunting lodge owned by the Gathercole family: East Anglian gentry. During the First World War they donated it to the army as a convalescent home for wounded men. It then became an administrative building, and thereafter an intelligence centre. Churchill is reputed to have stayed there once when he visited the test base at Orford Ness. I'd been looking out for a place like Wyldehope for years. When I learned that the military had no further use for the building, I made some enquiries and managed to pull a few strings.' Maitland took a drag from his cigarette. 'We have twenty-four beds. Two wards and a narcosis room. We also offer limited outpatient services and very occasionally home visits – something I had to agree to, in order to keep the Health Board happy.'

'Where do the patients come from?' I asked.

'The London teaching hospitals. But news travels fast. A treatment centre of this kind is a valuable resource. I've started to get referrals from much further afield. We're a small operation at the moment, but I'm sure we're going to expand. There are nine nurses. Eight of my nightingales and a local girl who's being trained up. Then there's Hartley – the caretaker – and his wife, who cooks and manages the kitchen.'

'And how many medical staff?'

'There is only one doctor.'

I hesitated before repeating his last words. 'One doctor?'

'Yes.'

'But—'

'I know what you're thinking. Don't worry. You're not expected to be there all the time. We have an arrangement with a cottage hospital just outside Saxmundham. A duty psychiatrist comes and holds the fort most weekends.'

Maitland pulled a bell cord and continued talking about Wyldehope: his eagerness to make it a centre of excellence, his plan to expand the facility by adding two more wards the following spring. I noticed that his manner had become less formal and he insisted that I take another cigarette. He was a trenchant critic of psycho-therapy and while enthusing about recent advances in drug treatment, he lambasted those whom he dismissively called 'couch merchants'.

'Freudian techniques are hopelessly ineffective. All that talk. All those wasted hours. Three hundred milli-grams of chlorpromazine is worth months of analysis! Don't you agree? Dreams, the unconscious, primitive urges! Psychiatry is a branch of medicine, not philosophy. Mental illness arises in the brain, a physical organ, and must be treated accordingly.'

He held my gaze, searching for signs of discomfort or dissent, before forging ahead with more rousing talk. I sensed that if Maitland hadn't chosen a career in medicine, he would have made a very good soldier. It was easy to imagine him commanding a garrison in some far-flung outpost of the Empire.

There was a knock on the door and a serving man entered carrying a tray with two whiskies. I thought it rather early for spirits. When we were alone again, Maitland picked up a glass and indicated that I should do the same. 'Congratulations!' he said, grinning broadly.

'I beg your pardon?'

'Congratulations. You've got the job.'

I had been seeing a girl called Sheila over the summer, a secretary who worked at the BBC. We didn't have much in common, but we generally had fun together, dancing or going to jazz clubs. We had arranged to meet at seven thirty, but as usual she was late (something I had learned to accept without complaint). I was sitting at a table in a cafe in Soho, observing the clientele: men in tweed jackets with leather elbow patches, women in white blouses and slacks. A scratchy recording of Neapolitan songs was playing on the gramophone.

Sheila arrived and we chatted about nothing in particular. It was peculiar how our lengthy, friendly conversations always remained shallow. There were never any meaningful disclosures – not even after sex. Our pillow talk was always sterile, an impartial exchange of views before the onset of sleep. Halfway through "O sole Mio', I summoned up the courage to make my announcement.

'I went for a job interview today.'

'Really? Did you get it?'

'I did.'

'Oh, well done.' She saw the reticence in my eyes, the qualm of conscience. 'What?'

'Unfortunately, it involves moving to Suffolk.'

'When are you going?'

'Quite soon.'

She accepted this news with characteristic, cheerful indifference. In actual fact, I suspect she was relieved. There would be no need to negotiate the terms of our separation, no awkwardness, no pretence. We were free to drift apart. When we had finished drinking our coffees, we went to see a comedy at the Astoria, and when the time came to say goodbye Sheila kissed me and said, 'Good luck. I hope it all goes well.' She jumped on a bus and waved through the window as it joined the traffic heading towards Euston.

I took the Northern line to Kentish Town and walked the short distance from the station to the house where I rented a third-floor bedsit. When I opened the front door, my nostrils filled with the all too familiar smell of boiled vegetables: an indelible smell that never dispersed. It was only half past eleven, but my landlady, a widow called Mrs Briggs, came out of her drawing room and glared at me. She was wearing a hairnet and her arms were folded.

'It's very late, Dr Richardson.'

'Yes. An emergency at the hospital.'

'Oh, I see.'

She tightened the belt of her dressing gown and said, 'Goodnight, then.'

'Goodnight, Mrs Briggs.'

'Don't forget to switch off the landing light.'

'I won't, Mrs Briggs. Sleep well.'

I tried to creep up the stairs quietly but it was impossible. Almost every step produced a loud creak. On entering my room, I placed a chair by the window and looked up into a cloudless sky. A full moon had risen above the chimney stacks and the slates were awash with a silvery brilliance. I didn't think about Sheila once. I thought about Maitland.

*

On the day I was due to make my departure, I had intended to catch an early train; however, an administrative error necessitated my immediate return to the Royal Free. There were some documents that had to be signed. My replacement, Dr Collins, had just arrived, and I foolishly allowed myself to be dragged into a protracted and rather tedious handover meeting. Collins asked me a ludicrous number of questions and I'm ashamed to say I grew quite impatient.

It was late afternoon when I arrived at Liverpool Street station, just in time to catch the six thirty-four to Ipswich. On reaching Ipswich, I telephoned the caretaker, Mr Hartley, to inform him of my delay. It had already been arranged that Mr Hartley would meet me at Wyldehope and show me to my quarters. He did not seem terribly inconvenienced and said, 'Call me again when you get to Darsham.' The branch line took me as far as Woodbridge, where a signal failure meant that I had to disembark and wait for another two hours, after which a small locomotive appeared, belching smoke, and pulling along two empty carriages. I picked up my suitcase, heaved it aboard, and after squeezing through the narrow corridor, entered the first compartment. Before I was seated, a whistle blew, and the train began to crawl forward.

Once the train was out of Woodbridge, I was able to

study the countryside – low, rolling hills and flat expanses. Night was falling and the windows soon became black and reflective. The train stopped at a couple more stations, Melton and Wickham Market, but my carriage remained empty. At Saxmundham, I heard a door slamming shut and a few seconds later I saw a man outside my compartment. He peered through the glass and our eyes met. Before I could look away, he slid the door aside and stepped over the metal track. Removing his hat, he nodded, before sitting down on the seat directly opposite. The train began to move and the station slipped away.

'Are you going to Lowestoft?' the man asked.

'No,' I replied. 'Darsham.'

'Darsham?' he repeated, his voice carrying a note of surprise.

'Well, not exactly,' I continued. 'Dunwich Heath? There's a new hospital there. I'm a doctor.'

'Wyldehope Hall.'

'Yes.'

I had supposed that, having chosen to enter the only occupied compartment in the train, my companion was in need of company. But my supposition was quite wrong. It was as though, having satisfied his curiosity concerning my identity, he had no more need of conversation. He sat very still, frowning slightly, his hands tightly gripping his kneecaps. I turned my face towards the window. A few minutes later he spoke again. 'It wasn't wanted.'

'I beg your pardon?'

'The hospital. Folk 'round here didn't want a madhouse on their doorstep.'

I was finding his behaviour and manner quite irritating.

'Well,' I replied, 'I'm sorry to hear that. There are many individuals who suffer from diseases of the mind and provision has to be made for their care. They have to be treated somewhere.'

The man bit his lower lip and fell silent again. I toyed with the idea of moving to a different compartment, but decided against it. Instead, I distracted myself by reading Maitland's textbook and when the train came into Darsham I was quick to leave the carriage.

I stepped down onto a platform shrouded in mist. Stressed metal groaned, flashes of firelight emanated from the cab, and glowing cinders formed chaotic constellations above the smokestack. The effect was vaguely diabolical. I glanced at my wristwatch and paused to observe the train pulling out. The wheels began to turn and I stood there, immobile, strangely captivated as the engine and carriages vanished into an opaque middle distance. I picked up my suitcase and walked to the end of the platform where a ramp descended to the road. There, a few yards ahead of me, I saw a telephone box. I stepped inside and lifted the receiver, but when I held it to my ear there was no dialling tone. Swearing loudly, I replaced the receiver and lifted it again. Still no tone. I took a deep breath and made my exit by leaning my back against the door.

Ribbons of mist were floating before my eyes. I ventured a short distance from the telephone box and noticed that the station had all but disappeared. Even so, I took a few more steps down the road with the intention of walking into the village. I remembered what Maitland had said about Wyldehope being 'somewhat off the beaten track' and his impression that the previous registrar, Palmer, had felt 'rather isolated'. At that moment, I heard the wail of a night animal, one of those melancholy calls that could easily be mistaken for the cry of a human child. The combination of the impenetrable mist and the eerie cry proved too much for my already tired nerves and I turned back.

I ascended the ramp and walked up and down the platform. The door to the ticket office was locked, all of the station windows were dark and the only illumination came from a row of lamp posts. There was, however, a waiting room, the door of which was open. I went inside, sat on a bench and considered my situation. It seemed to me that I had no choice but to wait for the mist to clear and then make another attempt at reaching the village.

A few minutes passed, during which time I stared hopelessly through the window. Then I heard footsteps. I got up, rushed out, and saw a bright light coming towards me, beams lancing through the haze. I raised my hand to protect my eyes from the glare. Someone called – 'Hello there!' – and a few seconds later a uniformed figure appeared in front of me. It was the stationmaster, wheeling a bicycle. I was so glad to see another person that I laughed out aloud with delight. 'Good evening.'

'Look at this!' said the stationmaster, creating a swirl of fog with a wave of his hand. 'It came in off the marshes about an hour ago.'

'Will it clear?'

'Who knows. Sometimes it does – sometimes it doesn't.'

'I wonder if you could help me. My name is Dr Richardson. I'm expected at Wyldehope Hall: the new hospital on Dunwich Heath?' The stationmaster showed no sign of recognition. 'The public telephone is out of order. Might I use yours instead? Otherwise I fear I might be stuck here all night.'

The stationmaster escorted me back to his office and I called Mr Hartley, who was, on this occasion, less understanding. 'I suppose I'd better come and get you,' he grumbled. The stationmaster informed me that Dunwich Heath was only five miles away: 'You won't have to wait for very long.'

He locked his office and we walked down the platform together. When we reached its end, he mounted his bicycle, said 'Goodnight, sir' and coasted down the ramp, ringing his bell.

I positioned myself beneath the projecting roof of the station and gazed out into a featureless expanse. The quiet was extraordinary. Dense and absolute. A car passed, driving very slowly, and I did not see another one until Mr Hartley arrived some thirty minutes later.

Mr Hartley was a big man with a pockmarked face and bulbous features. His hair was brushed to one side and he wore spectacles with circular lenses. He was not particularly talkative, although this was quite understandable given the circumstances. I apologized several times for my lateness, but this had no effect on his manner. He was still disinclined to make conversation. We passed through only one village on our way to the hospital, a place called Westleton, after which, thankfully, the mist began to lift and Mr Hartley was able to drive faster. A mile or so further on, the road became uneven and I had to press my palm against the dashboard so as to prevent myself from being thrown around. We passed between two square columns and I saw a cluster of faint lights ahead.

'Wyldehope,' said Hartley.

As we drew closer I realized that I was not looking at one building, but several – a central block flanked by outhouses. The car ground to a halt beside a stone porch, and when I got out, I took a few steps backwards to get a better look at my new home. It was too dark to see very much detail, but I was able to discern mullioned windows, mock battlements and a tower. A background noise was impinging on my awareness, and when I gave it my full attention, I realized that I was listening to the sea.

'This way, please,' said Mr Hartley. He was standing in front of the car with my suitcase.

We walked to the porch and the caretaker produced a bunch of keys from his coat pocket. He unlocked the door and we entered a spacious but dimly lit vestibule. It was decorated with wallpaper that I supposed must be Victorian – gloomy maroon stripes enlivened by a floral motif of faded gold. A suit of armour, evidently unpolished for centuries, stood guard by the stairs. I followed Mr Hartley up to the first-floor landing, where we passed beneath a stag's head with glassy black eyes. When we reached the second-floor landing, Mr Hartley unlocked another door, switched on a light, and invited me to enter a wide hallway which had rooms adjoining it on both sides. He handed me a key. 'You only need the one, sir. None of the other rooms on the second floor are occupied.' I was shown a bedroom, a study, a small kitchen and a bathroom. The furniture was solid and functional, except for an antique writing bureau which was elegant and beautifully crafted. I imagined myself seated at it, writing a monograph.

'Would you like your breakfast brought up, sir?' asked the caretaker. 'Or would you prefer to join the nurses in the staff canteen?'

'If it isn't any trouble, I think I'd like to eat here.'

'I'll tell Mrs Hartley. Seven o'clock suit you?'

'That would be very good.'

'Oh, I almost forgot – Dr Maitland called. He'll be arriving tomorrow at ten thirty. I think you were expecting to see him a little earlier.' Mr Hartley put the keys back in his pocket. 'Well, I think that's it, sir.'

I wanted a cup of tea, but dared not ask. 'Thank you so much. And thank you for collecting me from the station. That was most kind of you.'

The caretaker appeared indifferent to my gratitude and said, rather brusquely, 'Goodnight, sir.'

I locked the door to the landing and set about unpacking my suitcase. After hanging my shirts in the wardrobe, I filled a few drawers with the remainder of my clothes and distributed the rest of my possessions (mostly books and documents) in the study.

When I had finished, I walked down to the bathroom, where I washed my face and brushed my teeth. The sink was deep and its surface broken by fine cracks. Each of the taps had a circular enamel medallion at its centre, on which black letters spelled out the words 'hot' and 'cold'. Raising my head, I looked at my reflection. I placed a finger under one of my eyes and dragged the loose skin downwards, exposing a crescent of pale, pink flesh.

There was a sound – a familiar sound – a sigh, and it seemed to come from just behind me.

I stared into the mirror, registering the emptiness of the bathroom.

That someone might be lurking in the hallway seemed very unlikely. I had heard no approaching footsteps, only the curious, breathy exhalation. Nevertheless, I found myself checking, and even peered into a few of the adjacent rooms to make sure that I was truly alone.

The tap was still running, and I was about to go back to the sink in order to turn it off, when an obscure intuition made me hesitate. I was reminded of the superstitious wariness that arrests one's progress the instant one perceives that the path ahead proceeds beneath a ladder. Irritated by my own irrationality, I marched over the linoleum, grasped the tap handle, and rotated it until the flow of water stopped. I looked at my reflection again, perhaps more carefully than before, and I was forced to concede that I was not looking my best: my complexion was sallow and my eyes bloodshot. It had been a long day and I was clearly overtired. A painful throbbing in my head accompanied each beat of my heart.

I returned to the bedroom, put on my pyjamas, and got into bed. As I listened to the subtle music of waves on shingle, London seemed very distant. I thought again about what had happened in the bathroom. If the 'sigh' had been produced by natural means – an obstruction in the pipes, the acoustical properties of the environment, and so on – then it was remarkable how chance events and processes had duplicated the effect with such fidelity: an intake of breath, the slow release of air from the lungs, a suggestion of descending pitch. It had been most disconcerting.

I slid down further between the crisp, clean sheets, and reached out to turn off the lamp. Although I was exhausted, it was some time before I closed my eyes.

2

I will always remember entering the sleep room for the very first time: descending the stairs that led to the basement, Maitland at my side, immaculately dressed, talking energetically, cutting the air with his hands, the door opening and stepping across the threshold – a threshold that seemed not merely physical, but psychological. The nurse, seated at her station – a solitary desk lamp creating a well-defined pool of light in the darkness – the sound of the quivering EEG pens and, of course, the six occupied beds. All women – in white gowns – fast asleep: one of them with wires erupting from her scalp like a tribal headdress.

Narcosis, or deep-sleep treatment, had originally been developed in the 1920s, although, according to Maitland, prolonged sleep was one of the oldest treatment methods in psychiatry. Distressed individuals had been using alcohol to 'knock themselves out' for thousands of years, and in the nineteenth century a few enterprising doctors had attempted to treat insanity with opium and chloroform, but it wasn't until the arrival of barbiturates that narcosis gained wider acceptance. Maitland was pioneering a new form of the treatment, which combined continuous sleep with the latest drugs and electroconvulsive therapy.

On that first morning, Maitland explained the regimen he had devised. 'The aim is to maintain narcosis for at least twenty-one hours a day. Every six hours, patients are woken up, taken to the lavatory, washed, and given drugs, food and vitamins. ECT is administered weekly. Careful records are kept of blood pressure, temperature, pulse rate and respiration; fluid intake, urinary output and bowel function are also noted. Due to the risk of paralytic ileus, regular laxatives are used and abdominal girth measured daily. Enemas are given immediately if there is any suspicion of failing bowel activity.'

Maitland walked from bed to bed, examining the charts, and making comments. 'All of the patients receive six-hourly chlorpromazine: one hundred to four hundred milligrams. Lower doses are given if the patient is sleeping well, higher doses if the patient is agitated or not sleeping. In addition to chlorpromazine, the more agitated patients also receive sodium amylobarbitone. Because this drug has been associated with withdrawal fits, EEG measures are taken regularly to identify those who might be at risk.' He indicated the woman with the wires sprouting from her scalp.

I asked Maitland about the patients' diagnoses and he replied, 'Schizophrenia and schizophrenia with depression.' When I pressed him for more details, particularly concerning the individual cases, he was not very forthcoming. 'They are all very sick,' he said, in a tone that suggested the severity of their psychopathology made discussion of specific histories irrelevant. 'Treatment is our priority.'

It transpired that one of the patients was due to receive her ECT. 'We might as well do it now,' said Maitland, running his finger down the chart. 'I've made a few practical modifications to the standard procedure which might interest you.'

The patient was young, probably in her late teens. Her mousy hair had been cut short and her nose and cheeks were lightly freckled. She looked quite boyish.

Maitland rolled a trolley to the bedside. The flex that trailed across the floor tiles connected an electric shock machine to a wall socket. It was an old unit – older than I had expected. The outer case was made of a dark, reddish wood, and when the lid was lifted I saw a control panel of black plastic. White lettering identified each switch, two of which were surrounded by circles of ascending numbers. Through a crescent-shaped window it was possible to monitor the mains voltage. Bulky electrodes – Bakelite handles with rounded metal termini – were stored in a side compartment.

I was wondering why the nurse wasn't summoning her colleagues. Maitland registered my expression and said, 'I've invented a simple expedient which means that we will only be needing one nurse.' He drew my attention to a bolt of material suspended under the bed. He crossed the patient's arms and unrolled a canvas sheet, pulling it across the sleeping girl before securing it tightly so that no movement was possible. 'You see, it does the work of four nurses!' I looked at the patient's chart and saw that her name was Kathy Webb. The nurse was cleaning the girl's forehead. 'Of course,' Maitland continued, 'the great advantage of administering ECT while patients are asleep is that they experience no anxiety – which means one can prescribe longer and more intensive courses.' He picked up some lint pads and soaked them in a saline solution. He then deftly enclosed the electrodes in the pads and offered them to me, his hands raised slightly. There was something almost ceremonial about his attitude.

'Would you mind?'

'No. Not at all.'

I took the electrodes and positioned them on the girl's temples. Maitland rotated the mains switch and the needle in the meter window moved, tracing an arc from one extreme to the other. I noticed that the 'voltage' and 'time' controls had been set at their uppermost limits. When I remarked on this, Maitland replied that 'difficult cases' required a 'greater stimulus'. While we conversed, the nurse was inserting a rubber gag. This was done in order to prevent the patient from swallowing or biting her tongue.

'Are you ready?' Maitland asked his helper.

The nurse gripped the girl's jaw and nodded. Maitland then looked at me. 'Ready?'

'Yes,' I replied.

He smiled and his eyes directed my attention to a particular switch on the unit which could be flicked from left to right, between the words 'safety' and 'treat'. The switch moved easily and made a soft click. At which point, the needle in the meter window suddenly dropped and the patient grimaced. Maitland turned the machine off and I replaced the electrodes in their compartment.

A tendon stood out on the side of the girl's neck and she made an involuntary grunting sound. I could see the mounds of her knuckles beneath the canvas as she clenched her fists. After about ten seconds, there was some rhythmic twitching around her eyes, and both of her feet, which were poking out from beneath the sheet, began to jerk. The seizure lasted for at least a minute, during which time none of us spoke. When the girl's twitching and jerking had subsided, Maitland unfastened the canvas cover and wound it back onto its drum. Finally, he checked the patient's respiration and pulse.

'Good.'

The nurse returned to her station and Maitland and I walked to the door. Before leaving, something made me stop and I turned to look back.

'How long have they been asleep?' I asked.

'Some of them have been asleep for a few weeks, others for several months.'

'And how long will the treatment last?'

'At least three months. Possibly four.' I had never heard of sleep being artificially prolonged for that length of time. My surprise must have shown, because Maitland gave me a hearty slap on the shoulder and said, 'New ground! That's what we're doing here at Wyldehope, breaking new ground!' An echo returned his final word to us from walls that receded into shadow. One of the patients sighed and the nurse looked up. 'Now,' said Maitland, 'let me show you upstairs.'

There were two wards on the ground floor, one for men, the other for women, and all of the patients were accommodated in separate rooms with large windows. Unfortunately, the iron bars in the casements were rather ugly, dividing the otherwise fine view of the heath into mean, narrow segments. Both wards were very quiet, and when we reviewed the patient records the reason for this remarkable calm was immediately apparent. Maitland believed that if a patient did not respond to medication, then the dose should be doubled, and if there was still no improvement, the dose should be doubled again.

I had assumed that the ward patients would be less sick than those in the sleep room. If they were, it was only by a small margin. They had all been diagnosed with chronic forms of psychosis and depression and almost all of them had either contemplated or attempted suicide. While we were looking through the files, Maitland said: 'It's humbling to consider what these poor wretches must go through every day of their lives: the demons they must struggle to overcome, the abject terror, the appalling anguish.' Naturally, I agreed, and he continued, 'Have you ever known a patient, suffering from a physical illness, to be in so much pain that they killed themselves to escape it?' I hadn't. 'Can you imagine? To be in so much pain that putting your head in a gas oven seems to be the only solution? That is why our work here is so very important.'

In due course, I would become accustomed to such ardent asides, but on that first day I was somewhat taken aback. It was as though Maitland had been wearing a mask, and that it had suddenly slipped, revealing an altogether different person: a more emotional, compassionate person. I saw the 'doctor' rather than the bluff radio personality, or the social engineer who had made it his mission to eradicate mental illness by the end of the century. In years to come, I would hear cynics say that these impassioned speeches were calculated, all part of his 'act', but that isn't true. I think they were genuine and exposed a facet of his personality that he usually chose to conceal. He was a complex man – more complex than the obituary writers ever credited.

After we had finished our business on the wards, Maitland took me to the kitchen and dining area. I was introduced to Mrs Hartley, a plump, frantic woman, who was washing up pots and pans with a young assistant. She dried her hands on her pinafore, compressed my fingers in a raw, red clasp, and asked me about my culinary preferences. She seemed to approve of my likes and dislikes, and said with solemn pride, 'You can't beat Suffolk pork, doctor. Best there is!' As we were leaving, Maitland asked her to prepare some corned beef sandwiches and a pot of tea. She didn't quite tug her forelock, but she made a gesture that came very close to it.

When we reached the first floor, Maitland showed me a suite of rooms that had been set aside for 'outpatient' consultations. He was anxious to stress, as he had done in my interview, that we were only obliged to provide the local community with this service on an occasional basis. He wanted to reassure me that I would not be over-worked.

Further on we came to a shiny black door. 'Just a moment,' said Maitland, halting to remove a key from his pocket. 'My office.' I heard the bolt retreat and Maitland pushed the door open. 'After you,' he added, gesturing for me to enter ahead of him.

I stepped into a room that combined the dusty serenity of a museum with the ostentation of a royal apartment. The decor was high Victorian: a marble fireplace, stuffed birds beneath domes of glass, and a massive ox-blood Chesterfield; there were oil paintings, standard lamps, and clocks festooned with silver and gold foliage. The only incongruous feature was a drab grey filing cabinet. On his desktop, Maitland had placed two photographs. One was a formal portrait of an attractive woman in her mid to late twenties – an old photograph, taken before the war. The other showed Maitland standing with three men of a similar type in front of the Statue of Liberty. I guessed they were American colleagues.

We carried on talking and after ten minutes or so the kitchen girl arrived with our sandwiches and tea. While we were eating, Maitland handed me a typed manuscript. It was an as yet unpublished theoretical paper that sought to explain why prolonged sleep was therapeutic. 'I'd be grateful if you could read it,' he said, still chewing. 'If you think any of the arguments are weak, then please say so. There's no need to rush. Take your time.' I was flattered. When we had finished eating, Maitland announced that he had some administrative work to complete and that he would be driving back to London at four thirty.

He sought me out before his departure and I accompanied him to his car: a Bentley. The body shell was gleaming and our reflected images were distorted by its sleek curves. Maitland shook my hand and said, 'Delighted to have you on board. Any problems, feel free to give me a call.' As he opened the door I detected the mellow fragrance of soft leather and cigars. The car rolled down the drive and bounced a little where the track became uneven. I raised my hand. He must have been looking at me in his rear-view mirror because he responded by sounding his horn. The ground dipped and the car disappeared from view.

I had not been outside all day and paused to take in my surroundings. Wyldehope was situated on a bleak heath that stretched away to the horizon. There was nothing to see, apart from heather, gorse bushes and a few stunted trees. The ground to my immediate left descended to a wide grazing marsh, interspersed with reed beds that rippled in the breeze. An elevated bank followed the coastline, beyond which was a rough, churning sea. It was not blue, but a peculiar shade of brown, like ditch water. I registered some outbuildings: stables that had been converted into living quarters and a lonely whitewashed cottage. To the east, a low-lying seam of black cloud trailed delicate tendrils of rain. I might have dallied there longer, had it not occurred to me that I was now the only doctor present, directly responsible for the care of twenty-four patients. This sudden realization produced a curious mix of anxiety and pride: I had been judged capable of taking charge of Wyldehope by Hugh Maitland, the most influential psychiatrist of his generation. Turning abruptly on my heels, I hurried back inside.

*

I spent the remainder of the afternoon on the wards, introducing myself to the patients, or at least as many of them as was possible. The majority were either asleep or unresponsive. One of the exceptions was a man called Michael Chapman, who I found pacing around his room, raking his hair with his hands and mumbling distractedly. His notes informed me that he suffered from hallucinations and delusions of persecution.

'Mr Chapman,' I said. 'Is something troubling you? Perhaps I can get you something to calm your nerves.'

He marched over to one of the windows and gripped the bars tightly. Staring out onto the heath, he said, 'I want to go home, doctor. I want to go home.' His voice was thin and pathetic.

'I'm sorry. That isn't possible, Mr Chapman.'

'Please, doctor. I want to go home.'

'But you are unwell, Mr Chapman. You must stay here until you are feeling better. Now, let me get you something to help you relax.'

'I don't like this place.'

'Why ever not?'

He turned to look at me and his lower lip began to tremble. He was like a frightened child. 'I want to go home,' he repeated.

I went to his side and eased his fingers from the bars.

Then I led him back to his bed. He didn't resist and submitted to my ministrations without a word of protest.

'Please sit down, Mr Chapman. You'll feel better in a minute.'

I called the nurse and told her to prepare a syringe of sodium amytal.

'Something bad is going to happen,' said Mr Chapman, wringing his hands.

'What do you mean? Something bad?'

He shook his head. 'I can feel it.'

'Feel what, exactly?'

The poor fellow simply frowned and continued muttering. When the nurse returned, we helped Mr Chapman back into bed and I gave him the injection. 'You've had this drug many times before,' I said. 'It may make you feel a little dizzy.' He produced a heavy sigh, the first outward sign that the sedative was starting to take effect. I had expected him to breathe more deeply but, interestingly, this did not happen. Instead, his respiration continued as before – shallow and fast. I told the nurse to keep an eye on him and to call me if he became agitated again.

'Of course, Dr Richardson,' she responded. 'Where will you be?'

'In the sleep room.'

I had been so preoccupied that I hadn't noticed the nurse's appearance. She was wearing one of the newer uniforms: short sleeves, bibbed front, shoulder straps and a pillbox hat. The nipped waist showed off her trim figure. Although she was quite tall, her ankles and wrists were pleasingly slim. Her features were delicate and her eyes were a striking green.

'Thank you, Nurse . . .' My sentence trailed off awkwardly.

She came to my assistance: 'Turner. Jane Turner.'

As I was leaving the ward, I glanced back. She was still standing outside Mr Chapman's room, and when our eyes met she rewarded my interest with a subtle smile.

I stepped out into the vestibule and was in the process of locking the ward door when the kitchen girl appeared carrying a stack of trays. She nodded at me and then descended the basement stairs. I was curious to see how the sleep-room patients were managed when they were woken up, so I followed her down. A senior nurse, Sister Doris Jenkins, was directing two subordinates – another nightingale and an alarmingly young-looking trainee. Sister Jenkins was extremely deferential, and I had to stress that I was not there to interfere, but simply to observe their routine.

The patients were difficult to rouse. Indeed, they never

achieved what I would call lucid, waking consciousness. They remained heavy-eyed and extremely drowsy – even when they were eating. Their jaws moved with the slow determination of cows chewing cud. Out of bed, they needed the steady arm of at least one nurse for support, otherwise they would have simply fallen over. I tried introducing myself to Kathy Webb, the girl who had been given ECT, but she looked at me with vacant eyes and said nothing.

I was very impressed by the nurses. They worked together with machine-like efficiency. Their movements were so well coordinated, so well rehearsed, that I was reminded of a factory production line. The patients were fed, washed, and taken to the lavatory, before being guided back to their beds and given medication. In their long white gowns, they looked like compliant ghosts. When they were all properly asleep again, I became aware of an unpleasant stench. The smell of the voiding, the enemas, and food, had no means of escape and tainted the air.

Although Sister Jenkins was deferential with me, she was brusque with her juniors. I suspected that she must be a strict disciplinarian. When she was ready to leave she said to the trainee, 'I shall return at eleven o'clock. Do exactly as instructed.' She then left with the nightingale.

The trainee nurse sat behind the desk and took a copy of the *British National Formulary* from one of the drawers. After studying it for a few seconds she put it back and gazed into the darkness. Her expression soon became blank with boredom.

I walked around the beds, examining the latest entries on the charts, and decided to run an EEG on a patient called Sarah Blake – one of three being given sodium amylobarbitone in addition to chlorpromazine. She was in her early twenties and possessed an interesting face, with features that are often unsympathetically described as 'witchy': long black hair, a pointed chin and a bridged nose. Yet, cast in a certain complimentary light, one could imagine those same features transformed, becoming something closer to devilish beauty. Her most recent ECT had been administered almost a week earlier, so I judged that the recording would be interpretable – within reason. EEGs taken shortly after ECT are often spurious. The paper rolled beneath the twitching pens, producing irregular peaks and troughs, the big slow waves of sleep.

A curious hush descended and I was reminded of something that I had read many years before about the healing rituals of the ancient Greeks. The sick and troubled in those remote times were frequently instructed by a holy man to spend a night in an underground temple. There, they would have a dream that would cure them. It seemed to me that the sleep room was a modern-day equivalent.

I was familiar with sleep laboratories. I had studied and worked in Cambridge and Edinburgh and they all had in common a strange, unreal atmosphere. But the sleep room at Wyldehope was different. The atmosphere was more intense, almost religious. It evoked feelings in me that I associated with certain churches – experienced in solitude and usually at dusk. In the hush and the shadow that enveloped those six beds were unexpected registers and suggestions of something beyond the reach of the senses. The subterranean healing ritual of the ancient Greeks was called 'incubation'. An apposite word, because it is composed of elements that produce the literal translation 'lying in the ground'.

Before leaving the sleep room, I removed the electrodes from Sarah Blake's head and examined her EEG results. The red ink looked unusually vivid on the white paper, like thin trails of blood. There was nothing remarkable to see: slow waves with brief bursts of faster activity originating from the frontal lobe of the brain. I wrote some comments in her notes and said 'goodnight' to the nurse.

'Are you going already, doctor?'

It struck me as a rather peculiar thing for her to say.

'Yes,' I replied. 'Why? Did you want to ask me something?'

Her face reddened and she said, 'No. It's all right. Goodnight, Dr Richardson.'

I returned to the ground floor to make sure that all was well in the wards. Michael Chapman was still awake, but he had remained in bed and only his frown persisted from his former agitation. I may have spent a little more time on the men's ward than was strictly necessary, chatting with Nurse Turner. She had been at Wyldehope since its opening. I asked her if she missed London. 'Not really,' she replied. 'Although I do go back about once a month. To see my mother – and my friends. The summer here was lovely.' I wanted to ask her more questions, mainly about herself, but I was wary of seeming unprofessional and brought our conversation to an end.

As I ascended the stairs, I was quite preoccupied by the day's events, but not so inward-looking as to be oblivious of my surroundings. I heard what I thought was the sound of someone following close behind, and glanced back over my shoulder. I was surprised to discover that my senses had been comprehensively deceived. Nobody was there. This was confusing, but not confusing enough to halt my progress. I continued climbing to the top of the stairs and crossed the landing. I was just about to tackle the next flight when, once again, I heard a noise, but on this second occasion it was quite distinct and easily recognized. An initial impact had been succeeded by a second, suggesting that something had dropped onto the carpet and bounced.

Turning around, I noticed a pen on the floor. I assumed that it was mine, but when I picked it up, I saw that it was only a cheap biro. My own pen, a silver-plated Parker, was still in my pocket. I had no recollection of taking the biro from the sleep room or the wards, but that was surely what I must have done.

In the study, I set about getting my papers in order. I was placing some drafts of unfinished articles in the bureau when I discovered an air-tight container in the bottom drawer. It contained three scored white tablets. I read the label: *Reserpine. Protect from light.* I wasn't familiar with this drug, but at the same time I had an inkling that I had perhaps encountered it, or at least heard about it before. I tipped one of the pills out. It was careless of my predecessor, Palmer, to leave what must have been his own medication, here, for me to find. Particularly so, because I suspected that Reserpine was psychoactive. I was reminded, again, of what Maitland had said about Palmer having resigned unexpectedly. A vague disquiet – like an echo, arising out of silence – made me put the pill back in its container. The room must have been dusty, because my nose felt stuffed up and I couldn't breathe very easily. I opened the window and looked out across the sea. Its unusual colour was a darker shade of brown in the evening light. I closed the window, drew the curtains, and prepared for bed.

Dr Angus McWhirter
Maida Vale Hospital for Nervous Diseases
London W9

26th February 1955

Dr Hugh Maitland
Department of Psychological Medicine
St Thomas's Hospital
London SE1

Dear Hugh,

Re: Miss Kathy Webb (d.o.b. 3.1.1937)
      Walsingham House, 26 Lisson Grove NW1

I would be most grateful if you would see Miss Webb:
a young woman with a history of schizophrenia and
severe mood disturbance. She was born in West
London and is the youngest of four children and her
eldest brother, Charles, also has a history of psychotic
illness. Her father is a market stall holder and her

mother, originally from Dublin, is a housewife. Miss Webb attended a Roman Catholic primary school but was expelled at the age of nine on account of her truancy. Apparently, the nuns were staunch advocates of corporal punishment and she was beaten regularly. In her mid-teens, Miss Webb started running away from home and it was soon after this that she reported hearing voices for the first time, most of which were critical and accused her of committing sins. Her mother believed that her daughter was possessed by the devil and took her to see a priest, who, fortunately, recognized that the poor girl was unwell and made sure that she was seen by a psychiatrist at St Mary's. Over the next several months her condition rapidly deteriorated and she was transferred to Friern, where she spent over a year as an inpatient and was treated, in my view, somewhat conservatively, with a combination of sedative drugs and occupational therapy. Three months after her discharge the voices returned. She resumed her habit of running away from home and consequently became known to the police, who would discover her, usually in a confused and dishevelled state, wandering around Notting Hill in the small hours of the morning. One must assume that it was during one of these episodes that she was

taken advantage of, because in June last year she
was declared three months pregnant (although Miss
Webb herself claimed to have no memory of being
seduced or sexually assaulted and identified her
pregnancy as an instance of immaculate conception).
It was decided that it was probably in her best
interests if she had an abortion and this was
performed in due course by Mr Herbert at the City
of Westminster Clinic. By this time, Mr and Mrs Webb
could no longer cope, the eldest son having also
suffered a relapse, and Miss Webb was moved to
Walsingham House (a charitable hostel run by the
Catholic Church) in the autumn. Her condition
deteriorated again and she was referred to my
department by Dr Simmons, who works at St Mary's
and with whom I believe you are acquainted. Miss
Webb was hearing voices almost every day, some of
which were now telling her to 'end it all' and she was
also convinced that several of the staff were 'devils' in
disguise. I immediately reviewed her medication and
gave her a course of ECT; however, she is still very ill
and suicidal. She has also begun asking for her 'baby',
which she now believes was taken away from her.
Unfortunately, we are not equipped at Maida Vale to
offer Miss Webb the kind of help that she so clearly

needs. When we last met I recall you mentioning a
new treatment centre and your renewed interest in
deep sleep therapy and wondered whether Miss Webb
might be a suitable candidate? I would be most
grateful if you could assess her with this possibility in
mind. Her notes can be forwarded by my secretary on
request. Forgive me, Hugh, for being so brief, but I've
been rather tied up this last week with some people
from the Health Board who I have been obliged to
show around the hospital and I am now rather behind
with my paper work. You, more than anyone, will
appreciate what a nuisance all this red tape has
become for us. Thank you in advance for your
opinion.

Yours sincerely,

Angus

Dr Angus McWhirter
MB ChB, D.P.M.

3

Over the next two weeks, each day became more and more routine: I monitored patients, ran tests, administered ECT, and made sure that our pharmacy was well stocked. Due to Maitland's tendency to prescribe high doses of drugs, the patients were, on the whole, undemanding, and I frequently found myself at a loose end. When this happened I was tempted to go back to my room in order to write up the last of my Edinburgh experiments, but I thought it wise to remain visible, particularly when Sister Jenkins was abroad. If she suspected me of being work-shy I was sure that Maitland would be informed without delay. Life at Wyldehope might have become quite oppressive, if it wasn't for the fact that there was little else I could do. A rainy spell eradicated the possibility of enjoying any excursions, and when I looked through the windows, out onto the damp, blustery heath, I had no desire to brave the elements.

The majority of my time was spent on the wards,

attempting to familiarize myself with the patients. They were, by nature, solitary creatures, but sometimes two or three of them would emerge from their rooms and wander down to the recreation area – dressing gowns open, belts trailing along the floor. Once seated, they might initiate a cheerless game of dominoes, or engage in oblique conversations in which certain observations or phrases were repeated over and over again. Sometimes, they just stared at their slippers.

In my second week – I think it was on the Wednesday – something rather peculiar happened on the men's ward. I was with Sister Jenkins, undertaking an examination of a patient called Alan Foster. He was in his fifties and his predominant symptom was a very specific delusion of control. He believed that his actions were being manipulated by a reptilian civilization that had evolved on the rings of Saturn. Unfortunately, Mr Foster had developed bedsores and it was necessary to treat them with a topical antiseptic. I was putting the ointment and lint back on the trolley and Sister Jenkins was standing at the sink, scrubbing her hands. She turned the taps off and I was dimly aware of her crossing the room. There was a rummaging sound, some impatient tutting, and when I looked up Sister Jenkins was on her knees, peering under the bed. She leaped to her feet with surprising agility, placed her hands on her hips and said, 'All right, Mr Foster – where is it?'

'Where's what?' he responded.

'You know very well, Mr Foster.' I coughed to attract her attention. 'My ring,' she said, 'I took off my ring and left it here on the bedside cabinet before going to the sink to wash my hands. And now it's gone.'

'Mr Foster,' I said gravely, 'please give Sister Jenkins her ring back.'

'I haven't touched her ring!' he replied, opening his hands to show me that they were empty.

'It was there!' Sister Jenkins brought a rigid finger down on the cabinet. 'Right there!'

'Come now, Mr Foster,' I said. 'You really must co-operate.'

He continued to declare his innocence. I beckoned Sister Jenkins to my side and whispered, 'Are you quite sure about this?'

She bristled and replied, 'Yes, Dr Richardson. I am absolutely sure! Mr Foster is fond of doing things which he later says were nothing to do with him. It's always because of . . .' she rolled her eyes at the ceiling. 'Them!'

'Ah yes, of course,' I sighed, recalling the nature of Mr Foster's condition.

Addressing him sternly, I said, 'Now, Mr Foster. I'm

afraid if you don't return Sister Jenkins's ring this instant we will have to search you.'

And that – in the end – was exactly what we had to do. We stripped Mr Foster and then his bed. Nothing. Finally, I looked inside his mouth. Still nothing.

'He's swallowed it!' said Sister Jenkins.

'Oh dear,' I said, nodding sympathetically. 'I think you may be right. Was it a very expensive ring?'

'It was my wedding ring.'

I turned to Mr Foster and said, 'I'm afraid you won't be allowed use of the toilet for a few days. When you need to pass stools, you must use a chamber pot.'

'But why?' he asked.

'Because that is where, in due course, we're bound to find Sister Jenkins's ring.'

'But I didn't swallow her ring!' Mr Foster cried, exasperated. Then, by slow degrees, certainty was replaced with doubt. 'Not unless . . .' His eyes caught the light and glinted. 'Not unless *they* made me.'

Sister Jenkins's expression hardened. She took a deep breath and her ample bosom lifted. It was not necessary for her to say, 'There, I told you so!'

'Perhaps we need to increase his medication,' I said drily.

'That would certainly meet with Dr Maitland's approval,' Sister Jenkins replied, glaring at Mr Foster.

At midday, lunch was served in the dining room, and it was there that I got to know all the nurses. Jane Turner was usually sitting with Lillian Gray, a colleague with whom she had trained at St Thomas's. They were old friends and in the habit of exchanging complicit, sideways glances. This tendency to exclude would have become quite irritating, if their expressions – girlish and mischievous – hadn't aroused in me certain questionable sensations of pleasure.

Our conversations were relatively superficial. We talked about films we had seen – *Three Cases of Murder, Doctor at Sea, A Kid for Two Farthings* – popular comedy programmes on the wireless, and places to go dancing in London. I was surprised to discover that Jane and Lillian had been to most of the jazz clubs in Soho. Unlike my predecessor, neither of them seemed to have found adjusting to life at Wyldehope problematic, and I mentioned in passing what Maitland had said about Palmer. Lillian shrugged and said, 'He was very serious. You know the type. His suit was rather shabby and he smoked a pipe.' Her hand came up to her mouth as she cupped an imaginary bowl. She made some puffing sounds and adopted an intense, slightly deranged expression. The parody was cruelly funny and made Jane and me laugh. 'And he didn't get out very much. Even on weekends, when the sun was shining, he used to stay cooped up in his rooms.' She shrugged a second time. 'We enjoyed ourselves over the summer.'

'Where did you go?' I asked.

'We went cycling,' Jane replied. 'The hospital has three bicycles. If you want to use one, just ask Mr Hartley – the caretaker. Have you met him? He always says yes. The land's very flat around here, so you can go for miles without getting tired.'

Lillian chased some peas around her plate with a fork: 'And we went to Southwold.'

'Southwold?'

'It's a little seaside resort,' Jane cut in. 'There's a beach there that's good for swimming – or paddling, at any rate: the North Sea is always a bit chilly. It's got a promenade, shops and a pier. Although you can't walk very far along the pier because it's been damaged.'

'And there are some quaint pubs,' Lillian added.

'How far is it?' I enquired.

'Not far,' Jane answered. 'Although it's probably best to go by bus.'

Sister Jenkins entered the dining room and scanned the tables. Jane looked at her watch and said, 'Oops! We'd better get going.' The two friends stood up together and marched off. Their coordinated step, the synchronized sway of their hips, and the sight of their shapely calves captured and held my attention for far too long. When they were gone, I became self-conscious and looked around the room so as to make sure that no one had observed my impropriety. It was my good fortune that Sister Jenkins had been wholly occupied by her own concerns.

Maitland was true to his word. He visited Wyldehope at least once a week and occasionally we spoke on the telephone. I didn't feel as though he was checking up on me – quite the contrary; my impression was that he was calling only to make sure that I was settling in all right and had no complaints. On the second Friday after my arrival I awoke to find a note on the floor. It had been slipped beneath the door that separated my quarters from the landing. I recognized the cream laid paper and the bold handwriting: 'I'm in my office. Come down when you're ready. Hugh.' He must have left London at some unspeakably early hour. I entered one of the empty rooms and looked out of the window. The Bentley was parked outside, partially obscured by blankets of mist. It looked slightly surreal – a displaced exotic object.

I skipped breakfast and went directly to Maitland's office. He seemed delighted to see me and we sat together on the Chesterfield, discussing medicine like colleagues who had known each other not for weeks, but for decades. Maitland poured me a cup of tea and asked if I had read his manuscript. I had read it – and very thoroughly too.

The precise mechanisms underlying the beneficial effects of narcosis were not understood; however, in his paper, Maitland had proposed that prolonged sleep might result in the disintegration of personality, allowing – at some later stage – for a healthier reconstitution. He likened the process to breaking and re-setting a leg. His advocacy of ECT as an additional component of treatment was based on the idea that it could hasten recovery by obliterating unpleasant memories.

Extending his arms out along the backrest, Maitland seemed to occupy a physical space disproportionately greater than his actual size: 'There are those who say that ECT should be abolished, that it is associated with memory loss and must cause significant brain damage. But what if those memories are painful? What if those memories are distressing or traumatic? Getting rid of them can only be a good thing, surely? Who would

choose torment over tranquillity, suffering over the chance
to begin afresh?'

I offered Maitland a few tentative criticisms, which
he took in good part. He tested each argument with a
counter-argument and I was thankful that the atmosphere
remained friendly. When there was nothing more to discuss, he said, 'Thank you so much for your comments.' He
wasn't, as far as I could make out, being disingenuous.

The rest of the morning was spent on the wards, and
after lunch we made our way to the sleep room. I could
now identify all six patients: Sarah Blake, Elizabeth
Mason, Marian Powell, Kathy Webb, Isobelle Stevens and
Celia Jones. Apart from their names, dates of birth and
diagnoses I knew nothing else about them. Their notes
contained pages of blood-pressure readings, pulse-rates
and drug dosages, but no biographical details. I wanted
to know more about these women, as individuals, as
living, breathing human beings. In effect, I wanted to
know who they were, but when I pressed Maitland for
more information, he was, once again, quite evasive. A
shade of irritation had entered his voice and I thought it
best to let the matter rest. As far as Maitland was concerned, case histories were entirely irrelevant. The only
thing that mattered was treatment.

In those post-war years, men like Maitland wanted to

distance themselves from the past: the personal past as well as the historical. They didn't want to grub around in the unconscious, looking for horrors. They had seen enough of them already.

One of the women, Elizabeth Mason, had been talking in her sleep, and the night nurse had jotted down some of the things that she, Elizabeth, had said: *I won't take it off. No, I shan't. He's on his way.* None of these utterances made any sense. Even so, I couldn't help wondering whether such disconnected phrases might become more intelligible, if I only knew a little of her case history. Maitland wrote 'Sodium Amylobarbitone 400 mg' on the chart, and then pointed at Elizabeth Mason's face. 'See here,' he said, 'cracks in the skin, spreading out from each corner of her mouth. Angular stomatitis. A common complication of narcosis, but easily rectified with a B vitamin supplement.' Before leaving, Maitland paused at the door and emitted a soft grumble, as one might after a particularly satisfying meal. He turned to me and said, 'Cigarette?'

'Yes. Why not?'

'Let's go outside.' The fetor of the sleep room was tenacious: it clung to one's clothing, lingered in the nostrils, and made the prospect of a cleansing draught of fresh air most welcome.

Standing beside the Bentley, we smoked and admired the desolate landscape. Some distance away, a solitary doe appeared in a patch of dead fern. She stood very still, determining whether we represented a threat to her safety, then cantered down the incline that swept off to the marshes.

'I've been meaning to ask,' said Maitland. 'Would you mind doing an assessment?'

'Not at all.'

'It won't be for a while yet. I'll tell you when. The only snag is that you'll have to give up one of your weekends. There's a woman who lives down in the village' – he gestured towards Dunwich – 'Hilda Wright: a catatonic schizophrenic. She hasn't got out of bed or said a single word in years. Up until July she was being cared for in a private convalescent home, but the family can't afford the fees any more. Her sister looks after her now, with a little help from a nurse.' Maitland blew a stream of smoke into the air and his expression became contemplative. 'There were a lot of dissenting voices when it became known that Wyldehope was to become a mental hospital. If – pending the result of your assessment – we accepted this patient into our care, that would be good for our reputation.'

I remembered the man who had shared my carriage on the evening of my arrival, and his reference to people not wanting a 'madhouse' on their doorstep.

'The patient sounds very . . . appropriate.'

Maitland dropped his cigarette and crushed it with his heel. 'I knew you would appreciate the importance of good community relations.'

On the men's ward, everyone was comfortable apart from Michael Chapman, who was experiencing one of his agitated episodes. All psychiatric patients have sad histories, but Chapman's was, at least in my estimation, sadder than most. Although his origins were humble, he had possessed a natural gift for mathematics. He was awarded a scholarship and subsequently went to Cambridge, where, while preparing for his final examinations, he had suffered the first of several 'nervous breakdowns'. He was overwhelmed by dark thoughts and believed that one of his tutors, a renowned logician, was stealing his ideas. The college doctor made a diagnosis of monomania and Chapman was sent home, where he was treated at a local hospital as an outpatient. His recovery was slow and this period of ill health left him with significantly impaired powers of concentration. He was unable to return to Cambridge and instead found employment as a clerk in an accountant's office. Within a year he had started behaving strangely once again and was dismissed: a notebook had been discovered in which he had recorded the movements and whereabouts of his work associates in minute detail. Thereafter, the poor man was never able to hold down a job for more than a few weeks, for he was always convinced that his colleagues were conspiring against him, and the rest of his life was spent in hospitals or hostels.

Chapman's promising youth and descent into madness evoked in me a very particular sympathy. It was my good fortune to have been born with chemicals benignly balanced in my brain, otherwise my Cambridge career might have ended just as ignominiously. Individuals like Chapman demonstrated all too clearly the moral indifference of fate. Accidents of biology, rather than brilliance or hard work, are the real and haphazard determinants of success or failure.

I could have given Chapman more sodium amytal, but he had had so much of late, I decided not to. Instead, I tried to calm him down with common sense and good humour, two practical expedients that all hospital doctors rely upon from time to time.

Chapman was breathing heavily and beads of perspiration were visible on his brow. 'Am I going to be punished?' he demanded.

'No,' I replied. 'Whatever makes you say such a thing?'

He ignored my question and, wringing his hands, repeated the same phrase over and over again, until it dwindled to a whisper: 'What have I done? Oh, what have I done?'

'Certainly nothing that deserves punishment,' I said, affecting a jovial manner. He started biting his nails. 'What are you so worried about?'

Chapman spun around on his heels, reached the window in two long strides and pressed his forehead against the iron bars. 'I don't like it here.'

'Perhaps we could play a game of chess? Do you play chess, Mr Chapman?'

He sighed, a massive expulsion of air that seemed to make him shrivel like a collapsed balloon. 'I used to.'

'Come on then, let's go to the recreation area.'

'I don't know.'

'We can start a game and see how it goes, and if you get tired, we'll stop.'

His head jerked around and he looked at me with suspicion. 'Why are you so eager to play chess?'

'I'm not, Mr Chapman. I merely think that you are preoccupied and that a game of chess will provide you with some much needed distraction.'

He continued to study me and after a lengthy pause, asked: 'What do you think of Botvinnik?'

'Who?'

'Mikhail Botvinnik.'

'I'm sorry, Mr Chapman, I haven't the foggiest idea who you're talking about.'

'He is the world champion.' Chapman narrowed his eyes and there was something in his expression that suggested he expected me to say something more. When I did not react, he moved away from the window, but was careful to keep his back to the wall. The manoeuvre was ungainly and he almost tripped over. He steadied himself and said, 'Botvinnik's play is remarkable on account of its strategic depth. There are those who say that his opening repertoire is limited, but his endings are quite exceptional. Moreover, his understanding of queen's pawn openings and the French defence is second to none.'

'Mr Chapman,' I said, making an appeasing gesture. 'I fear that you have overestimated my knowledge of the game. I play very occasionally for pleasure – nothing more.'

'So you say.'

'So I say? What do you mean by that?'

He pressed his lips together and his expression became defiant.

'Mr Chapman?'

'Did *he* send you?'

'Who?'

'Botvinnik, of course.'

'I'm afraid you are very much mistaken if you think that I am acquainted with the world chess champion.'

'Tell him that I know what he's up to.'

'I'll tell him nothing of the sort, Mr Chapman, because – as I have already made quite clear – we are not familiar with each other.'

His expression changed in an instant from anger to confusion. 'You don't know him?'

'No. I don't know him.'

'You are quite sure?'

'Quite sure.'

'He didn't ask you to . . .' The sentence trailed off and Chapman appeared disorientated. He scratched his head and blinked at the ceiling.

'What?' I enquired.

Chapman shook his head, more an involuntary shudder than a controlled movement. 'It doesn't matter,' he muttered to himself, 'a misunderstanding, that's what we have here. A misunderstanding.'

I raised my hand to remind him of my presence. 'Shall we play then?'

'All right – but you must not make any notes while we play.'

'I give you my word, Mr Chapman. There will be no note-taking.'

Together we walked down the corridor to the empty recreation room. Beneath the dado rail, the heavily embossed wallpaper was painted dark brown and above, bottle green. The effect was dismal and cheerless. A vase of dead flowers stood in the middle of a circular table and a late bluebottle bounced against one of the window-panes. I pulled out a chair for Chapman and he sat down, but he was still agitated and perspiring.

The chess set was kept in a cabinet filled with other games such as Monopoly and snakes and ladders. Look-ing down the shelves I found a wooden box containing the pieces and a scuffed old board, and then I returned to the table where we prepared to play. It was decided, after tossing a coin, that I would go first. I pushed one of my pawns forward and Chapman gave my action unmerited consideration – rubbing his stubbly chin and emitting a continuous, low hum. Several minutes passed before he responded by doing exactly the same thing.

Given his earlier comments about Botvinnik, I had assumed that Chapman would be an accomplished player. But in fact, he was rather poor. It saddened me to see a man once capable of solving the most abstruse problems struggling to anticipate my mediocre game. I let him take one of my bishops, then a knight, and was mildly amused when he leered at me, as if he had triumphed through the exercise of exceptional cunning.

I looked around the room to alleviate my boredom. The fireplace was rather grand: a stone edifice with carved scrolls and decorative flowers. There was a teak radiogram, and beside it a stack of rarely touched long-playing records. The carpet was cratered with cigarette burns.

When I returned my attention to the board, Chapman had placed his king behind a knight for protection. In doing so, he had made it possible for me to take an exposed rook, but I did not have the heart to do so. Instead, I reversed my queen diagonally with no particular purpose in mind.

'Dr Richardson?' Chapman was staring at me, his eyes wide open.

'Yes?'

'Why do you move my bed around at night?'

'I don't.'

'Then the nurses. Why do *they* do it?'

'They don't, Mr Chapman.'

'I tell them to stop but they never listen.'

'Perhaps it is a dream, Mr Chapman. They would not move your bed while you are asleep.'

'It is the movement of the bed that wakes me up.'

I passed my hand over the chessboard. 'Your turn, Mr Chapman.'

He studied the pieces for a full two minutes and then nudged his rook out of harm's way. The muscles around his mouth twitched repeatedly until a tremulous smile came into existence. It could not be sustained, and a moment later Chapman's expression was, as usual, fearful and unhappy.

4

On Saturday morning I was relieved by Stewart Osborne, one of the doctors from Saxmundham. I had met Kenneth Price, the other Saxmundham doctor, the previous Saturday.

Osborne was a few years older than me and affected a particular style of grooming that was reminiscent of Clark Gable playing the part of Rhett Butler in *Gone with the Wind*. He possessed the same wavy black hair and thin moustache, but the general effect he hoped to achieve was spoiled by a weak, flabby mouth. We shook hands and exchanged civilities. Apparently, he had also worked at the Royal Free Hospital, although before my time. Osborne congratulated me on my appointment and we discussed some of the patients who had been showing signs of agitation, but as we were talking I found his manner rather irritating. He seemed to be permanently attempting to conceal (without great success) a sneer. Even his voice had a mocking edge. I soon identified him as one of those boorish individuals who have learned to escape censure by pretending that everything improper they say is meant as a harmless joke. On the women's ward, he questioned my judgement in front of a nurse, and when I readied myself to respond he laughed and said, 'Sorry, old boy, I was only being facetious. Please, don't take offence.' I was glad that I didn't have to spend very long in his company.

Although the weather could have been better, I decided that I would go out for a walk. Behind the hospital I discovered a path that descended to the beach. It was very steep and I almost lost my footing. As usual the sea was quite rough and the waves crashed loudly onto the shingle. I picked up a pebble and threw it out as far as I could. Once again I was struck by the sea's unusual colour – a dull, enervating brown. In spite of all the froth and spray, the air was not salty. Indeed, it was disappointingly inert and lacked the medicinal tang so strongly associated with health and convalescence. I climbed the raised bank that separated the beach from the grazing marsh and ambled along in a southerly direction. The views were expansive. Great rafts of cloud drifted apart, allowing shafts of sunlight to break through. The spectacle was magnificent but – because of the restless, ever-changing sky – all too fleeting. As the gaps in the heavens closed the luminous columns became faint and ghostly.

I was presented with a choice: to either continue along the bank and follow the coast towards Aldeburgh, or to turn right, onto an adjoining raised bank that crossed the marsh. I decided to take the latter course.

It was a bleak place: entirely flat and without trees. I passed a sluice mechanism with rusted iron wheels and some long, straight drainage channels. An upturned rowing boat, untouched for years, had all but rotted away. Further on, I saw a couple of mangy ponies in a waterlogged field, and later, a small herd of cows. Somewhere, a bird was producing a lonely, plaintive call. I persevered, and further inland came across a wooden boardwalk. The planks were sodden and creaked loudly when I stepped on them. Undeterred, I moved along the fragile timbers, until I came to a flooded depression, the muddy fringes of which were patrolled by wading birds with long beaks. In the distance I could see the roof, chimneys and tower of Wyldehope. I had walked further than I had originally intended. It was getting cold and I decided to return.

The rest of the weekend was spent mostly in my rooms. Mrs Hartley's kitchen girl brought me my meals, and I was perfectly happy reading, writing and listening to the wireless. The previous two weeks had been very demanding, more so, perhaps, than I had truly appreciated. It wasn't until I was properly relaxed that I realized how tense and wound-up I had been. I had been getting a lot of headaches.

By Sunday evening, I was effectively back on duty. I met briefly with Osborne, who informed me that the weekend had been 'uneventful'. During the twenty minutes or so we spent together, he did nothing to make me revise my first impressions. He was irritating throughout. At one point, Jane Turner walked by and he nudged me with his elbow: 'It's always a pleasure to work with Nurse Turner.' He clearly expected me to reciprocate, to make some crass remark about her prettiness or figure, but I ignored him. As he was leaving, he called out, 'Richardson, do you play golf?'

'No,' I replied.

'Pity.' He swung an imaginary five iron. 'I could have got you into my club. I'm on the membership committee. You don't want to end up like Palmer. All work and no play makes Jack a dull boy.' Before I could deliver a suitably barbed response he was chuckling loudly – 'See you in a few weeks.' I was very glad to see the back of him.

Jane Turner was going about her business on the ward. I took the liberty of occupying her chair and pretended to find something of interest in Alan Foster's notes.

'Has Dr Osborne gone?' she asked.

'Yes,' I replied. 'Why?'

'Oh, nothing important.'

I looked up. 'He's very . . .' I paused to select a suitable euphemism. 'Confident, don't you think?' I invested my chosen adjective with enough scorn to make its purpose quite transparent.

She looked around, as if to make sure that we weren't being overheard. 'Lillian thinks he's quite suave.'

'Suave!' I had repeated the word much louder than intended.

Jane perched herself on the side of the desk and crossed her legs. 'Well, I can see why Lilly might think that. Sometimes he wears a cravat.'

'And what do you think?'

'Of Dr Osborne? I think he's rather full of himself.'

'I'm inclined to agree.'

'Still, he can be quite funny – at times – and he's better company than the other doctor from Saxmundham.'

'Kenneth Price? He seemed a decent enough fellow to me.'

'Yes, but he's a little . . .' Her features contracted.

'Dull?'

'Either that or very shy.' She peeked over the top of the folder to see whose notes I was reading. 'Alan Foster?'

'Yes. I can't see anything about Sister Jenkins's ring.'

'That's because it hasn't arrived yet. Actually, Sister Jenkins gave him a laxative only yesterday.'

'Is that so?'

'But still no luck.'

'Well, some things can't be hurried.'

She laughed – a rather musical laugh – and pushed herself off the desk. I stood up and gestured for her to sit in the empty chair.

'Did you have a nice weekend?' she asked.

'Nice enough. I managed to go for a walk – along the beach and across the marshes.'

'That doesn't sound terribly exciting.'

'Perhaps not.'

She curled a wayward lock of blonde hair behind her flawless ear. 'It's nicer here in the summer.'

We carried on talking in a casual, easy manner, and occasionally our exchanges became mildly flirtatious. After nine o'clock, for the sake of maintaining some vestige of propriety, I dragged myself away.

Before retiring, I thought that I should check that all was well in the sleep room. The trainee nurse (whose name I had since found out to be Mary Williams) was on duty. As I entered I noticed that Mary was looking fixedly in my direction, as if she had been waiting for me to enter. She looked worried – perhaps even fearful – and this expression was sustained until a spark of recognition appeared in her eyes. Relief was followed by a broad smile. I felt a pang of sympathy for her, supposing that she had been expecting the redoubtable Sister Jenkins. As I advanced, she stood respectfully and made some small adjustments to her bib.

'Good evening, Mary.'

'Good evening, Dr Richardson.'

'Have you been here long?'

'Since lunchtime.'

'Any problems?'

'Isobelle Stevens was a bit restless earlier, but she seems to have settled down now.'

'Did you make a note on her chart?'

'Yes. Of course.' Her tone was indignant. A moment later her cheeks were burning with shame.

I touched her arm and said, 'It's all right, Mary – really. You must be tired.'

One of the patients spoke in her sleep: 'Don't! Don't! Please . . . no.'

Mary and I looked at each other – but made no comment.

I did my usual circuit of the beds, examining the charts, registering medication levels, and I made a mental note of who was due to receive ECT the next day: Celia

Jones, a middle-aged woman with short curly hair and a round face. Her eyes were rapidly oscillating from side to side beneath closed lids – a reliable indication that she was dreaming. As I was preparing to make my departure one of the nightingales arrived to relieve Mary Williams. Consequently, the trainee and I left the sleep room together.

Even though I had indicated that Mary should go first, her deferential nature made her fall in behind me. We were about halfway up the stairs when I heard her gasp: a sudden, sharp intake of breath. I stopped and turned around. Mary was looking back down the stairs, her right hand raised and covering the nape of her neck.

'Mary?' I enquired.

When our eyes met I saw that her pillbox hat was tilted at an angle.

'I'm sorry, Dr Richardson.' She glanced towards the sleep room again and stammered a few words that I did not hear properly. Even in the weak light that reached us from the vestibule, I could see that she was confused.

'Mary,' I pressed, 'whatever is the matter?'

Her mouth worked silently, opening and closing without producing words, until she finally managed to blurt out: 'My ankle. I twisted my ankle.' She doubled over and probed the joint.

'Here,' I said, offering her my arm, 'let me give you some support?'

She ignored my solicitation and made a great show of testing the foot with her weight. 'It's all right – I think. Yes. Yes. It's fine.'

'Perhaps I should take a look?'

'No. Honestly – it's nothing.' She tried to smile. 'I was being stupid . . .'

'Well,' I said, 'if you're quite sure?'

'I am,' she answered firmly. 'Quite sure.'

We completed our ascent and as soon as we were in the vestibule Mary said, 'Goodnight.' She let herself out by the front door and locked it behind her. Although she was a local girl, she had been allocated a room (like the other nurses) in the converted stable building. Given that she had not troubled to collect a coat before leaving, I assumed that this must be her destination. I listened to the sound of her step receding into the night. There was nothing about its determined regularity that suggested a 'twisted ankle'. The rhythm faded away into silence, a silence that yawned and gaped and felt deep enough to produce a sensation not unlike vertigo. Yet, I kept on listening. I don't know what I was listening for – but I kept on listening.

5

The following week I saw a great deal of Jane Turner, during which time my feelings for her began to grow stronger. Her absence became increasingly associated with a dull longing. There were, however, some hopeful indications that she might feel the same way. She was always cheerful in my presence and had a tendency to stand so close I could smell her perfume. In spite of all this, I had very real doubts about the wisdom of initiating a relationship with a colleague. If things didn't work out, or, even worse, turned sour, life might become very complicated.

I was sitting with Jane and Lillian in the dining room and it transpired that they planned to visit Southwold at the weekend. 'The weather forecast is very good,' said Jane. 'It'll probably be our last chance to enjoy some sunshine before the autumn sets in.'

Lillian looked up from her mashed potato and said to me, 'What are you doing? This weekend?'

'Oh, nothing much,' I said, pitifully.

'Then why don't you come with us?'

My usual doubts and reservations surfaced, but swiftly dissipated when I looked at Jane. Her expression was eager, expectant, and to have declined the offer would have appeared faint-hearted, or even cowardly.

'Well,' I ventured, 'if you wouldn't mind.'

'Of course we wouldn't mind,' said Lillian. 'We'll cycle into Westleton and get the bus.'

The thought of spending a whole day with Jane was somewhat distracting. I spent the remainder of the week in a rather restless state, and in the evenings, when I tried to write up my final Edinburgh experiment, I was unable to concentrate. Instead of working I smoked one cigarette after another and paced up and down the corridor until it was time to go to bed. On Saturday morning, Jane, Lillian and I collected three bicycles from Mr Hartley and we set off across the heath. Although there were more clouds in the sky than we had anticipated, the weather was mild for the season. It did not take us long to reach Westleton, where a publican – already known to Jane and Lillian – allowed us to leave our bicycles in his shed. Thankfully, the bus was on time and when we alighted the clouds had dispersed and the sun was blazing.

Southwold was a pretty seaside town, possessed of a sleepy, provincial charm, and largely free of the tawdry entertainments commonly associated with popular coastal resorts. The backstreets were lined with quaint little cottages and the wide, irregular green was encircled by more distinguished residences, some with wrought-iron balconies and tall, elegant windows. There were two outstanding landmarks: the first was a very large medieval church, the exterior of which was patterned with flint, and the second, a fully operational lighthouse. On a flat, grassy elevation close to the beach, six eighteen-pounder cannons pointed out to sea. The place was called, somewhat unimaginatively, Gun Hill.

We ate lunch at a hotel and drank far too much. When we had finished, Lillian rose from her chair and said that she was going off to do some shopping on the high street. 'I'll meet you by the pier in about an hour,' she added with breezy good humour. After her departure, Jane and I walked back to Gun Hill, where we sat together on a bench. She had put on a pair of sunglasses that made her look glamorous and continental.

I asked her a few questions, mostly about herself, and she warmed to the theme of her own history. Her mother was a schoolteacher and lived in North London. Her father, a pharmacist, had died when she was only thirteen. She disclosed this information without senti-mentality. Although her father had died young, his early demise did not result in financial hardship. A wealthy uncle had made sure that the needs of mother and daughter were always met. Jane spoke about her training at St Thomas's, meeting Lillian, and how much fun they had had going to the Festival of Britain; about a holiday that she had enjoyed in Wales with her cousins, Vanessa and Neville, and her plan to take driving lessons. Her confidences and revelations proceeded with effortless fluency.

My surroundings began to feel strangely unreal. The contrast between the brown sea and the blue sky was striking and otherworldly. A union flag snapped in the breeze and a flock of long-necked birds flew past in a perfect V-formation. I was aware that something had changed, but it took me a few seconds to identify what. Jane had stopped talking. I turned to look at her, and at that precise moment she also turned to look at me. I can remember seeing myself, miniaturized and suspended in her lenses, and watching with fascination as these pale copies of my face began to expand. And then, quite suddenly, we were kissing.

When we finally separated, she took off her sunglasses. The vivid green of her irises had the translucent depth of stained glass.

Ordinarily, some outmoded idea of gentlemanly conduct might have induced me to say, 'I'm sorry, I didn't mean to take advantage,' or some other expedient that allowed her to demur. But there was little point. The situation that we found ourselves in had been so obviously engineered that to pretend otherwise would have been insulting. We kissed again, and carried on kissing, until Jane glanced at her wristwatch and said with a sigh, 'Lillian.'

We walked along the promenade, past brightly coloured beach huts, hand in hand. It was only when we were close enough to the stunted pier to appreciate its decrepitude that the sense of a greater world beyond our mutual self-absorption impinged upon our senses. A little girl with blonde hair passed us by, holding a toffee apple which seemed to glow from within like a gemstone. On the horizon, I could see two large tanker ships.

'There's Lillian,' said Jane.

She was standing with her back to us.

'Do you think perhaps . . .' It was not necessary for me to say any more.

'Yes, of course,' Jane replied, releasing my fingers.

On Monday night, Maitland telephoned.

'James? It's Hugh.' I can't remember when, precisely,

but we had started to use each other's Christian names. 'Is everything all right?'

'Yes.'

'No problems.'

'None at all.'

'Good. Listen. I'm coming up early tomorrow morning. Walter Rosenberg is in London this week and he wants to see Wyldehope.'

'Walter Rosenberg?'

'An old friend.'

The name was familiar. 'Didn't he work with Kalinowsky?' Kalinowsky had championed the use of ECT in the United States.

'They published several important papers together.' Maitland paused and I heard him light a cigarette. 'I'd like you to be present when I show him around.'

We talked briefly about Rosenberg, who was in charge of a massive asylum on Long Island. 'Fifteen thousand beds!' Maitland exclaimed, permitting himself a dry chuckle. 'They do things differently in America. I'm afraid that British psychiatry will be left behind if the authorities don't learn from the American example.' Then, in a more lively tone: 'Good God! Is that the time? I was supposed to be dining at my club tonight. I'll see you tomorrow.'

When I got out of bed the following morning, I

crossed the corridor and looked out of one of the west-facing windows. Maitland's Bentley was already parked on the drive. I ate breakfast in the dining room and performed a quick circuit of the two wards and the sleep room to ensure that everything was in order. By half past ten a Jaguar – as long as a hearse – had appeared beside Maitland's Bentley. A chauffeur was standing next to it, holding a transistor radio up against his ear.

I had returned to the men's ward and was reading through the notes when I realized that Sister Jenkins's wedding ring had still not been recovered. The job of sifting through Alan Foster's faeces was, understandably, very unpopular, and I wondered if the trainee – eager to get the noisome task completed as quickly as possible – had failed to exercise due diligence. In which case, Sister Jenkins's precious ring would now be lost in the sewage system. As I contemplated the absurdity of the situation, a new nurse – just up from London – sidled up to me and said, 'Excuse me? Dr Richardson? Dr Maitland would like to see you in his office.' I hastily put the notes back in the filing cabinet and made my way upstairs.

Maitland greeted me with his characteristically firm handshake. 'James, do come in.'

I had expected to see only one guest, but when I entered I saw two men seated on the Chesterfield. The older of the pair I immediately recognized; he was one of the three 'American colleagues' in the framed photograph on Maitland's desk – ten years older, perhaps, but still slim, dapper and tanned. The other man was much younger, square-jawed, athletically built, and with hair cropped so short that it was little more than a shadowy cap of stubble. I was introduced to Walt Rosenberg first, and then to his companion, Buck Stratton, whom I later discovered was an employee of a US drug company.

Maitland and Rosenberg talked incessantly. Yet, I did not feel excluded. I was quite content to sit quietly and listen. Indeed, I considered it a privilege to be a spectator as these giants of psychiatry sparred and floated ideas. At one point I went to Maitland's desk to get Rosenberg an empty ashtray. The bottom drawer of the grey filing cabinet had been left open and I saw that it contained some files. I only had a moment, but it was enough to read one of the names. The bold capitals spelled out the name 'Kathy Webb'.

Rosenberg was an amusing raconteur, with a comedian's sense of timing, and I was still laughing at one of his jokes when, unexpectedly, Maitland asked me to summarize the results of my Edinburgh research. He was particularly keen for me to discuss my final study – a demonstration that the sleeping brain can still respond to emotionally meaningful stimuli. I had discovered that whispering the name of a person's wife or husband was all that it took to produce a surge of EEG activity, irrespective of how deeply they slept. Stratton, who had been silent until that point, suddenly sat up and asked me some very technical questions. I thought it odd that a drug company representative should be so well informed about sleep research.

'Is this study published yet?' asked Rosenberg.

'No,' I replied, 'I'm writing it up now.'

'Sir, I'd be grateful for an offprint,' said Stratton, who reached into his pocket and produced a business card. I was not accustomed to being addressed so respectfully by someone of my own age and felt a little awkward. The card showed only his name and an address on East 42nd Street, New York.

'Well, gentlemen,' said Maitland, clapping his hands together, 'shall we proceed?' There was a hum of general agreement and we followed him to the door.

We walked out onto the landing where Maitland halted and stroked the carved banisters. 'These charming woodland creatures are believed to be the work of Robert Greenford, a friend of William Morris and an associate of the Pre-Raphaelite Brotherhood.'

On the way down we found Hartley treating the

banisters with a clear, oily fluid. He was on his knees, with a rag in his hand, but as we approached he stood, almost to attention, and inclined his head as we passed. When we reached the ground floor, Maitland indicated the suit of armour and claimed that it was early fifteenth century. We visited the men's ward first, and then the women's ward, but it was the sleep room where we tarried longest. Over an hour, in fact.

Rosenberg asked numerous questions about our drugs, vitamin supplements, and whether or not we used insulin to stimulate appetite. He circled the beds, studying the faces of the sleeping women, occasionally listening to their hearts with a stethoscope. I felt possessive and wished that he would leave them alone. Stratton had positioned himself near one of the walls, deep in shadow, his legs slightly apart and his hands behind his back. It was one o'clock, and the nurses were preparing to wake and feed the patients. Rosenberg wanted to stay and watch.

Sister Jenkins managed the complex choreography of waking, feeding, administering drugs, voiding and exercising with her usual brisk efficiency. While the patients were eating, Rosenberg tried to engage Kathy Webb. He introduced himself and asked her to perform some simple arithmetic, but the young woman only sucked on her fork and stared into the distance.

'Yes,' Rosenberg said, looking up at Maitland. 'Ours are much the same.'

'How long have your cohort been asleep now?' asked Maitland. It was an unusual choice of word – 'cohort'.

'Five months,' Rosenberg replied.

Maitland started. 'Five months?'

'Yes,' Rosenberg replied. 'Though things haven't gone exactly to plan. We lost two.'

'Bowel problems?'

'Chest infections. We were unlucky.'

Maitland nodded. 'And how long do you think you'll keep them under this time?'

'As long as it takes,' Rosenberg replied. 'I'll let you know how things are progressing.'

When the patients were all back in their beds and asleep, Maitland congratulated Sister Jenkins. 'Well done,' he said softly. Again, his attitude reminded me of a military man. The Americans accompanied Maitland back to his office and I returned to the sleep room. Before parting, Rosenberg had seized my arm and said, 'If you ever come over to New York, be sure to call me up.' His eyes were bright with raw intelligence.

I thanked him for the invitation.

The Jaguar was still parked outside Wyldehope at half past three. When I looked out of a window two hours later, both vehicles – the Jaguar and the Bentley – were gone.

That evening I sat at the bureau and added a few more paragraphs to my unfinished paper, but I wasn't satisfied with what I had written. The language was too dense and the sentences didn't flow. Forcing myself to concentrate was giving me a headache. I smoked a cigarette and thought about Jane. When I closed my eyes, the recollection of her kiss became so vivid it was like a repetition of the actual experience. I could feel the pressure of her lips against mine and their slow parting; I could detect a trace of her perfume in the air.

Since returning from our trip to Southwold, only a single opportunity had arisen for private conversation. I had said that I wanted to see her again, preferably alone, the following weekend, but she had already made arrangements to visit her mother in London. She had squeezed my hand and said: 'Never mind. We'll sort something out.' I wasn't sure what she had in mind.

A blast of wind shook the windowpane and its loud rattle disturbed my musings. I drew diagonal lines across the two paragraphs I had just written. It simply wasn't good enough. I stubbed out my cigarette, tidied up my notes and put them in the bottom drawer. The Reserpine was still there. I hadn't bothered throwing it away. I picked up the container, looked at the wastepaper basket, but found myself oddly disinclined to complete the action I had started. Instead, I put the container back in its usual place. Consulting my watch, I noted that it was eleven thirty.

I shuffled along the hallway, yawning, until I came to my bedroom door. Reaching into the darkness, I slid my hand along the wall until I felt the light switch. It emitted a soft 'click' and the room instantly materialized: the large iron bedstead, the chest of drawers, the bulky wardrobe. In the middle of the carpet, about a yard or so in front of me, a metallic gleam caught my attention. I crouched down to take a closer look.

'It can't be . . .' I was conscious of my words as if they had been spoken by someone else. They sounded abnormally loud.

I picked up the object and let it roll into the palm of my hand. It was a wedding ring. I tried to slide it onto my index finger and found that it was too small to get past my knuckle. Without doubt, it belonged to a woman.

Was I the victim of a prank? Hartley possessed a spare key, identical to my own, but it was patently absurd (I realized after a moment's reflection) to suppose that he and Sister Jenkins shared a common interest in playing practical jokes. Had Hartley been persuaded then by Sister Jenkins to plant the ring in my bedroom in order to accuse me of theft? Again, the idea was totally absurd. My brain generated a number of equally unsatisfactory theories, which I promptly rejected on account of their utter implausibility, until only one remained: Alan Foster must have slipped Sister Jenkins's ring into the back pocket of my trousers, and it must have fallen out while I was getting dressed that morning. The fact that I had not detected its presence earlier was perhaps a measure of how distracted I had become.

I was about to call Sister Jenkins on the telephone, in order to inform her that I had recovered her ring, when it occurred to me that telling her the truth might not be such a good idea. She would think me unobservant or, even worse, absent-minded, and very likely share her views with Maitland. After giving the matter some thought, I decided that I would invent a harmless lie, something that would clear me of any fault or blame. I placed the ring on my bedside cabinet and pulled back the cover and blanket.

As I was falling asleep, listening to the sound of the sea, the memory of Jane's kiss returned. Great black waves rolled through the room and I was carried out across a vast ocean of forgetfulness.

Dr Joseph Grayson
Department of Psychological Medicine
London Hospital
Whitechapel
London E1

23rd June 1955

Dr Hugh Maitland
Department of Psychological Medicine
St Thomas's Hospital
London SE1

Dear Dr Maitland,

Re: Miss Isobelle Joyce Stevens (d.o.b. 12.10.1929)
     The Old Alms House, 28 Rope Street E2

Thank you for agreeing to see the above patient, who
we discussed today on the telephone. She has been in
my care now for fifteen months and I would value
your opinion with respect to her future treatment. She

is twenty-six years of age and in her relatively short
life she has managed to collect several diagnoses,
some of which are rather exotic. These include *folie
circulaire*, melancholy and catoptrophobia. My own
view is that she suffers from a severe manic
depressive illness with pronounced psychotic features.

Her background is as follows: her father cannot
work on account of a major injury he sustained
during the war, and her mother is a seamstress who is
employed by a clothes' manufacturer in Bethnal
Green. She has one sibling, Maude, who is her junior
by three years. Miss Stevens was a premature baby
and slow to develop. She did not talk or crawl until
quite late and she missed much of her early schooling
because of a recurrent chest complaint. Be that as it
may, she eventually caught up with her peers and on
leaving school she was able to get a job as a waitress
in a cafe.

Soon after her nineteenth birthday she is said to
have gone through a change of character, becoming, in
turns, increasingly indolent and impulsive. She also
became fearful of mirrors and insisted that her parents
cover all reflective surfaces in the house. When asked
what she was afraid of, her responses were
nonsensical. She was attended by her family doctor,

Dr Fletcher, a man sympathetic to Freud and psychoanalysis, who attempted a talking cure which was, as one would expect, wholly ineffective. Miss Stevens's behaviour became increasingly erratic and she lost her job as a consequence.

After a period of several months, during which she hardly stirred from her bed, Miss Stevens's mood improved and her fear of mirrors remitted; however, one set of symptoms was immediately replaced by another. Miss Stevens could not sleep, she became garrulous, and she began to express grandiose ideas: for example, that she had been in conversation with a representative from a New York casting agency and that she was going to be a successful actress in Hollywood. She took to wearing flamboyant clothes and frequented local public houses, where she received a great deal of attention from men. Needless to say, she became the subject of much gossip and when her parents learned of her behaviour there were heated arguments at home. Some of these altercations must have been quite ugly, because Dr Fletcher noted the appearance of bruises on her face and a swollen, twisted ankle. At last, recognizing the limitations of his chosen method, Dr Fletcher referred Miss Stevens to my predecessor, Dr Meadows, who admitted her to the Royal London for a period of two months and treated her with bromides. This approach was successful, insofar as she became less agitated and expansive, but a depression followed, and thereafter this pattern of alternating mood states was repeated, usually resulting in an admission during the manic phase of her illness.

At the age of twenty-three, Miss Stevens became pregnant and she was not able to identify the father (although it seems very likely that he was one of her drinking companions). This proved to be the final straw for her parents, who subsequently threw her out of their home. Miss Stevens was taken in by a women's refuge and the baby was removed for fostering three weeks after its birth. The sad consequence of this was a severe depression, which culminated in a suicide attempt by overdosing. Fortunately, Miss Stevens was discovered in the act and immediately given an emetic.

Since that time, Miss Stevens's condition has not improved. Indeed, I regret to say that (in spite of my own best efforts), if anything, her symptoms have got worse. During manic episodes, her delusions are more florid than ever – she talks incessantly about how beautiful she is and how she is destined to be an international starlet – and when she is low she feels utterly useless and wishes that she were dead.

When I took over the case from Dr Meadows, I discontinued her bromides and replaced them with lithium carbonate. This was very effective and her mood swings flattened out but, sadly, she developed several side effects – nausea, tinnitus, blurred vision and, more alarmingly, attacks of arm hyperextension. I was forced to reduce the dose from 1200 mg to 800 mg daily. The side effects disappeared but, alas, so did the benefit.

Once again, I am most grateful for your assistance. Miss Stevens is an interesting example of cyclical mood disturbance with accompanying delusions and I very much look forward to receiving your advice concerning her management.

Yours sincerely,

Joseph Grayson

Dr Joseph Grayson
MB BChir., MRCP., D.P.M.

6

I discovered Sister Jenkins in the sleep room. She was sitting behind the desk, scrutinizing a rota. One of the bathroom doors was ajar and I could see Mary Williams, through the opening, energetically mopping the tiles. The air smelled of disinfectant.

As I approached the desk, Sister Jenkins altered her position and said, 'Good morning, Dr Richardson.'

'Sister Jenkins,' I responded happily. 'I have something for you.'

She looked at me askance. 'Oh?'

I took the ring from my pocket and raised it up for her to see. She permitted herself a faint smile. 'Did it come out – finally?'

'No. I found it in Alan Foster's room.'

'Where?'

'Under the radiator.'

'How strange. I looked there myself.'

'It was behind the valve. Right in the corner.'

I gave her the ring and I was rather surprised by her

reaction. She didn't put it on immediately, as I had expected. Instead, she extended her arm into the cone of light that spread out beneath the lampshade. She manipulated the ring, turning it over – first one way, then the other. Her eyes showed suspicion and her brow creased. Then, pinching the ring in such a way as to suggest that it might be dirty, or contaminated, she placed it with a precise action on a pad of lined notepaper. Her expression was a combination of disappointment and irritation.

'Is there something wrong?' I asked.

'It isn't my ring,' she said bluntly.

'But it must be.'

'Dr Richardson, I know what my wedding ring looks like.' Sister Jenkins realized that I would need some persuading. She reached for the ring and pushed her fourth finger through its centre. It was clearly too tight. 'See?' she said. 'It doesn't fit. My ring was larger, the gold more yellow. This ring is much smaller and made from gold that is very pale – whitish.'

'Then whose ring is it?'

She shrugged and said, 'It doesn't belong to any of the patients, that's for sure. Only Mr Cook and Mr Murray are married and they are big, strapping fellows. And none of my nightingales are married – although Sandra Perkins and Margaret Thomas are engaged.' Her expression became uncharacteristically wistful when she added this afterthought.

For a few seconds I was speechless, but I felt obliged to continue my charade: 'Then I suppose this ring must have been lying behind the radiator for quite some time.'

'What an odd coincidence,' said Sister Jenkins. 'That I should lose my own ring in the same room.'

'Yes,' I replied, feeling distinctly uncomfortable and mindful of the fact that the telling of one lie invariably necessitates the telling of others.

Sister Jenkins shook her head. 'I can't believe that I missed it, and how remarkable that none of the nightingales came across it while cleaning?'

I felt the heat of embarrassment on my cheeks and my speech became disjointed. 'What a shame. I thought I'd sorted everything out. How very annoying. To be frank, Sister Jenkins, I don't think we're going to find *your* ring now.' I looked across the basement in the direction of Mary Williams. 'The trainee probably did her best, but . . .' Sister Jenkins gave a curt nod. I picked up the anonymous ring and added, 'Perhaps I should write to the previous occupants of Mr Foster's room – to see if I can find out who it belongs to.'

'There weren't any previous occupants. The room was empty before Mr Foster's arrival.'

'Very well. I shall sell the ring to a jeweller and donate the proceeds to the hospital.'

Again, Sister Jenkins shrugged: an implied 'As you wish.'

'How have the patients been?' I asked, eager to steer the conversation in a different direction.

'None have required additional drugs. They have all been sleeping very peacefully.'

'Excellent,' I said, dropping the ring into my pocket.

I walked off and circled the beds, stopping at the end of each to study the charts. It was difficult to concentrate, because I kept on thinking about the ring and trying to fathom how it had come to be on the floor of my bedroom. In the end, I had to accept that it had always been there, hidden from view, and that some unlikely sequence of events had caused it to suddenly appear. What that sequence of events might be was beyond my powers of deduction. Having reached this reasonable but unsatisfactory conclusion, I dismissed all further thoughts about the ring and got on with my work.

Marian Powell was due to receive ECT. She was one of the younger women, and, like Kathy Webb, still a teenager. There was something about her face – the angularity of the features, the weariness of her expression – that suggested extreme poverty and hardship. I had seen that same type of face many times before, particularly in the East End of London. It was a face that had known hunger, violence and cruel deprivations.

With Sister Jenkins's assistance, I administered the shock – 110 volts for almost half a second – and then turned my attention to Elizabeth Mason, who was scheduled for a routine EEG. I fixed the electrodes to her skull and watched as the jittery pens scribbled slow wave patterns. After a minute or so, the peaks and troughs became less pronounced. A transition was taking place. These new, low amplitude waves were similar to those associated with wakefulness; however, Elizabeth Mason was most definitely still asleep. She had started to dream, and her eyes were darting from side to side as if she were tracking the movements of a tennis ball.

It was then that I noticed, for the very first time, an interesting phenomenon. Although, on this particular occasion, it was not something that I dwelled upon. Indeed, it was only after I had seen it happen several times that I realized I was witnessing something out of the ordinary, something that merited special consideration. A single instance of the phenomenon was not, of itself, noteworthy and might be expected to arise by chance. What alerted me to its significance was the frequency with which it subsequently occurred.

The patient sleeping next to Elizabeth Mason was Celia Jones. She had started to dream too. Then I noticed that Sarah Blake was dreaming – as was Kathy Webb. In fact, apart from Marian Powell, they were all dreaming.

Stewart Osborne arrived on Saturday morning and was even more irritating than usual. He had bought a new car and insisted that I go outside and see it. I followed him through the porch and immediately understood why he was so pleased with himself. Parked on the drive was an exquisite red convertible. The hood was down and the chrome lamps and bumper seemed to shine with unnatural brilliance. 'It's a Midget,' said Osborne proudly, 'a TF fifteen hundred. The engine's bigger than earlier models and the cooling system has been thoroughly revamped. You just have to touch the accelerator and you're away.' He stroked and patted the bonnet as though he were grooming a thoroughbred mare. 'Take a look at the radiator grille. Stand by the side and crouch down a bit – notice how it slopes.' In order to ensure my full appreciation, he sliced a diagonal through the air with his open hand.

I must confess, I felt exceedingly jealous. It would be many years before I could afford anything quite so exciting. Where did he get the money to buy a car like that? In the end, I came to the conclusion that Osborne must be a man of independent means. A junior psychiatrist's salary did not stretch to sports cars.

'Very impressive,' I mumbled, 'very impressive indeed.'

Osborne winked at me and responded, 'No offence, old boy, but it wasn't you I was hoping to impress.' Nodding towards the building he added, 'Who's on this weekend?' He bent down to look at his reflection in one of the wing mirrors, repositioned some loose strands of hair, and brushed his moustache – two quick movements – with his fingertip. 'Nurse Gray? Nurse Turner?'

'I think Nurse Turner is away.'

'Really? Where's she gone?'

'I believe she has a mother in London.'

Osborne made a scoffing noise and brayed, 'A boyfriend, more like!'

'Possibly. I really don't know.'

'Aren't you interested?'

'I beg your pardon?'

'Aren't you curious?'

'Not really.'

Osborne looked at me with an exaggerated expression of disbelief. 'I'm afraid you'll have to do better than that, Richardson.'

I shook my head and said wearily, 'If you're quite finished checking your lipstick, perhaps we could get on with things?'

Osborne laughed. 'Very droll, Richardson! There's hope for you yet! So, what are you going to get up to this weekend? Made any plans?'

'Actually, I'm going to undertake an assessment: a local woman called Hilda Wright.' Maitland had left me some paperwork after Rosenberg's visit.

'I thought you had weekends off,' said Osborne, adjusting his cravat.

'Yes,' I replied, 'so did I.'

By mid-morning I was cycling to Dunwich, a tiny coastal village situated a mile or so north of the heath. On the way, I passed the ruins of an old abbey and stopped to investigate. There wasn't much left of the original edifice and what had survived looked functional. I guessed that I was viewing what might have once been a refectory. The roof and upper floor had fallen in, but the high walls still remained. I stepped though an arched opening and noticed some horses grazing at the far edge of the field. It was a romantic location: the land was elevated and a short walk brought the sea into view. I might have stayed there longer, had it not been for the punishing wind.

When I arrived in the village, I couldn't find Hilda Wright's cottage and I had to ask for directions at an inn. The landlord was surly and evidently suspicious of my motives. It wasn't until I declared that I was a doctor and held up my black bag for him to see that his manner changed and he spoke more freely. To make amends, perhaps, for his earlier recalcitrance, he obligingly sketched a map on a scrap of paper and marked my destination with a cross.

The cycling had made me thirsty and although, strictly speaking, I was at work, I found myself ordering a pint of bitter. It was a mellow brew that gave off a comforting, malty aroma. After a few minutes, spent in a state of meditative vacancy, my attention began to wander, and I noticed a sequence of sepia photographs hanging on the wall. They showed the gradual destruction of a church through coastal erosion. In the first photograph, the building was perched proudly on the edge of a cliff, but as the series progressed, and the cliff crumbled away, the knave was shortened – window by window – until eventually only the tower was left standing. The final photograph showed only a finger of stone, pointing up into a forbidding sky. I rose from my seat in order to inspect the images more closely.

Noticing my interest, the landlord explained that in

medieval times Dunwich had been a thriving seaport and one of the largest towns in England. The coastline had gradually receded until its harbour, warehouses, merchant palaces and market place were all lost to the sea. It seemed inconceivable to me that so great a catastrophe – a catastrophe of almost biblical proportion – should have befallen the people of Dunwich. The landlord assured me that everything he had said was true. He then told me that the bells of the submerged churches (of which there were once many) could still be heard in the dead of night. At which point I drained my glass, thanked him for his assistance, and made a speedy exit. I was not in the mood for old wives' tales.

With the aid of the landlord's map, it was relatively easy to find Hilda Wright's address. The door was opened by Mrs Baines, the patient's sister, who escorted me up a narrow staircase and into a bedroom with a low, beamed ceiling.

'Hilda,' said Mrs Baines, addressing a painfully thin woman whose head was supported by a pile of pillows. 'This is Dr Richardson. He's come to examine you.' Mrs Baines turned to me and said, 'I still talk to her. Even though she never answers.'

'Of course,' I said. 'I am sure the sound of your voice is a great comfort to her.'

'We were very close, you know,' Mrs Baines continued. 'Well, we still are – although it's different now, as you can imagine.' I nodded sympathetically. 'It's terrible what's happened. I hope you can do something to help her.'

Like many catatonic schizophrenics, Hilda Wright refused to eat, which meant that she had to be fed artificially. I asked Mrs Baines to demonstrate how she did this. Subsequently, she removed all the pillows and made sure that her sister was lying flat on the mattress. With great care, she inserted a rubber tube into Hilda's nose and kept pushing, until she was sure that it had passed all the way down the gullet and had reached the stomach. Then she poured a jug of gummy liquid into a funnel attached to the exposed end of the tube.

'What do you give her?' I asked.

Mrs Baines looked up, her brow still furrowed with concentration. 'Powdered vitamins, Horlicks, three eggs and two and a half pints of milk. Nurse Pirie told me how to make it up.'

When I examined Hilda Wright, I discovered that she was not in very good health. Indeed, she had symptoms of what appeared to be tuberculous peritonitis. Even so, I was confident that we could manage her condition at Wyldehope and told Mrs Baines that I would be recommending her admission.

'What are her chances, doctor?' asked Mrs Baines. 'Could she get better?'

'Catatonic schizophrenia is a very serious condition,' I replied. 'However, Dr Maitland has devoted his life to the development of revolutionary new treatments. Patients previously considered incurable have recovered in his care. I cannot make any promises, Mrs Baines. Psychiatry is an inexact science. But I can assure you that, at Wyldehope, Hilda will receive the very best that medicine has to offer.' It was difficult to read her expression, which seemed to blend fear with gratitude. I didn't want to alarm her by mentioning the peritonitis, but at the same time I thought it wise to give her some indication that her sister's physical health was failing. 'Mrs Baines, Hilda is very weak. She's running a slight fever and there is some abdominal swelling. If her transfer to Wyldehope is delayed, then I might have to come back again, just to see how she's getting on. Would that be all right?'

Mrs Baines thanked me for my assistance and I made my way back to the hospital. I had a late lunch (brought to my rooms by the kitchen girl) and wrote Hilda Wright's report, mentioning the peritonitis and recommending her prompt admission. I wasn't expecting to see Maitland again until the following Wednesday, so I left a message for him at St Thomas's, explaining what had transpired and summarizing my conclusions. The remainder of the weekend I spent writing letters, although I had to cease this activity because of another bad headache. I thought I might be developing a cold, but it amounted to nothing, and later I was well enough to go for a short walk on the beach.

On Monday, Jane was back at work, but Sister Jenkins chose to hover around the nurses' station and we didn't get a chance to speak. Then, just before lunchtime, Maitland made a surprise appearance. He gave me no explanation for his sudden arrival and I had to spend most of the day acting as his personal secretary. Eventually we went down to the men's ward where Jane was still on duty. Almost at once I was aware of a certain awkwardness. The fact that Jane and I had become intimates introduced tensions into what would have otherwise been a very ordinary situation. I found myself resenting Maitland's authority: the necessity to respond to his every word with deference, the obligation to laugh at his jokes. Jane also seemed uncomfortable and spent most of the time looking down at her feet. Obviously I was suffering from an inexcusable attack of masculine pride. I wasn't happy having a woman with whom I was now 'involved' seeing me being ordered about; however, I couldn't understand why Jane appeared so uneasy.

All I had wanted was an opportunity to be alone with her. Even a few minutes would have sufficed, but any hope of achieving this end was utterly dashed when Maitland announced that he was going to postpone his departure until the next day. Apparently a publisher's deadline was approaching and he needed to finish writing a chapter for a new book on the treatment of addictions. As far as I was aware, Maitland didn't have a bedroom at Wyldehope, which led me to suppose that he intended either to work through the night or to sleep on the Chesterfield in his office. At any rate, the following morning he was up early, looking spruce and showing no signs of fatigue. I joined him for breakfast. He was brimming over with muscular vitality and eager to share his thoughts concerning emetics and how they could be employed to create an aversion to alcohol – a conversation which, to say the very least, I found quite wearing at that delicate hour.

When we had consumed our eggs and bacon we proceeded to the sleep room and I helped him to administer ECT, after which we went directly to the pharmacy to inspect a recent delivery of drugs. He drew my attention to some trade names that I was unfamiliar with. 'New,' he said. 'From America.' Subsequently, he gave me a pharmaceutical company brochure which described how these novel compounds worked on the brain. It wasn't until twenty past five in the afternoon that he finally left.

I searched for Jane the instant he was gone and couldn't find her anywhere, but I did discover Lillian in the dining room, who told me that Jane had already finished her shift. It seemed to me that the fates were conspiring against us. Disappointed, I scribbled a note, expressing how much I was missing her. I put it in a sealed envelope and asked Lillian to give it to Jane when she next saw her (which was going to be later that evening). Afterwards I felt rather foolish and regretted my impulsivity. I did not want Jane to think me desperate.

That night, I read through the brochure Maitland had given me and went to bed early. I did not go to sleep, but instead sat up listening to a performance of Bach's *Goldberg Variations* on the Third Programme. The music was quite exquisite and was played on a harpsichord with great sensitivity. I was just about to turn the lamp off when I heard a tapping sound. It came in short bursts: groups of four separated by long pauses. I kept still and strained to hear more. There was the sea, of course, ever-present, and the wind moaning intermittently in the chimney flue, but nothing else. Then it started again. *Tap-tap-tap-tap.* Pause. *Tap-tap-tap-tap.*

I got out of bed and put on my dressing gown. The

sound seemed to be coming from within the building. Somewhat apprehensive, I entered the hallway and glanced up and down its length. Silence. Then again, the same rhythm. The quality of the sound had changed and I realized, with some relief, that someone was outside on the landing, knocking, but so ineffectually it might have been a child. I walked into the shadows, took the key off its peg, and opened the door. A meagre light spilled out of my bedroom, but it was enough to reveal the figure of a nurse. She raised a finger to her mouth, glanced down the stairs, and stepped towards me. It was Jane. I shut the door behind her and turned the key.

For a few seconds, we stood, gazing into each other's eyes, before she wrapped her arms around my neck and pulled my mouth close to hers.

'I missed you too,' she whispered.

A tentative brushing of the lips was followed by hungry, devouring kisses. Our passion was so intense it felt as if we were engaged in an act of mutual destruction.

Jane broke away and said breathlessly, 'I'm on tomorrow – early . . .'

I nodded, acknowledging the implication. She would stay with me all night and sneak downstairs in the morning.

Once again she pulled me close, her mouth already

opening. She raised her knee and the hem of her uniform travelled up her thigh, exposing the embroidered trim of a nylon stocking. I slid my hand around her waist and let it drop, its descent following the neat curve of her buttocks. Her leg twisted around my hip and our bodies became locked in a tight embrace. She tilted her head back and I rubbed my cheek against the taut skin of her neck. A sigh warmed my face as she shuddered with pleasure.

There was a loud thud, as if something, somewhere, had fallen to the floor. I felt a tremor through the soles of my feet. We stopped kissing and Jane said, 'What was that?'

This distraction could not have come at a more inopportune moment.

'I don't know,' I replied. 'It doesn't matter.'

Taking Jane's hand, I led her to the bedroom, where I immediately recognized the cause of the noise: a pile of my books had toppled over and they were scattered near the wardrobe. I quickly tidied them up and returned my attention to Jane. Her presence in my shabby quarters was as miraculous as an angelic visitation, and I was momentarily paralysed by a sense of unreality. My incredulous stare was too prolonged and Jane's expression became concerned, inquisitive. I apologized: 'I'm sorry. I can't quite believe that you're here.'

She smiled sweetly. 'Well, I am.'

Bending over, she turned off the lamp.

The curtains were drawn, but not touching, and the room was illuminated by a slither of moonlight. I discarded my dressing gown and attempted to remove my pyjamas so quickly that I almost tripped. Jane was less hurried. I got into bed and watched her draping items of clothing over the back of a chair. As she undressed she seemed to acquire more substance, her pale flesh being more reflective than her undergarments.

Jane slipped between the sheets and clambered on top of me. I gasped, surprised by the intensity of her heat. She perceived my imminence and stopped moving. 'Not yet,' she said, 'please, not yet.'

After we had made love, talk seemed unnecessary – no endearments or declarations, confessions or confidences. We simply lay there, on the rumpled sheet, limbs intertwined, exchanging languid caresses. I inhaled Jane's perfume and stroked her hair.

The murmuring sea cleansed my mind of all thoughts, and eventually I fell asleep.

I dreamt of a lighthouse, its beam passing over black waters: sluggish waves, with the consistency of crude oil. The sky was starless. With each sweep, the beam made a sound, harsh and industrial, like the noise of a blast furnace. When I woke up something of the dream seemed to persist, like an after-image, but it soon faded away. Its dissolution left me feeling inexplicably sad.

The room was still dark, apart from the moonlight entering between the parted curtains. I saw Jane pass in front of the window, her shadowy form moving across the luminous gap. She was obviously being considerate, trying very hard not to make any noise. 'Darling?' I said softly. But she did not reply. Again she blocked the moonlight. 'Darling?' I repeated, a little anxious, wondering if there was anything wrong.

It was at this point that Jane's arm encircled my chest and I realized that it was not her standing at the end of the bed, but someone else.

My body tensed and my first thought was that one of the patients had escaped from the wards. Yet I had a distinct memory of having turned the key in the landing door. Had they picked the lock? None of the patients had criminal records, and I couldn't imagine who (among the men or women) would do such a thing. I drew some consolation from the fact that, without exception, all were heavily sedated and therefore unlikely to be violent.

One anxiety was superseded by another. If the situation wasn't handled with extreme care, Jane might very easily have Sister Jenkins to answer to. I could hardly count on a patient being discreet! A number of compromising scenarios played out in my mind.

I disentangled myself from Jane's arms and legs and sat up.

'Who are you?' I asked, modulating my voice so that the patient would not be startled. The strip of moonlight reappeared, but I could not determine whether the movement had been to the left or right. 'Don't worry,' I continued, 'I'm not angry. Look, just stay where you are. I'm going to turn the lamp on.'

I found the switch. Even though the bulb was very dim, I had to squint and wait for my eyes to adapt.

There was no one in the room.

I jumped out of bed, put on my dressing gown, and searched along the hallway, in all of my rooms as well as those that were unoccupied. To my utter amazement, they were empty, and when I checked the landing door it was locked, just as I had remembered. I went to the toilet, relieved myself, and then returned to the bedroom where Jane was stirring.

'What is it?' she asked. Her hair was attractively tousled.

'Nothing,' I replied. 'Go back to sleep.'

I turned off the lamp and when I got back into bed Jane snuggled up against me and rested her head on my chest. Her hand fell casually between my legs. I tried to make sense of what had happened, and sought comfort in the reassuring intelligibility of science. There was a rational explanation: people frequently report seeing things soon after waking. The brain can continue dreaming, even though it is no longer asleep, and figments of the imagination will suddenly seem very real. This well-documented phenomenon is most likely to occur after intense excitement or emotion . . .

Yes, I told myself. *That must be it.*

I was consoled by Jane's warmth, her corporeality, the smoothness of her skin, the hard certainty of her bones. The world seemed solid once more – trustworthy, reliable. I abandoned my inner deliberations and went back to sleep.

On waking, I reached out for Jane but my hand met no resistance. She was gone. I opened my eyes and looked at the face of the alarm clock. It was six thirty and the room was suffused with the grey light of an indifferent dawn. I did not get up, but stretched my limbs and let my head fill with images of our lovemaking. Desire re-awakened and I hoped that it would not be very long before Jane came knocking on my door again. This state of lazy self-indulgence lasted until I remembered the phantom intruder. I had no cause to revise the explanation that I already favoured. Indeed, I was even minded to recall the technical term employed to describe such hallucinations. In textbooks they are commonly designated *hypnopompic*: from the Greek *hypnos*, meaning sleep, and *pompe*, meaning to send away. Still, something was troubling me, something unresolved, like a scruple or a niggling doubt.

I raised myself up and found my cigarettes. The first drag made me cough. I looked around the room and noticed the pile of books: the pile that had fallen over while Jane and I were kissing in the hallway. Now that I was at leisure to give the disturbance more detailed consideration, I couldn't help but notice (with some attendant perplexity) the pile's modest size. This was curious, because I remembered the thud produced by its collapse as having been extremely loud. The floorboards had actually vibrated. I got out of bed, crouched beside the pile and examined it closely. The brittle spines of two older volumes had cracked. It was damage that I had never noticed before. After a few seconds, I pushed the pile over. The books tumbled across the carpet and the noise they made was relatively muted.

It occurred to me that the method most likely to reproduce the effect of the previous evening would be to collect all the books together again and drop them from a great height. That – and that alone – would be sufficient to send a tremor through the floorboards.

I sat on the side of the bed, staring at the jumble of books, and when I had finished smoking my cigarette I lit another immediately after.

Maitland hadn't got back to me concerning Hilda Wright and I found myself worrying about her. In the end, I decided that I should probably return to Rose Cottage – if only to ensure my own peace of mind. I explained the situation to Sister Jenkins, who was very understanding and who suggested that I might ask Mr Hartley to give me a lift: I could then accomplish the round trip in less than an hour. Hartley was amenable to my request and I was soon standing at Hilda Wright's bedside conducting another examination. Fortunately, her condition had not deteriorated and I was able to offer some words of comfort to Mrs Baines. I knew, however, that I would be much happier once Hilda Wright was admitted onto the women's ward and being regularly monitored by nurses.

The following afternoon I received a phone call from Maitland and he came straight to the point. 'I'm afraid I've got some bad news. The patient you assessed on Saturday – Hilda Wright – she died last night. Must have been the peritonitis.'

I was shocked: 'How awful.'

'Yes, a terrible shame.'

'I went back to see her again only yesterday.'

'Did you?'

'Hartley was kind enough to give me a lift. She wasn't very strong, but all the same . . .' My sentence trailed off and I listened to the crackling of electricity in the earpiece.

'Well, you never know where you stand with tuberculous peritonitis.' Maitland's tone was benign, supportive. 'I'm sure you did everything you could.'

When Maitland arrived the next day, he invited me up to his office for tea and crumpets and asked me if I wouldn't mind going to Hilda Wright's funeral. Although I respected his wish to establish good community relations, I had only visited Hilda Wright twice, and I did not want to intrude upon the private grief of her family. Even so, I found it impossible to refuse him. 'Oh, and one other thing,' Maitland continued, 'perhaps it would be a good idea to call the coroner? I've already had a word with him. There's nothing to be concerned about, he's a sensible chap.'

I did as I was instructed and the coroner proved to be exactly as Maitland had described: a practical, efficient

and eminently reasonable man. After a short but considered discussion, he said, 'If you are satisfied that the
cause of death was tuberculous peritonitis then I will issue
a death certificate without recommending an inquest.'

'Yes,' I responded, 'I am quite satisfied.'

'Dr Richardson,' he said with polite distinction, 'you
have been most helpful.'

On the morning of the funeral, Hartley dropped me off
outside St James's Church in Dunwich and said that he
would wait for me at the inn. The service was a modest
affair, attended by only close relatives and a handful of
villagers. After the burial I sought out Mrs Baines in order
to offer her my condolences, which she accepted with
earnest gratitude. She even invited me back to Rose
Cottage for sandwiches, but I made my excuses and, after
exchanging a few mannered words with the vicar, I dis-
creetly exited the churchyard. Hartley's car was parked
close to the inn, but when I went inside I couldn't find
him anywhere. He had warned me that he might go for a
short stroll along the beach, so I was not very surprised
by his absence. The landlord recognized me and I ordered
another pint of the same bitter I had enjoyed on my first
visit.

'Been to the funeral?' he asked.

'Yes.'

'How did it go?'

'All right I suppose.'

'If you don't mind me asking . . .' He held the glass under the tap and it began to fill with dark liquid. 'What did she die of?'

'An illness called tuberculous peritonitis.'

He passed me my drink and I couldn't help but notice the peculiarity of his expression. There was something suggestive about the cast of his features.

I tilted my head to one side, tacitly requesting clarification.

'Is that so?' he responded, 'tuberculous peritonitis?' This time I could detect a definite critical undertone.

'Yes,' I said, somewhat bemused. I had not expected him to challenge the accuracy of my diagnosis! 'It is an inflammatory disease – and not *that* uncommon.'

He nodded and lit a cigarette.

'I suppose the Bainses will be leaving Rose Cottage now, off to somewhere much grander.'

'I beg your pardon?'

'Well, they won't be short of a few bob. Not now.'

The landlord looked at me, eyebrows raised, as if willing me to draw some specific conclusion. Suddenly,

I understood what he was implying. He observed my reaction with obvious satisfaction, smiled and added, 'Something to consider, eh?'

I shook my head and feigning indifference replied, 'I don't think so.' He was about to say something else, but I turned my back on him and walked away from the bar. I sat down and gazed into the fire. My frosty dismissal had been disingenuous, and by the time Mr Hartley appeared I was becoming quite concerned.

At our next meeting I discussed the matter with Maitland. 'The symptoms of arsenical poisoning are easily confounded with tuberculous peritonitis and Mrs Baines always prepared the tube feed.'

Maitland stood and walked to the window. He rested his hand on a massive, antique globe, and then set it spinning. 'My advice – for what it's worth – is to let sleeping dogs lie.'

'But shouldn't I speak to the coroner again?'

'If there's an inquiry, you might be asked some problematic questions.' There was an uncomfortable silence and I loosened my collar. I was expecting some sort of reprimand, but instead Maitland continued in a much lighter voice: 'This landlord of yours said nothing consequential. He made a few oblique insinuations, that's all. You know what people who live in villages like Dunwich

are like, how parochial they can be, how small-minded –
and how fond they are of idle gossip.'

'Yes,' I replied. 'That's very true.' I felt as though I had
exposed a flaw in my character, a fragile seam of gulli-
bility.

Maitland waved away my apology with his hand. I
felt relieved – or perhaps it would be more accurate to
say absolved. I should have known better than to accept a
dispensation granted with such casual disregard. I should
have been less easily persuaded.

That evening I went to see Michael Chapman. He was a
little agitated, but I managed to engage him in some
casual talk about chess and this seemed to calm him
down. For several minutes he spoke in a measured way
about diversionary and eliminatory sacrifices. I told
Nurse Page to look in on him and to call me if he became
restless again. 'Yes, doctor,' she replied, while emptying a
jar of pills into a silver kidney dish.

On leaving the men's ward I descended the stairs to
the sleep room. As soon as I opened the door, I was aware
of the sound of someone crying. The nurse seated behind
the desk immediately turned away from me so that she
was facing in the opposite direction. I could tell by the

fullness of her figure and the colour of her hair that it was Mary Williams. Even though she was making valiant efforts to stifle her sobs, the acoustic properties of the basement amplified each gasp and sniff. I didn't want to intrude and cause the girl embarrassment but, equally, I didn't want to appear callous or indifferent. After a momentary hesitation, I decided that it would be wrong to abandon her when she was exhibiting such obvious signs of distress. Moreover, I was disinclined to enact a shoddy pantomime, however well intentioned, of having just remembered something very important that would necessitate my prompt withdrawal.

I crossed the floor and halted in the halo of half-light emanating from the desk lamp. Mary did not acknowledge my approach. She remained very still, although her shoulders, which were broad for a woman of her height, shook intermittently.

'What's the matter?' I asked. She did not respond. 'Mary?'

I heard her swallow and she shifted on her chair. 'They won't leave me alone.' Her voice had a shrill, hysterical quality.

An atavistic instinct made me peer uneasily into the darkness. 'Who won't?'

I touched her shoulder and she turned around. Her

eyes were moist and unfocused. Indeed, she looked dazed and there was a lengthy interlude before she registered my presence: 'Dr Richardson.' Her intonation was dull; even so, a gentle ascending gradient introduced a suggestion of uncertainty.

'Mary,' I repeated. 'Who won't leave you alone?'

She took a deep breath. 'I'm sorry, Dr Richardson. I thought . . .' She stopped, quite suddenly, and her compressed expression betrayed the exercise of mental effort. 'I must have fallen asleep.' Her face went blank and she took another deep breath. 'I had a nightmare.'

'I see.'

On the desk was a time-worn volume bound in black leather. Mary saw my interest and quickly picked it up and placed it in one of the drawers. She then made a show of tidying some other objects: pens, a paperweight, a ruler. Her bungled attempt at concealment was so clumsy, so misconceived, that I found myself pitying the poor girl. The embossed gilt cross on the black leather cover, faded, but still conspicuously reflective, strongly suggested that Mary had been reading a book of prayers.

'Are you all right now?' I asked.

'Yes,' Mary replied. 'I'm sorry.'

I could sense that she wanted to ask me something and it was easy to guess what that might be. 'Don't worry,' I said, anticipating the cause of her anxiety. 'I won't tell Sister Jenkins.' Mary sighed with relief. I picked up a formulary and pretended to study the index. 'It must have been a very bad dream.' I heard Mary fidgeting before she replied. 'Yes. It was very bad.' Then she stood up with peremptory haste and marched over to the beds. Clearly, she did not wish to continue our conversation.

Marian Powell groaned and Mary was at the patient's bedside in an instant. I watched as Mary reversed Marian's pillow, then gathered the loose sheets and tucked them beneath the mattress.

Why, I asked myself, did Mary think it was necessary to bring a prayer book with her whenever she was on night duty in the sleep room? She did not know that I had glimpsed the prayer book on two previous occasions. She was a simple soul and possessed no talent for deception.

Dr Peter Bevington
Oak Lodge
Nr Biggleswade
Bedfordshire

30th April 1955

Dr Hugh Maitland
The Braxton Club
Carlton House Terrace
St James's
City of Westminster
London SW1

Dear Hugh,

Forgive me for writing to you at the club regarding
a professional matter, but it feels more appropriate
given the circumstances. A tricky situation has arisen
and I think you might be able to help. I won't supply
you with all the details now; however, if after reading
this letter, you can see a way forward, then do give
me a call. Elspeth and I will be going to Norfolk for a

few weeks with Moira and Geoffrey, but I'll be back in harness on Monday the 16th of May.

We have a patient at Oak Lodge known as Celia Jones. The reason why I say 'known as' will become apparent shortly. She is a lady, probably in her mid-fifties, who has been in a stuporous state for over a decade. Since my appointment last September, she hasn't uttered a single word. She rarely moves and occasionally demonstrates waxy rigidity.

Nevertheless, she is able to eat, particularly so when her appetite has been stimulated with insulin (5 soluble units). Abdominal scarring suggests that she once had a Caesarian section. I've tried pretty much everything with this woman. Benzedrine, Drinamyl, 3 courses of ECT, even metrazol, without any effect.

Now, here's the rub: it turns out that a patient called Celia Jones was killed when St Dunstan's Asylum in Stepney was destroyed by the Luftwaffe back in January 1941. I worked there once and have fond memories of the Superintendent, a Dr Wilson, who sported bushy side-whiskers and dressed like an eminent Victorian. All of the staff were killed, including dear old Wilson. As you can imagine, things must have been pretty chaotic that night, and what with survivors being shunted here, there and everywhere, I suppose it isn't surprising that errors were made. All the documentation must have been lost in the fire. Anyway, I have very good reason to believe that the patient I have hitherto called Celia Jones is in fact an unknown person, who was mistaken for the real Celia Jones after the tragedy. If her stuporous state persists, then her true identity will remain a complete mystery – and I can't abide mysteries: this one more so than others, because even a negligible improvement in her condition would probably result in her being able to tell us who she really is. Any suggestions?

I hope that you and Daphne are both well. Elspeth sends her love.

Kind regards

Peter

Dr Peter Bevington
Director of Services

PS I heard you on the wireless last night. I'm so glad you showed that couch merchant up to be such a

fraud. You could hear the panic in his voice.
Personifications in the unconscious! What clap-trap!
I thought Freudians were bad enough but these
Jungians really take the biscuit!

7

The heath seemed to darken earlier with each passing day. Flocks of birds rose up from the grazing marsh, creating living whirlpools that unravelled in a southerly direction, the trailblazers peeling off shadowy pennants of concentrated activity. The softly undulating horizon, hazy and indistinct, was tinged with russet and magenta, like pigment diffusing through the saturated paper of a watercolour.

As the new season advanced, Jane and I continued to meet in secret. She would creep up to my rooms at least twice a week, and on one occasion we dared to spend an entire Sunday together.

We were lying in bed, enjoying the lazy, self-satisfied torpor of exhausted lovers, and talking in short, unconnected bursts, when I mentioned the patients in the sleep room and how I wanted to know more about their histories. Jane rolled over on to her front and looked at me with her exquisite green eyes: some mascara had fallen onto one of her cheeks and she was looking irresistibly sluttish.

'Interesting,' she said, maintaining her steady gaze.

'What is?'

'That you should be so curious about the lives of others.'

'I'm a psychiatrist,' I laughed.

'Yes, but . . .' She reached out for her packet of cigarettes. After lighting one she placed the filtered tip between my parted lips. 'You know a lot about me, but I don't know anything about you.'

'Well, there's not a lot to tell.'

'You never mention your parents, your family.'

'Girlfriends?' I cut in, playfully.

She snatched the cigarette out of my mouth, inhaled deeply and blew smoke in my face. 'Not necessarily.'

'All right, what do you want to hear?'

'The usual things – the things that people talk about when they're getting to know each other.'

'I think we're pretty well acquainted already,' I teased, squeezing her buttocks. 'Don't you?'

She looked upwards and assumed an expression of mock exasperation. 'You know exactly what I mean!'

'And I thought I was doing you a favour.'

'A favour?'

'Sparing you the detail. It's pretty boring stuff.'

'I don't care if it's boring.'

'You're just saying that.'

'No, I'm not.'

I sighed. 'Very well then. If you insist. But when I'm done, don't say I didn't warn you.' She offered me the cigarette again and I took a few more drags. After collecting my thoughts, I said, 'To begin at the beginning.' I was quoting the first line of a play that I had listened to on the wireless. For some reason it had become lodged in my memory. I repeated it again, 'To begin at the beginning.' Jane knocked my ribs, as she might a gramophone player when the record on the turntable gets stuck. 'I don't remember a great deal about growing up, but I think I was a reasonably happy child. We lived in Canterbury, where my father was a GP. He was well-liked by his patients but he could be rather reserved at home: not cold exactly, but not terribly demonstrative either. I don't think he was unusual in this respect. It's just the way men of his generation are. What else can I say about him? He's a decent man, dependable, hardworking – a safe pair of hands. My mother is a very different kind of person. Lively, capricious, a little on the nervy side perhaps, with a dry sense of humour that often escapes my father's notice: they're an unlikely match really. She left school when she was only fourteen. Even so, she's a great reader and passionate about poetry. She used to make me rote-learn screeds of

Keats and Coleridge: "In Xanadu did Kubla Khan, A stately pleasure-dome decree . . ." and so on. I haven't forgotten a word. When the war ended my mother and father moved to Bournemouth. My father still practises.'

'Do you see them very often?'

'Not as much as I should.'

'Don't you get on?'

'They're perfectly pleasant. It's just . . .'

'What?'

'There's so little time.'

'Would I like your mother?'

'Yes. Actually she's quite amusing. Some would say eccentric, and getting more so as she gets older.'

I talked about school, Cambridge, national service and Edinburgh. As I spoke, I became acutely aware of the fact that my rather studious life was, by and large, embarrassingly void of significant incident, and it occurred to me that I was probably more like my earnest, reliable father than I cared to acknowledge. I omitted mention of any girlfriends and Jane didn't press me to make any revelations – which was refreshing. My former lovers were positively obsessed with the subject. Even Sheila had displayed some curiosity, albeit of an oddly detached variety.

When I had finished, I folded my arms and said, 'There. Are you satisfied now?'

Jane leaned forward and kissed me.

Then after a lengthy pause she said, 'You don't find it easy talking about yourself, do you?'

She was more perceptive than I had given her credit for.

'Is it such a bad thing,' I smiled, somewhat insincerely, 'to be interested in other people – other lives – rather than your own?'

'No,' she said, 'I suppose not.'

Before she could ask me any more questions, I returned her kiss, and continued kissing her until our mutual excitement made further conversation impossible.

When night fell I made sure that nobody was on the stairs, or in the vestibule, and signalled for Jane to follow. She pecked me on the cheek and tiptoed to the front door. A moment later, she was gone.

Although Jane continued to occupy my thoughts for much of the time, I was still troubled by what had happened when we had spent our first night together. The shadowy figure that I had observed blocking the moonlight could be reasoned away with the help of a medical dictionary, but the sound of twelve volumes hitting the floor with great force (which both of us had heard) and the circumstantial evidence of the broken spines could not be so easily dismissed. There seemed to be no natural explanation.

I knew all about poltergeists or 'noisy spirits'. Their defining feature was the power to move physical objects. I had read about them with naive relish and uncritical enthusiasm as a boy; however, I had never expected in my wildest imaginings to experience such phenomena myself.

As I tentatively opened my mind to possibilities beyond the remit of science, I found myself recalling a number of perplexing incidents that I had hitherto ignored, or more accurately failed to give proper consideration: the sigh that I had heard in the bathroom, the biro that had dropped on the landing, Mary Williams's odd behaviour, and the two wedding rings – one having vanished, the other having suddenly appeared. I was even prepared to reconsider Michael Chapman's claim that his bed moved.

The idea of the dead returning to annoy the living by performing small acts of mischief had always struck me as being faintly absurd. Even so, I was obliged to reserve judgement because, no matter how hard I tried, I could not think of a plausible alternative that would account equally well for all of the facts. To my surprise, arriving at this conclusion was accompanied by a sense of relief. It was as though I had been inadvertently (or dare I say unconsciously) resisting a supernatural explanation, and that maintaining this attitude had been effortful. At the same time, I was not willing to abandon logic altogether. I had generated a hypothesis and now, by rights, it should be tested. Undertaking some sort of experiment was, of course, out of the question, but I could still gather information and look for meaningful connections.

I remembered how Maitland had acted like a tour guide when the two Americans had visited Wyldehope: how he had drawn Rosenberg and Stratton's attention to the carved banisters on the main staircase, and pointed out the suit of armour from the 'fifteenth century'. And back in London, during my interview at the Braxton Club, Maitland had spoken knowledgeably about the building's recent past. Consequently, the next time I saw him I pretended to be interested in the carvings, and asked him how he had come to discover that they were the work of Robert Greenford. My intention had been to steer the conversation towards the topic of Wyldehope's history, so that any further questions concerning the hospital's previous occupants would not appear conspicuous. As it turned out, such artful premeditation was completely unnecessary.

'I learned about Greenford from a book,' said Maitland.

'About the Pre-Raphaelites?'

'No. They don't appeal to me. I find their choice of subjects rather whimsical, don't you? Knights, angels, fairies!'

He seemed to sink into a state of contemptuous abstraction and I had to remind him of my initial question: 'This book . . . the one that mentioned Greenford. What was it about?'

'Wyldehope,' he replied. 'I found it stuffed behind a row of cricketing almanacs in the men's recreation room.'

'Who wrote it?'

'A chap who was convalescing here during the Great War, a historian by profession. I suppose he must have been bored stiff and in need of diversion. You can borrow it if you wish. But it's very dry.'

Later that day, Maitland handed me a slim volume bound in faded yellow cloth. The title was barely legible: *Wyldehope Hall: A Victorian Hunting Lodge.* Below this was the author's name, Hubert Spence. It was published by George G. Harrap & Company, Kingsway, London.

A brief introduction explained the author's circumstances and this was followed by a description of the building and its principal features. There was a section on 'House Contents' which, at the time of writing, included canvases by Rossetti and Burne-Jones, a rare Chinese cabinet and a seventeenth-century Swiss clock mounted

in a case of gilded bronze, but the majority of the text concerned Sir Gerald Gathercole, the man who had built
Wyldehope, and his architect, Robert Lyle. The story of
the Gathercole family, from humble beginnings in the
seventeenth century to ennoblement by the time of the
Great War, was detailed in a torturously dull 'Appendix';
however, I read nothing that would account for the persistent return of restless or vengeful spirits. There were no
murders, suspicious deaths, broken promises or dubious
ancestors known to have dabbled in the dark arts. Only a
tiresome chronicle of merchant-class industry, commercial
success, philanthropy, and eventual admission into the
upper echelons of society. It was very disappointing.

Even so, I was not discouraged from pursuing other
lines of enquiry.

The following Friday, Jane came up to my rooms
again. We were lying in bed, gossiping about the other
nurses, when I made some comments concerning Mary
Williams. 'Have you noticed how jittery she is? How
she's always on edge?' I then went on to describe how
Mary had wheeled around on the sleep-room staircase,
acting as if someone had pulled her hair. I was hoping
that this account of the incident would encourage Jane to
make some relevant disclosures of her own, but all she
said was, 'You are kind, worrying about Mary. Yes, she is

a bit nervous. I'll try to talk to her more, be more friendly, and look out for her when Sister Jenkins is on the war-path.'

'Did you know,' I tried again, 'that she brings a prayer book with her when she's doing night shifts in the sleep room?'

'No,' Jane said, 'I didn't.' She sounded a little puzzled. 'I wonder why?'

'She's religious,' said Jane, in a tone of voice that carried a hint of impatience. 'Isn't it obvious?'

I was tempted to tell Jane about the evening I had found Mary crying, but this seemed too disrespectful, an unwarranted violation of the girl's privacy.

Still undeterred, I sought out Michael Chapman.

We had continued to play chess together on a regular basis, and as a result Chapman's game had improved dramatically. It was no longer necessary to let him win: he was quite capable of beating me even when I was doing my best. This I took to be a good sign, indicative of increased powers of concentration and the restoration of ordered thought. He was still a very sick man, but I was now inclined to take what he said more seriously.

As usual, the recreation room was empty. Someone was snoring loudly on the ward.

Chapman eyed the board, twitched a few times, and

said, 'To establish a rook on the seventh rank is a great advantage; to get two rooks on that rank is deadly.' He rubbed his hands together as if the friction he produced would hasten my demise. His rooks had been sweeping up and down, annihilating my pawns and threatening checkmate.

'Yes,' I said. 'My prospects are not good.'

Chapman chuckled. 'Dr Richardson, they are non-existent. Will you concede defeat now?'

'No, not just yet.' Chapman shook his head. His expression combined impatience with mirth. I attempted to get my king out of danger and Chapman removed another pawn. It took him only two more moves to achieve a decisive victory.

'Well done, Michael,' I said, shaking his hand. 'An impressive performance.'

He dismissed my congratulatory remarks and toyed with the cord of his dressing gown. A low sun revealed every detail of his deeply creviced face. I offered him a cigarette, which he accepted, and we smoked for a while in companionable silence.

Eventually, I cleared my throat and said, 'Michael?' He turned to look at me. 'Some time ago you asked me why it was that the nurses moved your bed at night.'

'Yes,' he replied, extending the syllable warily.

'I told you that you must have been dreaming. Does it still happen?'

His head jerked to one side before it returned to its original position. 'Yes.'

'Tell me about it. Tell me what happens.'

'I wake up . . . it's dark . . . and the bed is moving.'

'How?'

'Backwards and forwards.'

'If it's dark, how do you know that it's a nurse?'

He rested a finger on his lower lip: 'Who else would come into my room and move my bed?'

'Have you ever thought it might be . . .' I hesitated before saying, 'Someone else?'

'Another patient?'

'No. Not exactly.'

'Then who?' Chapman's brow creased and I realized I might be confusing him. The conversation was proving more difficult than I had expected.

'I'm sorry,' I apologized. 'I just wanted to . . .' Again I hesitated before concluding, 'I just wanted to make sure that you were getting enough sleep. That's all. I'll have a word with the nurses.'

Chapman seemed to shrink. A tic appeared on his cheek and he glanced back over his shoulder. I had clearly upset him and I felt ashamed of myself for putting my own needs before those of my patient.

That evening, seated in my study, I was still feeling guilty about Chapman. Moreover, I began to doubt the wisdom of having embarked upon an ad-hoc psychical investigation. I had learned nothing new, and if I continued asking odd questions, there was a risk that I might end up looking like a fool. It is ironic – given what happened next – that by the time I went to bed I had convinced myself that I should forget about poltergeists, put more effort into my relationship with Jane, begin a new research project, and get on with my job.

Sleep came gently, lapping at the fringes of consciousness, taking away my thoughts until all that remained was the pleasing absence of mind that precedes extinction.

I awoke with a start. There was absolute silence, but I was sure that there had been a sound: a sound loud enough to rouse me. A reverberation of some kind seemed to persist in the air. I switched on the lamp and sat still for a moment, listening. Timbers creaked and I may have heard the scuttling of tiny clawed feet behind the skirting. I got out of bed and stood in the hallway. A loose door handle opposite began to rattle and I reached out to touch it. When my fingers made contact with the brass, it stopped – but when I let go again the vibration continued. There was nothing remarkable about this. The effect was clearly attributable to currents of air; however, I then noticed that the door of my study was ajar – and this was less easily explained. I had shut it before going to bed. Indeed, I could remember pushing the divide between the sunken panels and the satisfying 'click' of the spring mechanism engaging. Wyldehope was a draughty old building, but I had never known a shut door to be blown open. My progress down the hallway seemed to take far too long, as if I had overestimated the length of my stride. As I positioned myself just outside the study, the darkness within did not give up any of its secrets.

'Hello?' I said softly. 'Hello. Is there anybody there?'

I stepped over the threshold and turned the light on. My lower jaw dropped, and I stood there, gaping like an idiot. It was as if the room had been recently occupied by drunken revellers. The chair by the bureau had toppled over and the floor was covered with what at first sight appeared to be confetti. I knelt down, scooped up a handful, and immediately realized it wasn't confetti at all, but ordinary writing paper that had been torn into tiny squares. Fragments of my handwriting were clearly visible. I was looking at the fair copy of my final Edinburgh experiment.

'Christ!' I said out aloud. 'Jesus Christ!'

I tipped my hand and watched the shreds fall to the carpet. Once again, I heard movement in the skirting.

My nostrils flared and I identified a pungent odour that, under normal circumstances, would have captured my attention earlier. I could smell burning. After rising to my feet I began searching for its cause. The cigarettes in the ashtray had been extinguished hours ago. I buried a fingertip in the white-grey flakes of tobacco and after stirring them felt no warmth. In the wastebin, I found two used matches with blackened tips, but none of the discarded balls of paper were scorched or discoloured.

I wanted answers. And it occurred to me – in a rare, jolting moment of insight – that there was someone who could very probably supply them. I needed to find my predecessor. I needed to find Palmer.

8

The Royal Medico-Psychological Association was most helpful. I discovered that Dr Benjamin Palmer, formerly based at Wyldehope Hall, was now part of a small team attached to the maternity services at the Whittington Hospital, not very far from where I used to live in Kentish Town. I wrote to him, requesting a meeting, and he responded, saying that – in principle – he was agreeable, but that he would appreciate a little more clarification concerning my purpose. The tone of his reply was civil and solicitous: 'I wouldn't want you to come all the way down to London for nothing.' It was impossible to test someone's willingness to talk about bizarre experiences in a letter. I needed Palmer sitting right in front of me, close enough to see his eyes and gauge his reactions. Consequently, I was obliged to fabricate a pretext.

Maitland had been critical of Palmer and I suspected that their relationship must have been quite difficult towards the end. With this in mind, I wrote to Palmer a second time, suggesting that I was not particularly happy at Wyldehope and quite worried about my prospects. I was certain that Palmer, being a junior doctor, would interpret this as meaning that I was thinking about resigning and anxious to know what sort of reference I could expect from Maitland.

The ruse worked. Palmer wrote back, assuring me of his discretion, and as luck would have it we were both free the following Saturday. I cycled to Darsham, caught the train to Liverpool Street, and then travelled by underground to Archway. We had arranged to meet in a pub on Highgate Hill.

I arrived early, bought myself a pint of Guinness, and sat next to a window. There were only two other patrons, red-faced regulars with swollen features, who occasionally consulted the horse-racing pages of a newspaper and conferred in hushed voices. A man wearing an apron entered and sold the pair some jellied eels. When the transaction was completed, the vendor approached my table, but I communicated my lack of interest with a shake of the head. He raised a densely tattooed arm, saluted the barman and made his exit, whistling a popular ballad that – at that time – was being played incessantly on the wireless.

When Palmer appeared, we recognized each other immediately.

'Richardson?'

'Palmer.' I extended my hand. 'Thank you so much for coming.'

'My pleasure. Can I get you anything?'

I indicated my stout: 'I'm fine, thanks.'

He nodded and went off to the bar.

When he returned, he draped his coat over the back of his chair and placed a dimpled glass tankard, filled with pale ale, on a cardboard beer mat. We made some small talk about the weather and the east coast trains, and while we were chatting Palmer produced a pipe. He tamped a plug of tobacco into the bowl and struck a match. I was reminded of Lillian's cruel impression of Palmer smoking, and had to make efforts to conceal a smile.

He was just the man I had expected him to be: early thirties, somewhat gaunt, bearded. His suit did not fit him very well, his hair was a shade too long, and his maroon cardigan clashed with a blue shirt and green tie. These sartorial defects were compounded by oversized spectacles that created an impression of owlish eccentricity.

Our conversation progressed from trivia to professional matters and I asked him about his new position.

'I was very fortunate,' he replied. 'I learned of the vacancy as soon as I got back to London. It's psychosomatic medicine, really. I see mothers suffering from post-natal depression and, when the need arises, other family members: husbands and occasionally older children.' He spoke with enthusiasm, but there was something clerical about his delivery, a particular cadence that recalled sermons and church halls.

'There wasn't any trouble then?' I ventured.

'With my reference? No.' Palmer took a temperate sip of his ale. 'Maitland's a difficult customer, but he's not vindictive. I know for a fact that he thought I'd let him down – he as good as told me so – and in a way I suppose that's true. I *did* let him down.'

'Everyone has the right to resign.'

Palmer winced. 'The situation was complicated. You see, when I was at St Thomas's . . .' He looked away for a moment and mumbled, 'How can I put this?' Then looking back again: 'Maitland took what you might call a fatherly interest in me. I haven't a clue why. I'm quite conscientious, I suppose, but that's all – I didn't do anything to make myself stand out. The job at Wyldehope came up and it was as good as handed to me on a plate. So, as you can imagine, when I resigned Maitland was none too pleased. I must have appeared very ungrateful.'

'How did he respond, when you told him you wanted to leave?'

Palmer shivered a little at the recollection. 'He was

pretty fearsome. And when I left his office I was having serious doubts about whether I'd done the right thing, let me tell you.'

'What did he say?'

'It wasn't so much what he said, but how he said it.' I was about to ask another question but Palmer stopped me with a gesture. 'Richardson. I wouldn't get too het up over all this. What you need to remember about Maitland is that he's always got bigger fish to fry. Once you're off his radar he simply forgets you. He doesn't have time for vendettas. If there *was* anything prejudicial in my reference, it wasn't enough to stop me from getting another job.'

Palmer bit the stem of his pipe and rocked his head sagely.

Two more customers arrived, labourers in flat caps, who perched themselves on high stools and greeted the barman with strong Welsh accents.

It seemed to me that Palmer and I were getting along well enough, so I decided to ask him a more direct question.

'Why *did* you resign?'

Palmer frowned. 'I felt the same as you do now. I wasn't happy. Although, thinking about it, I should never have gone to Wyldehope in the first place.'

'Why?'

'Bad timing. Six months – or maybe a year later – and I think I might have found the place less irksome. I thought it was what I wanted – to be given responsibilities, to immerse myself in work, without any distractions – but I was wrong.' He produced a crooked, pained smile. 'And I didn't get on with the nurses.' He was weighing up in his mind whether to proceed. The mental scales tipped in favour of disclosure and he added, 'They used to make fun of me – and laugh behind my back. I mean, really! How bloody childish!' I could see that he regretted this final admission as soon as the words were out of his mouth. When he spoke again he sounded embarrassed, beaten: 'You must think me a dolt. To let that sort of thing get to me.'

'No,' I said sympathetically. 'Not at all. Situations of that kind can be very tricky. If you object, you're accused of not being able to take a joke.'

'But if you say nothing . . .'

'They'll continue to take advantage of your forbearance.'

'Quite,' Palmer agreed.

I lit a cigarette and endeavoured to establish more common ground: 'I had similar good intentions.' Palmer looked at me quizzically. 'I imagined myself working, reading, writing. As you say – no distractions. But I've found it very hard. I miss the city more than I expected. My friends, Soho. And as for the accommodation . . .'

'Second floor?'

'Yes.' Simulating perplexity, I continued, 'The rooms are spacious enough. But I find the atmosphere rather . . .' I hesitated on purpose and watched Palmer's expression intensify. He was impatient for me to complete the sentence. 'Unsettling.' Palmer gave me a hard, penetrating look, as if he were trying to read my thoughts. I went on: 'I don't feel comfortable there.'

For a fleeting moment it appeared that he was about to say something relevant to my real concerns; however, his courage failed him at the last instant and instead he said, 'Then there's the sleep room, of course.' Returning the conversation to his own reasons for leaving Wyldehope, he continued, 'Between you and me, I'm not sure that narcosis is anywhere near as effective as Maitland says.' Palmer leaned across the table and whispered, 'Patients have died, you know.'

'Not at Wyldehope?'

My companion shook his head. 'No. Not at Wyldehope. Even so, the possibility always worried me.'

'Did Maitland ever let you read their histories – the sleep room patients'?'

'I was instructed to give them ECT and keep an eye on their measures. We never discussed particular cases.'

'Odd – don't you think?'

Palmer fussed with his pipe. 'I gave up trying to fathom Maitland a long time ago.'

An hour had passed and I hadn't got anywhere. Allusive language and knowing glances had not tempted Palmer to take me into his confidence. Yet I was absolutely certain that he was holding something back. I decided that I would have to abandon innuendo and speak more plainly.

'There's a trainee nurse called Mary Williams. She clearly hates working in the sleep room.'

'I'm not surprised. Only the nightingales seem inured to the smell. It can be quite dreadful.'

'No – it's nothing to do with the smell. She's frightened.'

'Frightened?'

'Yes. She acts as if she's seen something.'

'Whatever do you mean?'

'You know. Something supernatural – a ghost.'

A pulse appeared on Palmer's temple.

'Old houses . . .' he said, non-committally. Then, after a long pause, he said it again, 'Old houses.' But it was obvious that he was struggling to conceal a more violent reaction. His pipe had gone out, and when he tried to light it again I thought I detected a slight tremor. He stood up and said, 'Let me get you another stout,' and before I could decline he turned away and marched briskly to the bar.

When he returned, he was restless and our conversation flowed less easily. There were a few lengthy pauses during which he simply stared into his glass, and he might have stayed like that indefinitely had I not reminded him of my presence with a tactful cough. Eventually, he shifted in his seat and said something entirely unconnected with our ongoing talk. 'Look, Richardson. I don't suppose you've come across a ring by any chance?' Palmer saw me start. 'You have?'

'Yes,' I replied.

I watched him grasp the edge of the table. There were only two jackets in my wardrobe, and the jacket I happened to be wearing was the same one that I had worn when I had spoken to Sister Jenkins about my find. Although I had said to her that I intended to sell the ring and donate the proceeds to the hospital, I hadn't touched it since that day. I reached into my pocket and handed the shining object to Palmer.

'Where did you find this?' he asked.

'In the bedroom.'

'But where?'

'On the carpet.'

He was staring at the ring as if he had fallen into a trance.

'Palmer, who does it belong to?'

He hesitated before replying: 'My wife.'

'I didn't know you were married, Palmer?'

'She died last year.'

'Oh. I'm so sorry.'

He looked up and said, 'Leukaemia.' It was said with such tender melancholy he might have been telling me her name. 'That's why Wyldehope wasn't such a good idea. I wasn't ready.' He continued staring at the ring, fascinated. 'Extraordinary. I never thought I'd see this again. Before they closed the casket, I removed the ring from her finger. I wanted something that had been close to her – to hang on to.'

'Palmer,' I said gently. 'How did you come to lose an item of such enormous sentimental value?'

'I don't know. I put it down and . . .' His voice carried a trace of irritation. 'Look, I just lost it – all right?'

'No. You didn't just lose it, Palmer. It disappeared. That's what really happened.' His head changed position sharply and the lenses of his spectacles caught the light. I couldn't see his eyes, but I detected a certain hardening of his attitude – a suggestion of 'squaring up'. I continued. 'And I suspect other things happened too – strange things that were difficult to explain.'

'Listen, Richardson,' Palmer replied. 'If you're not happy at Wyldehope then leave. I've done what I can to help you – and there really is nothing more to say.' He stood up abruptly and offered me his hand. 'Thank you for the ring.'

'But Palmer—'

'Good luck with everything.' He picked up his coat and took a few steps towards the door. Then he stopped and turned to face me. His expression had softened again. 'Remember what you do for a living, Richardson. Be careful what you say – and to whom you say it. You don't want to find yourself hauled up in front of an RMPA disciplinary committee, being assessed with regard to your fitness to practise.'

I watched Palmer cross the floor and crash through the doors. One of them remained open for a few moments, and I saw a line of buses and lorries struggling up the hill. Diesel engines roared and a blast of cold air carried exhaust fumes and a few autumn leaves into the pub. The barman was looking at me, and I wondered if I had inadvertently attracted attention by raising my voice. I ignored his inquisitive gaze and lit another cigarette.

Palmer's refusal to speak freely about what he had seen, or heard, was extremely frustrating, and at first I was annoyed with him, irritated by his caution. His concerns about professional embarrassment were so exaggerated that they were almost paranoid! But as I sat there, smoking and thinking, I could not sustain my anger. Palmer didn't know me – he had no idea what sort of person I might be – and I had not demonstrated much integrity by inventing a pretext for our meeting. I am sure that Palmer must have realized something was amiss quite early on. And it was impossible not to pity the man. The loss of his wife at such a young age must have been devastating. I pictured Palmer at Wyldehope, sitting at my bureau, lonely, miserable, and – on occasion – scared. Taking his little white tablets to steady his nerves. No wonder he resigned and no wonder he didn't want to talk about his experiences.

While on the train, returning to Suffolk, the movement of the carriage rocked me to sleep and I had a disturbing dream. I had entered my study, and there standing directly in front of me was a young woman in a gauzy nightdress. An endless shower of confetti fell around her. 'What have you done with my wedding ring?' she demanded.

'I gave it to your husband,' I replied.

'You had no right to do that!' she howled. Then she picked up a pile of my books and threw them to the floor. The impact was so loud that I awoke.

'Just a dream,' I said to myself. Then, as if I was not quite convinced, I repeated the words more firmly. 'Just a dream.'

THE HAWTHORNE TRUST
Est'd 1928

Dr Margery Garrett
Hawthorne House
Tulip Crescent
East Dulwich
London SE22

11th February 1955

Dr Hugh Maitland
The Institute of Psychiatry
Maudsley Hospital
Denmark Hill
London SE5

Dear Dr Maitland,

It was a great pleasure to meet you and Dr Palmer last week and your talk was much appreciated. Thank you once again for interrupting your doubtless busy

schedule to keep us abreast of the latest developments
in somatic psychiatry. We live in exciting times and
the new treatments you discussed will bring hope to
many young people who have been, until very
recently, poorly served by our profession. I couldn't
agree with you more: psychiatry is a branch of
medicine, not philosophy. If only there were more
practitioners willing to acknowledge this simple truth,
then the mental health of our nation would be greatly
improved. I would also like to thank you for agreeing
to accept direct referrals. The trustees were overjoyed
when I gave them the news. We simply do not have
the facilities at Hawthorne House to undertake the
treatments you recommend. The London County
Council medical advisory committee refused to give
us permission to purchase a shock machine on the
grounds that ECT is yet to be proved effective for
young men and women. So, your kind offer is as
timely as it is welcome.

I have now reviewed all of our residents and would
very much like you to assess a young lady called
Marian Powell. You may recall we talked about her
very briefly before your departure.

Marian is sixteen years of age and has been living
in foster homes almost all of her life. She was born in

Hackney. Her mother worked in a munitions factory
but died when Marian was five. Her father, who was
apparently a music-hall performer, abandoned his
wife and infant daughter at the outbreak of the war.
Marian was adopted by her maternal aunt, Mrs
Mildred Hurst, and her husband, Mr Raymond Hurst,
but sadly, shortly after, both were killed in a fire.

Marian spent the next four years in Nazareth
House, Epping, which has since been closed. You may
have heard rumours concerning the scandalous
conditions that prevailed there. Children were
underfed, frequently beaten and, if the official inquiry
is to be believed, molested. A sorry state of affairs,
and one that thankfully escaped public notice. If the
iniquitous Mr Gilbert, who was as canny as he was
unprincipled, had not fallen down the stairs and
broken his neck, I fear that Nazareth House would
still be operating today. It is highly likely that Marian
was one of the many children who had to endure
Gilbert's shameful improprieties. She has never
spoken of her time at Nazareth House and if pressed,
becomes electively mute.

Marian was subsequently moved to a foster home
on the outskirts of Dartford, where she seems to have
been reasonably contented. She attended a local

school and made what is described as 'good progress'. There is a curious entry in her notes dating from this period. A teacher by the name of Mr Joshua Armstrong became convinced that Marian possessed psychic powers and had her investigated by members of the Society for Psychical Research. I have asked Marian what the test procedure involved and, although she has only the dimmest memory of what transpired, she was able to remember being encouraged by two 'gentlemen' to influence the fall of a die. There is no record of whether the experiment was successful or not. I only mention this, because the test date may give us some indication as to when Marian's illness began. The credulous Armstrong very probably mistook her auditory hallucinations for some kind of 'spirit communication'. (It never ceases to amaze me how many seemingly educated individuals still believe in such arrant nonsense.)

Marian was not officially diagnosed as suffering from childhood schizophrenia until a full year later, in 1951, when she was thirteen years of age. Her symptoms were mainly of the leaden, lumpish variety: lack of motivation, blunted emotion, social withdrawal, poor self-care and poverty of speech – a presentation that has, in fact, changed little since the onset of her illness to the present day. For the next few years, due to a combination of administrative changes and closures, Marian was moved around several homes in South London, and finally came to us last summer. As far as I can tell, she was given no medication before her arrival at Hawthorne House. There are references in her notes to occupational therapy only.

Her general behaviour is unremarkable, with the single exception of a recurring delusion concerning her rag doll (a very ancient and tattered specimen), which she insists is her daughter. She calls it 'Little Marian' and comforts it and talks to it as though it were real. Her tenderness is quite affecting and she will become enraged if anyone tries to remove 'Little Marian' before the fantasy has run its course; however, between delusional episodes, she is quite happy to concede that the doll is nothing more than a toy.

I very much hope that you will be able to admit Marian onto one of your treatment programmes. She has had a wretched life and deserves so much better. Given the extensive armamentarium at your disposal, I have every confidence that you will be able to help her.

Finally, concerning another matter: the trustees responded very favourably to your suggestion vis-à-vis the creation of a Hawthorne Annexe. Sir Philip Ostler was particularly keen and will be writing to you shortly. A document must be prepared before the AGM, but there is plenty of time (the AGM is scheduled for late September). Sir Philip's fundraising achievements are second to none and with his support the prospects for the Annexe are very good indeed. He is already talking about architects!

I very much hope we will not have to wait too long before you visit us again.

Yours Sincerely,

Margery Garrett

Dr M. Garrett
Senior Medical Officer

9

Jane knew that I had been down to London, but I had not told her the real purpose of my visit. I had fabricated some excuse about a reunion with old college friends. When she asked me how things had gone I described an enjoyable day spent in Soho, reminiscing and eating cheap but authentic Italian food, but all the time I was thinking of Palmer, and in particular what he had said about how the nurses had made fun of him. I hoped that Jane wasn't one of them. Or at least I hoped that, if she had made jokes at his expense, her humour had not been too heartless.

It must have been two or three in the morning. I was sitting up in bed, smoking and staring at Jane's back, admiring the length of her spine, its long, smooth descent to a dimpled depression that always seemed to invite the weight of my hand. Unable to resist, I reached out, rested my palm on her cool skin and felt a curious sense of satisfaction – almost relief. The upper half of Jane's body was propped up on her elbows, and she held a steaming cup of tea a few inches beneath her chin.

I am not sure why it was that I had not told Jane the truth: perhaps there was a part of me that feared she would think me ridiculous, and that I would suddenly find myself being mocked, just like Palmer.

On returning to Wyldehope, I had entered my apartment and found one of Maitland's notes. He had written that he wanted me to keep a Saturday free in March. There was going to be a fundraising event at the Savoy Hotel in aid of the Hawthorne Trust, a mental illness charity for young people. Maitland had become involved in one of their projects and he had decided that I should be on hand to explain 'modern psychiatry' to anyone who expressed an interest: 'Sir Philip Ostler is the organizer, so there will be no shortage of worthies.' I was familiar with the name Ostler on account of its regular appearance in the society pages of newspapers and magazines.

I read the note out aloud to Jane and when I had finished she exclaimed with undisguised envy, 'A dinner and dance at the Savoy!'

'Yes. A crying shame you can't come. But . . .'

She affected an excessively glum expression. 'I know . . .'

'It'll be a black tie do, of course, so I'll have to hire a formal suit and all the trimmings. I hope Maitland doesn't expect me to pay.'

'I'd like to see you dressed up.' Jane looked at me with devouring eyes and blew the surface of her tea. 'Who's Sir Philip Ostler?'

'An industrialist. Immensely rich and a great champion of children's causes. He had a daughter who suffered from depression and she committed suicide when she was only fifteen.'

'Poor man.'

I slid the note under the ashtray. 'I wonder how it is that Maitland is so well connected? He seems to mix in such exalted circles. Only a few weeks ago, he told me that he was at a private function attended by Princess Margaret.'

'Were they introduced?'

'I didn't ask. And while he was interviewing me for this job, he said something that, on reflection, strikes me as rather odd. He said that when he learned that Wylde-hope wasn't needed by the military, he was able to pull a few strings. Why would the military do Maitland any favours? I mean, he's distinguished, obviously, a public figure, but at the end of the day he's still only a doctor.'

Jane raised her eyebrows. 'Oh, surely you must have guessed.'

'Guessed what?'

'He used to work for British intelligence.'

'How on earth do you know that?'

There had been something in her tone of voice, the merest suggestion that I was being slow or dim-witted, but it had been enough to make me overreact. My voice had sounded accusatory instead of surprised.

Jane blushed and seemed flustered. Before I could apologize, she blurted out, 'Oh, back at St Thomas's . . . You know how vain he is. He could be very indiscreet.' Thankfully she had not taken offence. Indeed, she didn't even seem to have noticed that I had raised my voice. 'I think he used to say things to impress us girls.'

'What?' I said incredulously. 'That he was a spy?'

'Oh no, nothing like that. I think he had some sort of advisory role with MI5 – or is it MI6? One of them anyway. He used to speak a lot about foreign travel. I think he wanted to give us the impression that he had been sent on missions.' Jane placed her teacup on the floor and turned over. She folded her arms over her breasts and the compression made them rise. I found their taught luminescence somewhat distracting. 'There were always Americans coming to visit the department at St Thomas's. I think they had something to do with intelligence. One of them was a colonel. Maitland used to show him around the sleep room at St Thomas's. He would observe our routine, the feeding and voiding – the exercises.'

Jane was tired and her speech became more fragmented and digressive. I lit another cigarette and once or twice the world seemed to fall away. We yawned simultaneously and exchanged forgiving glances. After a long silence Jane said, 'Have you heard about Mary?'

'No.'

'You were right. She isn't very happy here. She handed in her notice. I'm sorry, I didn't get the chance to speak to her like I promised. I'm really very sorry.'

'Oh, that's all right,' I said, stubbing out my cigarette. 'It can't be helped. I'll have a word with her myself if I get the chance.'

Jane glanced at my alarm clock. 'I really should be getting some sleep.' Her eyelids looked heavy. 'I've got to be up in a couple of hours.'

'Yes, of course,' I said, leaning sideways and turning off the lamp. Jane stretched an arm across my chest and pulled me closer. She made small wriggling movements and emitted a contented purr as she settled. Our limbs discovered mutual accommodations and shoals of darkness seemed to swim before my eyes. I did not expect their perpetual motion to relieve me of my thoughts quite so easily.

That night I had a most peculiar dream. I was descending the staircase at Wyldehope, carrying some records under my arm. The mellow, sentimental melody of a big band serenade was wafting up from below, accompanied by the babble of conversation. I leaned over the banister-rail and saw that the vestibule had been festooned with bunting, paper garlands and Union Jack flags. Golden crowns, made from cardboard and gift paper, had been mounted over the doors. Patients were dancing. The majority had dressed for the occasion, but some were still wearing their hospital gowns and pyjamas. I didn't recognize any of the faces, but I was overwhelmed by a curious impression of familiarity. Beneath a large, framed photograph of the Queen was a trellis table, piled high with sandwiches, scones and cakes. I saw bowls of jam and heaps of clotted cream. Two nurses were arranging cups and saucers in neat rows by a tea urn. One of them opened her mouth and produced a peal of theatrical laughter. Clearly, the purpose of the gathering was to celebrate the coronation.

When I reached the bottom of the stairs, I discovered my father standing next to the suit of armour. He was surveying the festivities with a benign smile. On noticing me his expression became solemn and he said, 'Good boy.' Then he lit a cigarette and blew an aromatic cloud of smoke over my head. I could read the tiny red writing that curled around the cigarette paper: 'Abdulla No.7'.

Even the punctuation was clearly visible. My father started to cough and it struck me that he didn't look very well. His skin was grey and he had lost a lot of weight. 'Run along then,' said my father, still coughing into his hand. 'Give those records to your mother.' He gave me a gentle push and I began to walk away from him. I took a few steps and narrowly missed a woman in a pink frock, whose solitary dance consisted of fast revolutions followed by a reckless leap.

My mother was sitting beside a table on which a gramophone had been set up. Her hair had been combed and lacquered into a fixed bell-shape and a double string of pearls dangled from her neck. I made my way around the edge of the dance floor, and when I reached my mother she took the records I was carrying and said, 'Thank you, Jimmy.'

'What a helpful child,' said a cheerful ward sister.

My mother looked up, acknowledged the compliment and began searching through the discs.

Two patients, holding each other close, shuffled past. The man was extremely tall, with wiry hair that looked knotted and windblown. He wore a dark suit and he stared into space with moist, fearful eyes. Clinging to him was a tiny woman, as fragile as a hummingbird, wrapped in a quilted housecoat. Her lipstick had smeared and she was grinning madly.

'What shall we listen to while we're eating?' said my mother. 'Some Elgar, perhaps?'

'That would be splendid,' said the ward sister. 'Do you have his Pomp and Circumstance Marches?'

'Just what I was thinking,' said my mother.

The gramophone was covered with what appeared to be crocodile skin. On the inside of the open lid, I could see the 'His Master's Voice' trademark, the little white dog with brown ears looking into an old-fashioned brass horn. Again, I was oddly conscious of how clear everything was.

'My husband has a recording of Malcolm Sargent conducting *The Dream of Gerontius*,' the ward sister continued, evidently anxious to impress upon my mother that her husband was a man who appreciated good music.

'Ah yes,' said my mother wistfully. 'The dream.'

I woke up. The sound of the sea brought me to my senses and I turned my head to see Jane lying at my side. Yet it seemed to me that I could still detect a trace of my mother's perfume lingering in the air. I found myself thinking about my parent's bedroom and the glass bottle on my mother's dressing table, the words 'Chanel' and

'Paris' on the label. It wasn't until I had washed and dressed that I felt the cloying atmosphere of the dream beginning to dispel, and it wasn't until my second cup of coffee that my emotional equilibrium was fully restored.

The first thing I did that morning was make a close inspection of the sleep-room rota. Mary had been allocated a late shift. The day passed uneventfully and I went down to see her at ten o'clock.

As I stepped into the basement, my expectations were confirmed. Mary was seated behind the desk, hunched close to the desk light, as if its cone of brilliance was in some way protective. She suddenly looked up, eyes wide – apprehensive. Then: recognition, a sigh, the slow release of tension from her shoulders. I walked towards her, dimly aware of the sleepers, half-hidden in shadow. A faint smiled appeared on the trainee's face.

'Dr Richardson?'

'Mary.'

She closed the book she was reading and hastily put it away in one of the drawers. I suspected that it was her prayer book.

'Everything all right?' I asked. She nodded. 'Good.'

I pretended to study the notes and made some inconsequential remarks about Kathy Webb's blood pressure, after which I circled the beds and returned to the desk.

'Mary,' I began. 'I was so sorry to hear that you are leaving us.'

She shifted position. 'It's because of my boyfriend. You see, he's got a job in Ipswich and I'd like to be near him.'

'Are you engaged?' I asked.

'Yes.'

'I didn't realize. Congratulations.' She murmured something that I supposed must be thanks and looked away, unable to sustain eye contact. 'And is that the only reason?'

She turned to face me again: 'The only reason?'

'For leaving us?'

'Yes.'

One of the patients moaned. Another answered in the same register and the two voices overlapped to produce a discordant, guttural duet.

'It's just . . .' I paused and wished that I had given my line of questioning prior consideration. The sentences that formed in my mind seemed unfit for purpose. Tentative, faltering. 'I was wondering whether there was more to it?' She did not respond and I noticed that her lips were pressed tightly together. 'Is it possible that you haven't been very happy here?'

She shook her head, denying my suggestion. 'No. I *have* been happy here, Dr Richardson.'

'Forgive me, Mary,' I made an appeasing gesture, 'I don't mean to be presumptuous, but are you quite sure?'

Her response was slightly delayed. 'Sister Jenkins has been very thoughtful.'

'Indeed – a little severe, on occasion, but her heart is in the right place.' I offered Mary a smile, but her features did not soften and the set of her jaw remained rigidly defiant. 'Although, to be frank, I wasn't really thinking about Sister Jenkins.' I picked up a pencil, twirled it in my fingers and put it down again. 'I was thinking more about the house.' I looked up at the wooden beams that crossed the ceiling. They were dark and oppressive. 'The atmosphere. It does have an atmosphere – doesn't it?'

Mary responded with a jarring non sequitur. 'I think they'll take me at the Ipswich General.'

'Yes,' I replied. 'I'm sure they will.' There was an awkward break in our conversation, and I realized that I would have to be more blunt. 'Mary, there's something I've been meaning to ask you for some time. Shortly after my arrival, we were leaving the basement together, do you remember? You gasped, and when I turned round you had your hand raised, covering the back of your neck. You said that you'd twisted your ankle, but that wasn't true, was it? You were only saying that. In actual fact, something had either struck you on the back of the head, or pulled your hair.' She looked confused, fright-ened. 'Mary. Listen,' I continued, trying not to sound too inquisitorial. 'I understand your reluctance to speak about it. Really I do. You think that people won't believe you, or, even worse, they'll assume you're going crazy. But I'm not like that. Please. Can you tell me – honestly – what happened? I won't say a word to anyone else.'

She looked at me with uncharacteristic intensity, as if she possessed some auxiliary sense that allowed her to gauge my intentions and judge the extent to which I could be trusted. I was willing her to speak, to confide in me, and she seemed to be on the verge of disclosing something, when the door flew open and Sister Jenkins entered. Such was my frustration that an inwardly voiced expletive almost found expression.

'Dr Richardson? What are *you* doing here?' Her emphasis carried a subtle demand: my presence in the sleep room at that late hour required justification.

'I was a little concerned about Kathy Webb's blood pressure.'

Sister Jenkins advanced, her shoes sounding a lively staccato on the tiled floor. 'Really? I wasn't aware that there was a problem.'

'It's been a little low.'

'But nothing to worry about, surely?'

'Indeed. I was just being . . . thorough.'

She communicated her approval with a nod.

I became aware of a thrumming sound followed by a series of jangling impacts. The pencil I had left on the table had rolled across the desk and fallen to the floor. Sister Jenkins crouched down and picked it up. As she placed the pencil back on the desk, she threw a stern look at Mary. The trainee quickly apologized: 'I'm sorry, Sister.' But she had not been responsible. I had placed the pencil on my side of the desk, out of her reach. When I caught Mary's eye, she gave no indication that anything out of the ordinary had happened. Her gaze was level and the cast of her features inscrutable.

Turning around, I strolled off into the gloom. I did not look back, but I could hear Sister Jenkins talking to Mary in a low, confidential tone. Positioning myself next to Marian Powell, I studied her hollow cheeks, the sharpness of her bones, her scarecrow hair. She was dreaming. In fact, they were all dreaming: eyeballs oscillating beneath dry, papery lids; limbs occasionally twitching. Elizabeth Mason was the first among them to stop. Then, within a minute, they had all stopped.

Sister Jenkins had entered the bathroom, but she had left the door open, and a yellow trapezium of illumination had appeared on the floor outside.

I made my way back to Mary.

'When are you leaving?' I asked.

'Not just yet. I'm here for another three weeks.'

'Good. Perhaps we can have another talk?'

She bit her lower lip and after a lengthy pause, she said, 'I don't think there's anything to discuss, Dr Richardson.'

I picked up the pencil and held it in front of her nose. 'Yes, there is.'

The bathroom door closed and the trapezium of light vanished. Sister Jenkins was making her way towards us. I put the pencil in my pocket and said, 'Goodnight, Mary.'

Chapman was seated at the table in the recreation room. He did not hear me approach and he was unaware that I was standing in the doorway. His head was tilted back and he appeared to be pinching the loose flesh of his left forearm. Each movement was accompanied by a pained vocalization.

'Michael?'

He looked over his shoulder, and then changed his position so that he could see me more easily.

'Ah, Dr Richardson.'

'What are you doing?' I asked.

'Nothing,' he replied. 'Nothing in particular.'

I entered the room and sat on the empty chair beside him. 'May I look at your arm please?'

The sleeves of his dressing gown and pyjama jacket had been rolled up and his skin was covered in small purple bruises.

'Michael?' I enquired, conducting a cursory examination. 'Why are you doing this?'

He shrugged and pulled his sleeves down. I tried to get him to talk, but he was unresponsive. Self-injurious behaviour is frequently observed in patients with depression, and naturally that is what I assumed was going on; however, a few days later, I had reason to doubt whether I had understood Chapman's motives correctly. I realized that Chapman's 'pinching' might not be an instance of self-harm after all.

We were playing chess and something of a stalemate had developed. As I was contemplating yet another uninspired move, Chapman said, 'Reality.' He managed to invest each of the four syllables with increasing amounts of pathos.

Raising my eyes from the board, I enquired, 'What about it?'

'When I was at Cambridge, we used to discuss the nature of reality.'

'And . . .'

'There was a philosophy tutor. Halperin – G.K. Halperin. He was very keen on a Chinese conundrum. Third or second century BC, I believe.' Chapman made a steeple with his fingers and acquired a donnish mien. 'A man dreams that he is a butterfly, and in the dream he has no knowledge of his life as a human being. When he wakes up he asks himself two questions: am I a man, who has just dreamed that he was a butterfly? Or am I really a butterfly, now dreaming that I am a man?'

'Is that why you've been pinching yourself, Michael? To see if you can wake yourself up?'

He collapsed the steeple, curling his fingers into clenched fists, and replied, 'Lately, I've been dreaming a lot about Cambridge.'

'I see. Are you a patient in a hospital, who frequently dreams that he is an undergraduate at Trinity? Or are you an undergraduate at Trinity, who is now dreaming that he is a patient in a hospital?'

He prodded the edge of the table, as if testing the stability of the material universe. 'There's no way of knowing. That's what Halperin taught us.'

'Well, pinching yourself won't resolve the issue,' I said.

'No,' Chapman sighed. 'I suppose not.'

Over the next few days, Chapman became distant –

his speech vague. It was as though he was constantly distracted by some troublesome internal process. We played
another game of chess, but he wasn't concentrating. I beat
him easily and he responded with indifference. I began to
worry about his mental state and made efforts to see him
more frequently. He was usually sitting up in bed, staring
blankly into space. Then, one afternoon, I found him positioned by the window, his fingers gripping the iron bars.
It was something I hadn't seen him do for a while. The
view was dismal – low-slung hammocks of grey cloud,
merciless rain. Chapman didn't turn round but said, 'I
had stopped sleeping. No, that's wrong. I *could* get to
sleep but I found myself wide awake in the early hours
of the morning. I used to feel lonely and claustrophobic
in my little college room, so I went for long walks. More
often than not I took the footpath to the meadows.'

Chapman let go of the bars and thrust his hands deep
into the baggy pockets of his dressing gown. He continued looking out onto the heath.

'I came across a bicycle lying on its side in the grass.
There wasn't anyone around, but I could hear someone
singing, a woman's voice, and then I noticed a swimmer
in the river. I crouched behind a bush, and when this
woman, this girl, this slip of a thing, climbed onto the
bank I saw that she was quite naked – not a stitch of

clothing. I went back again the next morning, and the morning after that, and the morning after that. I went back again and again, to the same place, and she was always there. It was obvious that she wasn't quite right.' He stopped and screwed a finger into his temple. 'Mentally, I mean. She was like a child. She would pick flowers and talk to the moon. When the sun appeared she would greet it with a wave, and when she was swimming she would sing that nursery rhyme.' Chapman began humming a simple melody. 'Do you know it?'

'Yes,' I replied. '"Row your boat".'

'That's it. "Row your boat".' He raised his arm and swung it from side to side, a little like a conductor beating time. 'Row, row, row your boat, gently down the stream. Merrily, merrily, merrily, merrily, life is but a dream.' Then, emitting a dry, humourless cackle, he repeated the final words. 'Life is but a dream.' Chapman turned to face me and in a voice that trembled with anguish he said, 'Naked. Innocent. And . . . I . . .' His face crumpled and his chest heaved. 'Will I be punished, Dr Richardson?'

'What happened, Michael?'

'Will I be punished?'

'What happened? Tell me.'

Chapman's eyes darted shiftily from side to side. 'Nothing happened!' he snapped.

I tried to coax him to say more, but he turned his back on me and gripped the window bars again. When I looked in on him later he was still in the same position, softly humming the tune of 'Row your boat'.

When I told Maitland about Chapman's confession he was rather dismissive. 'I don't think we can give it much weight.' The attitude he struck reminded me of how he had behaved after I had asked him about the histories of the sleep-room patients: surprise at my naivety was mingled with a definite undercurrent of irritation, and he insisted that I put Chapman on one of the new antidepressants from America. I felt slighted. I had worked hard to build a relationship with Chapman. Even if his confession was nothing more than a fantasy, it still felt to me like a breakthrough, an expression – albeit a cautious expression – of trust. 'Might I suggest a little less talk,' said Maitland, failing to sweeten the reprimand with a counterfeit smile.

I should have watched Chapman more closely, especially so after I had changed his medication. But that very same week, Wyldehope became the focus of a police investigation and I forgot all about Chapman and his confession. It was an oversight that, in months to come, I would bitterly regret.

10

I removed a circle of condensation from the kitchen window with the cuff of my shirt and peered out into a featureless void. An opaque haze obscured the view. I made myself a cup of tea, smoked a cigarette, and then descended the stairs. When I reached the first-floor landing, I saw Lillian Gray rushing from one side of the vestibule to the other. She looked harried.

'Good morning!' I called out.

Lillian spun round and instead of returning my greeting she asked, 'Have you just got up?'

'Yes. Why?'

'Mary Williams has run off. Sister Jenkins is fuming.'

'What do you mean, run off?'

'Sorry, can't talk. Ask Sister Jenkins, she's downstairs.' Lillian unlocked the door to the women's ward and vanished inside.

I continued my descent, all the way down to the sleep room, where Sister Jenkins was studying papers which were spread over the entire surface of the desk.

'What's happened?' I asked.

'That stupid girl!' Sister Jenkins hissed.

'Mary Williams?'

'She relieved Nurse Aldrich at one o'clock. When Nurse Page arrived at six she had gone. Can you believe it?' Sister Jenkins snorted in disgust. 'I've never known such irresponsibility. To leave the sleep-room patients unattended! And if that isn't bad enough, she failed to lock the front door!'

I was dumbfounded: 'How very odd.'

'Dr Maitland will be furious.'

'Where is she now?'

'God knows!'

'Have you checked her room?'

'Yes.'

'And she wasn't there?'

Sister Jenkins's tone was impatient. 'Obviously not.'

'Then where is she?'

'Dr Richardson, Nurse Thomas is on leave, Nurse Perkins has gastric flu, and now, thanks to that foolish girl, I've got to reorganize all of these rotas again. The whereabouts of Mary Williams is the least of my concerns.'

'But it was still dark at six o'clock.'

Sister Jenkins's brow furrowed. She was too preoccupied with her task to recognize the significance of this fact. 'Indeed it was,' she replied, not bothering to look up.

'She couldn't have crossed the heath. It would have been pitch-black, and there's a thick mist this morning.'

Sister Jenkins stopped writing. 'You think she's still here?'

'I think that's very likely. Perhaps we should look for her.'

'With respect, Dr Richardson, I have to get these rotas completed as a matter of urgency. And – before you ask – I can't spare any nurses.'

'I'll speak to Mr Hartley.'

The caretaker listened to the news of Mary Williams's disappearance without showing much emotion. He nodded, collected some keys, and we commenced our search. We looked everywhere, or at least everywhere that the missing trainee might choose to hide: the first-floor outpatient suite, the rooms adjoining the kitchen, the laundry. Then we trudged through a cold mizzle to the outhouses. None of the bicycles were missing and she was not in Hartley's car. I had hoped we would dis-cover Mary, lying on the back seat, curled safely under a blanket, but when I looked through the rear window, I saw only stitched leather and a crumpled shopping bag.

In Mary's room, we found a coat hanging in the

wardrobe. Hartley pulled back the curtains and looked out onto a landscape of undulating fog. He didn't say anything; he didn't need to. It was obvious that we had both reached the same disquieting conclusion. When we had completed our tour, Hartley went back to his cottage, and I walked round the main building and down to the beach. The dull brown waves crashed on the shingle and a spiteful wind scoured my face. I made a funnel with my hands and shouted, 'Mary? Mary?' But her name was immediately swallowed by the noise.

Thirty minutes later I was standing next to Sister Jenkins as she spoke to Mary's mother on the telephone. Although I could only hear half of the conversation, it was enough. 'Not there? And she hasn't been in touch? Is there anywhere else she might have gone? No? Mrs Williams, what about Mary's boyfriend? Where does *he* live?' It was then that we learned that there was no boyfriend. He had been a piece of creative licence, a device for deflecting difficult questions.

'She lied to us,' said Sister Jenkins, raising her eyebrows and handing me the receiver. Reluctantly, I dialled St Thomas's and asked to be put through to the Department of Psychological Medicine.

Maitland's foremost concern was the welfare of the sleep-room patients. 'They are all right, aren't they? I take

it nothing happened to them during the girl's absence?'
He didn't seem at all worried about Mary. When I pointed
out that she had very probably left the hospital in the
middle of the night and set off over the heath his only
comment was, 'Oh dear.'

At about two o'clock in the afternoon, the police
arrived. Inspector Cooper was a big-boned man who
wore a long black raincoat and a felt trilby hat. He was
accompanied by an assistant who he introduced as Davis.
Although I suggested that they would get much more
information about Mary Williams from Sister Jenkins,
they ignored my advice, and insisted on interviewing me.
I was, as Cooper put it, 'The man in charge.' His questions were fairly straightforward. How long had Miss
Williams been working at Wyldehope? Who saw her last?
Did I have any theories that might account for her disappearance?

'You're a psychiatrist, Dr Richardson,' said the inspector, 'better qualified than most to judge a person's state
of mind.' He invited me to speculate with a sweeping
gesture.

'She wasn't very happy,' I replied. 'In fact, she only
recently handed in her notice.'

'Why wasn't she happy? Do you have any idea?'

'It's a demanding job, working with the mentally ill.'

Cooper nodded sympathetically. 'Do you think she might have been . . . perhaps . . . unwell herself?'

'I never thought that. No.'

'But what she did . . .'

'It's very irregular, certainly.'

At the end of our conversation I could tell that Cooper was unsatisfied, and possibly even a little irritated by the brevity of my answers. He had wanted more.

The next day, Cooper was back again, his black saloon leading a fleet of police vans up the drive. Constables and dogs disgorged onto the gravel, assembled into groups, and dispersed on the heath. Another party headed off towards the wetlands.

Two hours later, one of the nightingales came to inform me that Cooper had returned. He was waiting in the vestibule, standing next to the suit of armour, his hat positioned over his heart.

'Dr Richardson.'

'Inspector.'

'We've found her.' His expression was grave.

'Where?'

'In the reed beds.'

'How dreadful.'

'We'll have to wait for the autopsy results, but it looks to me like she drowned.'

'Is there any suspicion of . . .'

'Foul play?' He shook his head. 'We found shreds of her uniform in the bushes. I'd say she scrambled down the bank, lost her bearings, and ran on to the marshes.'

'Ran?'

'She'd lost her shoes. There were footprints in the mud – widely spaced.'

'I see.'

Cooper paused, studied the suit of armour for a few moments and then said, 'She wasn't well, was she, Dr Richardson?'

'Evidently not.'

'Just as I thought.' He looked at me in such a way as to suggest that I might have been more forthcoming the previous day.

A journalist from a local newspaper telephoned later that week, but I refused to speak to him. When the story appeared, it was, thankfully, a sober piece. No attempt was made to sensationalize the facts. Mary's parents had been anxious about her health for several months. They had said that she had become increasingly withdrawn and tearful. A sentence at the end of the article caught my attention and gave me pause for thought – a reference to the family being members of a Christian spiritualist congregation known as the 'Monmouth Brotherhood'.

The funeral was a modest affair and only friends and family were invited. I composed a letter of condolence and arranged for a wreath to be sent. Maitland had expected some unpleasantness to follow: 'They'll say we should have noticed she was ill. They'll say we should have prevented this from happening.' But there were no complaints or demands for an inquiry.

For several weeks, the atmosphere in the hospital was subdued. Everyone made an effort to be more considerate, the incidence of small acts of kindness increased, and in the dining room conversations were conducted in a respectful whisper. Even Osborne refrained from his usual jokes and boasts. 'She was a sweet person,' he said with uncharacteristic feeling. 'What a terrible waste, eh?'

When it was all over, and life was getting back to normal, Jane took my hand and said, 'I'm sorry I didn't talk to Mary. I really am. I feel so guilty now.'

'There's nothing you could have done,' I replied, returning the pressure. 'Not really.'

'I still can't believe it.'

Brushing her cheek with my knuckle, I said, 'Don't punish yourself. There's no point.'

It was impossible for me to enter the sleep room without thinking of Mary. I would picture her, hunched close to the desk lamp, looking up to see who had arrived.

Sometimes my recollection of her was so vivid that the nurse who had taken her place would be transformed by a ghostly superimposition. Memory and reality would elide and I would see Mary's face, once again, hovering in the darkness.

She had raced up the basement stairs and exited the building without pausing to lock the door. She had scrambled down a steep bank, tearing her clothes and losing her shoes. In absolute darkness, she had attempted to cross the reed beds, running, blindly, until she had tripped and fallen into deep, freezing cold water. Every night, as I passed from wakefulness into the shallows of sleep, I asked myself the same question: what had Mary Williams been running away from?

11

Maitland handed me the referral letter as we were leaving his office. 'I wonder if you would be so kind as to assess this gentleman for me?' His manner was casual, almost careless, but I wasn't fooled. He was keen to repair any damage done to our reputation by the Mary Williams affair. The provision of outpatient services at Wyldehope was long overdue, and if we offered them now this would not only improve our standing among local GPs but it would also mollify the Health Board.

Our new patient's name was Edward Burgess. During the war he had spent four years as an army driver and had never reported sick. He then became an infantryman and was sent to the front line, where he and his comrades came under fire. Heavy shelling and mortar bombs precipitated a rapid mental collapse, and he was transported to an aid post on the Normandy beachhead. In due course he was evacuated to England and given various treatments. Although outwardly he appeared to improve, he was constantly on edge and prone to attacks of anxiety.

He was allocated a desk job and after being demobbed he started a haulage business in Lowestoft that subsequently became very lucrative. Within a relatively short period of time he had become a well-respected member of a regional trade association and his contribution was recognized when he was voted its president. Yet he continued to be tormented by traumatic memories and his sleep was disturbed by vivid nightmares of the battlefield and all of its attendant horrors. He would wake up, several times a week, screaming and drenched with perspiration. Occasionally, he would be crippled by a loss of sensation in his legs. His nervous condition was placing a considerable strain on his marriage, and after years of resistance and procrastination he was finally persuaded by his wife to consult his GP.

I was waiting for Mr Burgess in one of the first-floor outpatient rooms, reading and rereading the referral letter. A nurse had been instructed to receive him in the vestibule, and I knew that he had arrived when I heard the heavy iron knocker sounding downstairs, three unhurried strikes that were amplified by the resonant space of the vestibule. Shortly after, there were footsteps in the corridor and Mr Burgess was ushered in. I recognized his face at once – the sloping brow, sunken eyes and lean features – but it took me a few moments to establish where, exactly, I had seen that grim, haunted visage before.

'Doctor,' he said, offering me his hand.

'Mr Burgess.' And then it came to me. 'I believe we've already met.'

'Briefly, yes. We shared a train compartment.'

I recalled my first, interminable journey to Wyldehope: the man sitting opposite, gripping his kneecaps. *Folk 'round here didn't want a madhouse on their doorstep.* I had misunderstood him completely. Mr Burgess had not been expressing his own view but, rather, forewarning me of local hostility.

'Please,' I gestured, indicating an empty seat.

'I'm still not sure whether I've done the right thing, coming here today.'

'Why's that?'

'There are others who have far greater need of your help than me.'

'Suffering is not easily quantified, Mr Burgess. I make no such distinctions.'

He considered my words, nodded, and sat down without removing his coat.

After some preliminary discussion, I encouraged him to talk about his wartime experiences, and discovered that when Burgess had joined the front line the shelling and mortar fire had lasted continuously for eight days. He was then ordered to cross a river and mount an attack on the enemy in a densely wooded forest.

'My friends were falling all around me. I remember the noise, the cries and the explosions. I lost my voice, started to sob, and my legs stopped working. Two chaps got me back to an ambulance, but I was stunned, and just lay there, gibbering.'

'You must have been very frightened.'

'I'm not sure what I felt. In a way, it was like I wasn't there.' Later he sighed and said, 'Doctor, I did a lot of talking when I got back to England. I was admitted to a hospital down in Surrey, where they made me go over what had happened every day. It didn't do me any good then, and I don't think it'll do me any good now.'

After undertaking the assessment, I wasn't at all sure how to proceed. Mr Burgess was not only disenchanted with talking cures, but also medication. The barbiturates his GP had prescribed were equally ineffective. I discussed our new patient with Maitland, who recommended 'excitatory abreaction', a treatment that he had developed during the war precisely for veterans like Mr Burgess, that is to say men suffering from nervous shock. I had, of course, read about this procedure; however, I had no direct experience of carrying it out myself. The

opportunity had never arisen. Maitland detected my hesi-
tancy, and said, 'Perhaps I should conduct the session.'
I was grateful that he was willing to do so and eager to
learn from example.

The following week, Mr Burgess returned. I introduced him to Maitland, who sat by his side and explained
in layman's terms how the treatment was going to work.

'Your symptoms are caused by pent-up emotions, a
blockage if you like, but a blockage that can be removed.
To this end, we must get you into the right state of mind,
and we'll achieve this by giving you some ether to inhale.
It's quite harmless and you have no need to worry. You'll
feel light-headed and a little intoxicated, but the ether will
also increase the clarity of your memories. It is essential
for us to arouse strong feelings, particularly those associated with your experiences in Normandy, if the treatment
is to succeed.' Maitland asked Burgess to remove his
jacket and his tie and to unfasten the top button of his
shirt. He then poured some ether onto a mask and helped
Burgess to put it on. 'Breathe normally,' said Maitland,
resting a reassuring hand on the man's shoulder. The
strong, chemical smell filled the room, and I began to feel
a dull ache behind my eyes. 'Now,' Maitland continued, 'I
want you to tell me about what transpired on the front
line?'

Burgess told his story again. As he spoke, his delivery gathered momentum and he became more and more agitated. The words tumbled out of his mouth, his eyes darted around the room, and his index finger wound around a phantom trigger. At one point he began to panic and he tried to tear off his mask. Maitland took a firm hold of Burgess's wrist, looked him in the eye, and barked, 'No!' Burgess seemed to come to his senses and fell back in his chair. 'You are in the forest,' Maitland continued, 'there are loud detonations, screams and shouts. What do you see ahead of you, Mr Burgess? Tell me? What do you see?'

'Jack!' said Burgess, his eyes swelling out of their sockets in terror. He raised his hand and pointed. 'I can see Jack. He's standing there, right in front of me, and I can see straight through his head.'

'How is that possible, Mr Burgess?'

'There's a hole, a big one, big enough to put your arm through – and a red mist in the air that tastes of iron – and his brains are on my face.' Burgess was hyperventilating and his forehead was beaded with perspiration. 'Harry turns round and he hasn't got a chin any more, but he's still making sounds, horrible sounds. He wants me to advance, but I can't – my legs won't move. Blood is dripping on me and when I look up I see soldiers hiding in the trees. But they aren't hiding and they're not really soldiers. What I'm seeing is parts of soldiers – arms, legs, torsos – and I think to myself, this isn't happening. This can't be happening.'

'But it is happening,' Maitland interjected.

'No. It isn't real.'

'Oh, but it *is* real,' Maitland insisted with stern authority. 'And there is no escape.'

Burgess started to beat the air wildly and he pitched forward onto the floor. I immediately leapt to his assistance, but Maitland barred my way; he looked at me severely and shook his head. Burgess had curled up into a ball and tears were streaming down his cheeks. He was producing an infantile, mewling noise.

'Bombs are exploding,' Maitland intoned, exploiting the deeper registers of his voice with plangent theatricality, 'and the ground beneath your feet is trembling and shaking.' Burgess moaned and thrashed about from side to side, throwing gangly, uncoordinated punches and kicking without purpose. Maitland caught my attention and mimed a pinning down action. Our patient was enfeebled by a combination of ether and exhaustion and it was relatively easy to restrict his movements. 'It does not end,' Maitland continued. 'The earth is convulsing and you are being showered with dirt and rock. You can smell burnt flesh, gunpowder. All around you, men are dead or dying.'

'No more,' gasped Burgess. He wrenched one of his hands free and clawed at the mask. 'Please. No more.'

'There is no escape,' Maitland repeated.

I recovered Burgess's flailing arm and crossed it over the other, which I was already holding against his chest. He tried to heave me off, but the effort seemed to drain some last reserve of strength, and suddenly he became limp and his eyes closed. We lifted him up from the floor and carried him over to a rest bed, where we tried to make him comfortable by supporting his head on some pillows. Maitland removed the mask and wiped away two threads of mucous from beneath Burgess's nose.

'Typically, patients lie quietly for one or two minutes, and when they come round their manner is composed and rational and there are no signs of persisting excitement or intoxication. If the treatment has been successful, Mr Burgess will be able to tell us immediately.' Maitland adopted a more familiar tone of voice, 'James, would you mind awfully if I asked you to fetch some tea from the kitchen?' When I returned Burgess had regained consciousness. He looked very tired but his manner was curiously calm and untroubled.

'How are you feeling?' Maitland enquired.

'Better. More myself.' Burgess looked puzzled, per-
plexed. 'Everything feels different.'

'Do you remember what happened on the front line?'

'Yes, of course. Jack – the hole in his head – and Harry
– the legs and arms in the trees. Even so . . .' He produced
a lengthy sigh. 'It's sort of lifted. It's lighter. I feel unbur-
dened.'

'Good,' said Maitland, 'very good.' He was smiling,
but his smile was a little too self-satisfied to give off any
warmth. 'I want you to rest for a couple of hours. Then, if
Dr Richardson has no objection, you'll be free to go home.'

After lunch, I found Burgess standing by the window.
He had put on his tie and jacket and he was looking up
into a sky of bright white cloud. He glanced at his wristwatch. 'Half past one already. I came with a driver. He's
been waiting for me outside.'

'Perhaps we could meet again in a fortnight?'

'Thank you,' said Burgess, studying his reflection and
tightening the knot of his tie.

Later that same day, I encountered Maitland in the
vestibule. He was carrying a briefcase and I guessed from
his ink-stained fingers that he had been writing. We
swapped a few remarks about Mr Burgess and then I

accompanied Maitland outside. The heath was unusually still. Dusk had decanted pools of darkness into the hollows and even the sea was silent. Maitland opened the nearside door of his car and tossed the briefcase onto the passenger seat. Looking at me across the roof, he said, 'James, I'd like to propose something. You don't have to give me an answer now. Obviously, you'll want to think about it first. The second edition of my textbook was published in the spring, but Churchill-Livingstone are already asking me when they can expect the third. Producing such a comprehensive review of the literature is very time-consuming – too much really for one man. I was wondering, would you be interested in helping out with the next edition? Naturally, you'd be credited. You would be joint-author.'

It was an extraordinary offer.

'Why, yes, of course I'd be interested.'

'It's a considerable undertaking.'

'Indeed, but I can tell you right now, even after I've thought about it, my answer will be yes.'

Maitland walked around the front of the car and said, 'Excellent.' Before I could express my gratitude he was behind the steering wheel and the engine had begun to purr. I watched him drive off, and as was his custom he hooted his horn just before the road descended and the Bentley disappeared from view.

I was due to drop in on the sleep room, but instead I ascended the stairs to my apartment and found my copy of Maitland's textbook in the bureau. Sitting down, I balanced it on my knees and stroked the dust jacket. I formed a mental image of how the cover would appear in future, the simple black font on the pale-blue background: *An Introduction to Physical Methods of Treatment in Psychiatry, Third Edition, by Hugh Maitland and James Richardson.* Something like an electric charge of excitement seemed to travel up and down my spine. In another few years I could reasonably expect offers of employment from prestigious institutions, early promotion and a much better salary. Life would be very different.

It is a measure of how my feelings towards Jane were deepening that I immediately thought of her. I drifted into a kind of daydream and pictured us living together in London, somewhere genteel, like Hampstead. I saw us ensconced in a spacious mansion flat with tall windows through which the distant city could be seen over treetops. I saw us going into town to see films, frequenting jazz clubs and catching the last bus home. And all the while I was conscious of the fact that in this fantasy all of the usual social conventions, such as proposal, engagement and marriage, had already been observed.

I told Jane about Maitland's proposition and she was

very happy for me. 'How wonderful,' she said, squeezing my hand. I explained how joint authorship of the text-book would greatly improve my prospects and I was disappointed when she didn't reflect on what this might mean for her too. A regrettably mean-spirited response on my part because in actual fact I should have applauded her lack of self-interest.

It was about this time that a particular issue began to surface during the course of our conversations: whether or not we should make it clear to our colleagues that she and I were going steady. Apart from Lillian, no one was supposed to know, although I was sure that at least two of the nightingales suspected that there was something going on between us. Fortunately, they had chosen to be discreet. I was tiring of all the secrecy and felt that our lives would be a great deal simpler if we were more transparent. Jane was less keen. She was concerned about how Sister Jenkins and the other nurses would react. I didn't foresee any problems, but Jane was fairly resistant to the idea and I didn't want to pressure her. It occurred to me, somewhat belatedly, that Jane might have another, quite straightforward reason for being cautious. Men and women are judged according to very different standards of morality and perhaps I was being a little naive. If we made it known that we were a couple then, inevitably, there would be those who would see fit to ask how it was that, under such unpromising conditions, we had found opportunities to become intimate? The thought of clandestine meetings in the hospital would, no doubt, cause some to voice their disapproval. Old slurs were easily aired when it came to the conduct of women.

The fantasy of our life together in London became a persistent part of my mental activity. I had even begun to calculate the time it would take to make my dreams a reality: a year or two to complete the textbook, then publication, then another six months before taking up a hospital appointment with academic affiliations.

When I held Jane in my arms and she nestled against my chest, I was tempted to share my thoughts with her, to describe my vision. I had even started to imagine the interior decor of our Hampstead abode: art nouveau lampstands, a rug by the fire, a chintz settee. But I didn't say a word. I didn't want to frighten her off.

Too much, too soon, I chastised myself. *Not yet. Not now.*

It is difficult to account for this failure of confidence. Jane was a demonstrative lover. She would dig her fingers into my flesh and repeat the words 'I love you' again and again, until mounting waves of pleasure made her breathy and inarticulate.

Eventually I would muster enough courage to tell her of my hopes for our future – or so I thought. As it turned out, she never got to hear about the mansion block, the view, or the chintz settee.

Mrs Matilda Mason
88 Lordship Road
Stoke Newington
London N16

2nd June 1955

Dr H. Maitland
BBC
Broadcasting House
Portland Place
London W1

Dear Dr Maitland,

I hope you don't mind me writing to you like this and
I am sorry if I have done the wrong thing. I know you
must be a very busy man and that you must get many
letters like this one. If you don't have time to answer
then I will understand. I was listening to the wireless
last night and you were on a programme called *What
is Madness?* You mentioned a new sleeping cure and I

was wondering how I can get this treatment for my daughter, Elizabeth. She hasn't been well for many years and our doctor, Dr Stott, says she has had a psychotic breakdown. It all started when something terrible happened to her. She was jilted on her wedding day and the man who was going to be her husband ran away and he hasn't been seen since. Lizzie loved him very much and it's so sad, because she wanted to get married more than anything and start a family. All she talked about was having kids. Lizzie wouldn't take off her wedding dress. She kept it on for months. She was like the old lady in that film with John Mills and Jean Simmons. The dress got so dirty we had to cut it off her body when she was asleep. When she woke up she was livid and smashed the furniture in her room. The landlord threatened to throw us out when he saw what had happened and I had to sell my grandmother's silver brooch to pay for the repairs. I don't know why Mick, the man Elizabeth was supposed to marry, jilted her. His uncle said it was because he saw some awful things during the war. But we all did. I don't see what that's got to do with it. It was probably the usual story and there must have been another woman. My friend Doreen thinks he got someone in the family way.

Elizabeth won't go outside any more. She's frightened. I've tried taking her to Ridley Road market, but she starts shaking and crying and she runs back home. You can't talk sense to her. It's as if she doesn't really understand what you're saying. Sometimes she acts like things are just the same as they were before. She wants to sit down and plan her wedding and she talks about what kind of dress she wants. It's heartbreaking and I can barely stop myself from crying.

I know that her doctor is a clever man, but I can't say, hand on heart, that he's been able to help Lizzie very much. He talks to her and gives her injections but she doesn't get any better. A specialist from the Hackney Hospital came to see her and gave her some pills, but they didn't work either. Lizzie does seem to get a bit better when she's had a long sleep. Which makes me think that your sleeping treatment might be good for her?

I hope this letter gets to you. When you were introduced on the wireless, they said you worked at a lot of hospitals, but I wasn't really listening properly and so can't remember their names. If you think you can cure Lizzie, then please write and let me know how she can get to see you. My husband, poor Jack, was killed in Normandy and these days I'm not very well myself. I've lost a lot of weight and have a very bad cough. The doctor says I smoke too much but it's one of the few pleasures I've got left. Should anything happen to me, God forbid, I don't know what will happen to Lizzie.

Thank you for reading my letter.

God Bless

Mrs Matilda Mason

12

In the weeks running up to Christmas the hospital was generally more animated. There was, undeniably, if not excitement in the air, then at least a sense of expectation. Some of the nurses, Jane among them, were preparing to go home and replacement nightingales had started to appear in readiness for their departure. Unforeseen problems had arisen with respect to the secondment of staff from St Thomas's and Sister Jenkins was constantly fretting over her rotas. In the end, we had to accept that on Christmas Day and Boxing Day we would just have to get by with reduced numbers.

Maitland arrived early on the Thursday before Christmas. He spent the entire morning on the wards and made a point of talking to each nurse individually. The compliments of the season were declared and he distributed gift bags of Fortnum & Mason chocolates. It was a kind gesture, but not entirely selfless, as he so clearly enjoyed playing the role of paterfamilias. At two o'clock, I was summoned to his office, where we consumed a significant amount of brandy and several of Mrs Hartley's cinnamon biscuits. Maitland informed me that he and his wife were going to spend Christmas in Norfolk with friends. He wrote down a name and telephone number and urged me to call him if the need arose. We touched glasses and toasted Wyldehope.

As I was leaving the office, Maitland indicated a large cardboard box and suggested that I take it with me.

'What is it?' I asked.

'A sort of present,' he said. When I looked inside I discovered that it was full of offprints. 'You may as well start thinking about how we're going to revise the first chapter. Merry Christmas, James.'

I received a more traditional gift from Jane. She handed me a beribboned parcel and insisted that I open it at once. The wrapping fell away to reveal the title of the latest Agatha Christie novel: *Hickory Dickory Dock.*

'Something to keep you occupied while I'm away.'

She was not expecting me to reciprocate. I passed her an envelope of red crêpe paper, inside which was a pair of delicately fashioned silver earrings that I had obtained through a mail-order company. Jane was delighted and immediately held them up to her earlobes and examined her reflection in the window glass.

'Will you telephone me on Christmas Day?' she asked, pushing her hair aside and tilting her head back.

'Yes, of course,' I said.

'How do they look?'

'Beautiful,' I replied – thinking also of how much I would miss her.

On Christmas Eve, efforts were made to make the interior of the hospital more cheerful. Paper chains were hung around the windows and Mr Hartley erected a tree in the vestibule. I happened to be passing just as he was tidying up. He had dressed the branches with decorations that looked extremely old, most probably Victorian: miniature dolls, tin stars, wooden animals and porcelain trinkets. I commented on their quaint appearance, their antique charm, and Hartley said that he had found them in the tower attic while mending the roof. I scrutinized one of the little dolls and was slightly disturbed by the sinister vacancy of her expression.

As we were talking, I noticed that Hartley was looking distinctly off-colour. A film of perspiration covered his forehead and he was shivering. His complexion was pale and his eyes had a watery, glazed appearance.

'Are you feeling all right, Hartley?' I asked.

'I think I've caught a chill, sir,' he replied.

'Then perhaps you'd better spend the afternoon in bed.'

'Oh, that won't be necessary, sir,' he replied with gruff civility. 'I'm sure to shake it off.'

Unfortunately, his constitution did not prove to be as robust as he had hoped. Later in the day I was accosted by Mrs Hartley. 'Dr Richardson, I know you're very busy, but would you mind popping over to take a look at Mr Hartley. He's taken a turn for the worse. He's very poorly. Very poorly indeed.'

As soon as I entered the caretaker's cottage I could smell sickness and I found Hartley in bed with a raging temperature. He had clearly come down with a very bad flu. I gave him some aspirin and commiserated. 'What bad luck. On Christmas Eve as well. I'm so sorry.'

On returning to the men's ward, I discovered Sister Jenkins massaging her temples and wincing.

'What's the matter?' I asked.

'A headache,' she replied.

'Perhaps you should take an aspirin?' I ventured.

She pointed at a pill jar. 'I already have.'

An hour passed and Sister Jenkins's condition got considerably worse. She could hardly keep her head up without support and she was feeling nauseous.

'Look,' I said, 'there's no point in you being here. You're too ill to work.'

'But I've only got four nurses! How can I take time off?'

I ignored her protest and studied the rota. 'Nurse Fraser will have to do a double shift.'

Three of the male patients were looking peaky and their temperatures were raised. One of the female patients threw up and was clearly very unwell. The six sleepers, thankfully, were as yet unaffected.

As the evening progressed, I lost another nurse to the contagion and several of the women patients started to complain of aches and pains. I attempted to contact Maitland, but he had already left London for Norfolk, and when I called the Norfolk number no one was there to pick up the telephone. Subsequently, I rang Saxmundham, only to discover that they too were understaffed and stricken by an outbreak of flu. They couldn't spare any nurses – and neither could Ipswich.

Sister Jenkins and I had planned a modest Christmas celebration for the patients. We were going to move the radiogram into the vestibule, play seasonal records, and allow the men and women to mix. I had envisaged parlour games, carol singing and pyramids of mince pies; however, when I entered the sleep room and found Nurse Brewer mopping up her own vomit, I realized it wasn't to be.

*

By four o'clock in the morning I was managing Wylde-hope on my own. I spent the whole night rushing between the wards and the sleep room. For much of the time I was changing bed sheets and scrubbing the floor with disinfectant. The air was fouled by various forms of bodily elimination and the revolting smell got into my clothes and hair. Without assistance, it was going to be impossible for me to accomplish the feeding and the voiding of the sleep-room patients. There was always Mrs Hartley, of course, but she was not medically qualified and I did not feel that it was appropriate to seek her involvement. I decided that the best course of action would be to keep the sleepers sedated for the next twenty-four hours. After which I hoped some of the nurses might be, if not fully recovered, then at least well enough to provide essential support. I set up intravenous drips to ensure that the sleepers were properly hydrated and used the ECT canvas restraints to restrict their movements.

Suspension of the usual routine, I recognized, might produce a few problems – constipation, haemorrhoids and so on – but, conversely, it could also save lives. If any of the sleepers became infected, they might choke on their own vomit. This wasn't going to happen if their stomachs were empty. Only one favourable contingency was required to ensure the success of my stewardship: this was that I should not succumb to infection myself.

Dawn broke over a frosty heath and I picked my way along a slippery path to the nurses' accommodation, where I was admitted by a very weak Sister Jenkins. She could only stand by leaning against a door jamb. All of the nurses, I was informed, had had a very bad night. After the briefest of discussions, she cut short my solicitous enquiries and said, with gravelly insistence, 'Get back to the hospital. If you're needed, I'll give you a call.' Thus, I was summarily dismissed. It was only when I got back to the hospital that I realized neither of us had troubled to acknowledge the day's significance with the customary greetings.

At seven o'clock, Mrs Hartley arrived. Her plump cheeks had been pinched by the cold and she looked as strong as an ox.

'Merry Christmas, Dr Richardson,' she said, striking a defiant pose. She was not going to be cowed by circumstance.

'And a Merry Christmas to you too, Mrs Hartley. How is Mr Hartley?'

'A bit better. He's stopped being sick but he still gets dizzy when he gets out of bed.'

'Don't forget to give him plenty to drink.'

'I won't, Doctor. Can I get you some breakfast?'

'Yes, thank you, Mrs Hartley. That would be excellent.'

I telephoned Maitland in Norfolk and explained what had happened. He approved of the measures I had taken with the sleep-room patients and applauded my initiative.

'Do you think you can cope?' he asked.

I took the question too personally. It sounded like a challenge and rather stupidly I answered, 'Yes. Providing I don't get ill.'

'Good man. If you start to get any symptoms, I'll come down without delay.'

When the receiver was back in its cradle, I wondered why I was always quite so eager to impress him.

My Christmas Day was spent serving meals, checking on the sleepers, and mopping up vomit. In the evening, after Mrs Hartley's departure, I allowed myself a few moments of repose under the porch. The air was refreshing and overhead a clear winter sky was dense with stars. I was exhausted.

In the sleep room, the patients were dreaming. I passed between the beds, registering the rapid-eye movements. Marian Powell's lips were opening and closing. I stood beside her and studied her face: the sharp flint of her nose and her gingery lashes. She was trying to say something. I leaned closer and turned my ear towards her mouth. All that I could hear at first was a kind of inflected breathing, but gradually consonants were introduced and words became intelligible. 'Wake up . . . wake up.' It was as if her brain had recognized a departure from the usual routine and was sounding an alarm. Although sleep-talking is common enough, it is relatively rare while dreaming. I wondered if her sedation had stopped working, and said, 'Marian? Can you hear me?'

'Wake up!' she repeated. 'Wake up!' It sounded like a command and I was left with the curious impression that she was speaking specifically to me. The effect was quite unnerving.

Immediately after, Sarah Blake's lips began to tremble and she produced a lengthy exhalation. It was not continuous, but modulated. I walked from Marian Powell's bed over to Sarah Blake's, and caught a faint whisper: 'Wake up . . . wake up.' Again, there was a note of irritation, or perhaps urgency in this exhortation.

Had Sarah Blake actually heard Marian Powell and copied her? It was just possible, I supposed, but I had never observed anything like it before. Not even in a sleep laboratory. Subsequently, I began to worry about the sedation. Perhaps the sleep-room patients were becoming inured to its effects? Perhaps they weren't as deeply asleep as I had intended. I couldn't risk them waking up in my absence, so I gave them all an extra 15 millilitres of intramuscular paraldehyde.

As I was updating their notes I kept on experiencing brief absences. I really was very tired. Staying awake through a second night was going to be extremely difficult and I desperately needed to shave and freshen up. A quick bath and a change of clothes would, so I told myself, be entirely justified.

I ascended the stairs and when I reached the vestibule I became conscious of a delicate jangling sound. Looking around, I couldn't determine its source and it quickly faded. Then I noticed the Christmas tree. A number of the decorations were in motion, swinging gently from side to side. I was aware that there was something odd about what I was seeing, but a second or two passed before I realized what it was. Only some of the baubles were affected. It was as if half had been touched or prodded, while the other half had been left alone. A draught would not have been quite so selective. Two of the decorations had fallen to the floor and both were miniature dolls. At any other time I might have stopped to investigate, but I was simply too weary. I wanted my bath. Not another encounter with the supernatural.

After bathing and shaving I changed my clothes and

felt much better. As I was putting on a clean, starched shirt, I remembered that I had not called Jane as I had promised, and when I looked at my wristwatch I realized that it was now far too late.

Then I did something very foolish.

I went to the bedroom, laid down on the mattress, and lit a cigarette. I don't remember finishing the cigarette, because I fell asleep.

13

When I woke up, an hour later, everything was black. I had a feeling that I should be doing something, but no idea what it might be. My stupor lifted and, startled into activity by the sudden recollection of my circumstances, I launched myself out of bed and reached for the light switch. I did this instinctively, and it was only when the switch 'clicked' and nothing happened that I remembered: prior to falling asleep I had been lying on the bed and smoking a cigarette with the light on. I worked the switch up and down, but the room remained stubbornly dark. Blaspheming loudly, I felt my way into the hallway and swept my hand across the wallpaper until I encountered the protruding Bakelite fixture. Again, when I flicked the switch, there was no light, and no sound to suggest that the bulb had blown. A power cut. That seemed to be the only explanation. I shook my head in disbelief and groaned, 'What luck!' There was an emergency generator in one of the outbuildings, but I had no idea how to operate it, which meant that I would have to wake poor Mr Hartley and drag him from his sickbed.

I located my matches. A ribbon of smoke twisted in the air and the smell of phosphorus made me cough. Shielding the flame with my hand, I walked briskly to the kitchen where I knew I would find a candle in one of the drawers. I lit the wick and stepped back out into the hallway. A noise halted my progress. The door to one of the empty rooms had started to swing backwards and forwards, wringing out a slow, creaky scale from obstinate hinges: it ascended and descended as the door went this way, then that, and there was something about the tempo, and the length of each note, that suggested the exercise of control, a certain musicality. It was as though the sounds were being produced for pleasure, and I was reminded of the kind of games that children play – their capacity to find repetition endlessly amusing. There was no draught. No obvious, natural cause. Taking small, cautious steps, I approached the swinging door and, when I was close enough, I quickly grabbed the handle and pushed it shut. The action was too forceful, too nervous, and I almost extinguished the light. The flame danced and shadows jumped across the ceiling. For a few moments I stood very still, half expecting the handle to turn and the door to spring open again.

On the landing, the candle light was too weak to repel the darkness, which pressed at the edges of a pathetically small sphere of illumination. It was a darkness that made me feel utterly alone. I could sense its enormity, its infinite expansion beyond the walls, across the heath and the grazing marsh and the sea. Midwinter darkness. It awakened primordial fears, and I was returned to a primitive state of trembling ignorance: huddled in some ancestral cave, gazing out of its mouth at a night that concealed unimaginable terrors. I wanted that dreadful feeling of aloneness to end, because its indefinite extension seemed to present a very real threat to my sanity. Yet, only an instant later, I was thinking the very opposite, because to my shock and surprise it transpired that I wasn't alone after all. I had company.

The silence had been broken by a dull, repetitive thudding. Someone was climbing the stairs. The footfall was quite distinct and followed by an echo. There was a pause, a sigh, and the climber continued. My first thought was that it might be Hartley, but I knew that this was extremely unlikely. Hartley would be fast asleep. And if he had woken up and discovered that we had no electricity, he would have gone straight to the outhouses to start the generator. He wouldn't have come to the main building without a torch to light his way.

A querulous floorboard protested somewhere below.
I peered into the emptiness and the roar of my own
blood became louder. Nothing was discernible. I held
out the candle and waved it over the void, but all that
this achieved was a rearrangement of the shadows. The
magnified silhouettes of woodland creatures circled me
like predators. My eyes strained against the darkness and
I detected subtle suggestions of form and movement. I
found myself looking at a figure, engaged in the task of
slow, effortful ascent. Its pale hand slid along the banister
rail, producing a soft hiss, and the looseness of its gar-
ment reminded me of monkish robes. Fear rendered me
insensible, and a kind of strangulated cry escaped from
my open mouth.

'Dr Richardson? Is that you?'

The lambency of the flame assembled Michael Chapman's face in the stairwell. What I had mistaken for a
habit was, in fact, his baggy dressing gown.

'Michael!' Relief was instantly replaced by anxiety.
'What on earth are you doing here?'

'My bed,' Chapman said. 'It was moving so much, I
couldn't stand it any more.'

'But Michael, how did you get off the ward? The door
was locked.'

'No, it wasn't. It was open.'

'That's impossible.' I would never have made such an error. 'Did you find a key in the nurses' desk?'

'No.' He moistened his upper lip with the tip of his tongue. 'The lights aren't working. I couldn't see a thing. Why aren't the lights working, Dr Richardson?'

'A power cut.'

'I could tell that someone was upstairs with a candle. I was hoping it would be you. The bed was shaking and rolling from one side of the room to the other. It was making me feel sick. Mr Morley was sick earlier, perhaps his bed was moving too.'

'He has the flu. Come on, Michael. Let's go down-stairs.'

'That new medication you've put me on isn't doing me any good. I feel different. Not quite myself.'

'Michael. Listen. You really must go back to your room.'

'I'd rather not if you don't mind.'

I ignored his objection. 'I'll get Mr Hartley to start up the generator, and then I'll return at once. Come on, Michael, let's go.'

'No,' Chapman repeated. It was unlike him to be so stubborn.

He hauled himself up the last few steps and stood beside me on the landing. I saw something glinting in his hand. It was a carving knife. He must have seen me recoil, because he made a furtive attempt to slip it into his dress-ing-gown pocket.

'Michael?' I said, trying to remain calm. 'What have you got there?'

'Nothing.'

'It looks like a knife to me. Where did you get it from?' He shook his head. I guessed that he must have wan-dered through the dining room and into Mrs Hartley's kitchen. 'Michael' – I extended my hand – 'that could be very dangerous. Please, give it to me.'

'No.'

'Why do you want a knife, Michael?'

'To protect myself.'

'Against what? You don't need to protect yourself here.'

'I disagree, Dr Richardson.'

'Michael, give me the knife. Please.'

'Do you think it's her? Come back to torment me?'

'Who?'

'The swimmer. The girl.'

'What do you mean, come back? Come back from where?'

'She was so . . .' His fingers contracted. An odd, slow squeeze, as if they were meeting with some form of weak resistance. 'Soft.'

'We'll talk about the girl when we get downstairs,' I said, addressing him more firmly. 'Now, give me the knife.'

He wasn't a strong man and I was confident that I could disarm him. I was working out how I was going to achieve this, rehearsing manoeuvres in my mind when, quite suddenly, Chapman tensed. His whole body stiffened. He was evidently staring at something behind my back. His eyes were wide open and protruding slightly, his irises fully exposed and the whites gleaming. Everything about him was taut, coiled and alert. I wheeled round and followed his gaze. He was looking through the wooden arch of the door frame, at some distant point at the far end of the hallway.

'It's coming,' said Chapman.

There was something about his choice of words, the non-specificity of the pronoun, that chilled me to the bone. There is nothing more frightening than that which cannot be identified, no engine of fear more powerful than the unknown. If I had been more composed (and less prone to professional prejudices), I might have realized that Chapman's pronoun was not merely a part of speech, but the key; however, at that precise moment, I was incapable of meaningful insight.

'Please, Michael. Let's go downstairs.'

'It's coming,' he repeated.

I pointed into the gloom of the hallway and said, rather unconvincingly, 'There's nothing there. Come on, Michael. Please. Give me the knife and we'll go—'

My sentence was interrupted by a thunderous noise. Chapman and I ducked and cringed as if we were being shelled. Every door in the hallway was being repeatedly opened and shut with superhuman speed and violence. This crashing and banging was sustained for about ten seconds, after which it came to an end as abruptly as it had started. Chapman and I were so stunned we remained rooted to the spot, frozen in attitudes of cowering disbelief.

A flurry of 'confetti' blew out onto the landing; some of the flakes swirled in the air before dropping to my feet. I bent my knees and picked up one of the pieces. Holding it close to the candle, I saw that it was covered in closely printed text. I noticed the name of an American pharmaceutical company and realized that I was holding the remains of one of Maitland's offprints.

'Dr Richardson.'

Chapman's voice was wary, uncertain. I let the square of paper fall to the floor and looked up. A tongue of flame had appeared. It was difficult to judge its position, but I estimated that it must be hovering just outside the bathroom. I wanted to believe that it was an illusion, a reflection of my own candle on the panel of an open door. But there was something inconsistent about its elevation. It was far too low.

As I studied the flame, it seemed to be getting brighter. Then I realized I was mistaken. It wasn't getting brighter, but coming towards us.

Chapman took the carving knife from his pocket and thrust it forward like a sword.

'Put it away,' I barked.

'No,' said Chapman. 'I won't.'

As the flame advanced, Chapman and I retreated a few steps backwards. Perhaps my eyes were deceived, but I thought that I could see a shape behind the glare, an outline that encouraged the brain to supply missing details. I am still not sure what it was that I saw. But the darkness seemed to become textured. It moulded itself around a face: a small, rounded face with blank, doll-like features. Confusion became horror, I lost my nerve, and I was about to flee down the stairs, when the landing door slammed shut, displacing a large volume of air in the process. Its forceful closure sent a tremor through the whole building, my candle went out, and we were plunged into total darkness.

Chapman panicked: 'Stay away from me, stay away.'

I could hear the blade swishing nearby.

'No, Michael,' I called out. 'Keep still!'

I took the matches from my pocket, but before I could produce any light, Chapman's knife sliced into the flesh below my thumb. The matchbox dropped to the floor and I leapt away, hoping to place myself beyond his reach.

The swishing stopped and he began to whimper.

'That's better,' I said, trying to calm him down. 'Everything's going to be all right. Put the knife away. Do you hear me, Michael?'

I went down on my knees and felt for the matchbox. I couldn't find it on the landing, so I started to work my way down the staircase, undertaking a systematic search of each step from left to right. The cut began to hurt and my fingers were wet with blood.

The landing door swung open again with a mighty crash. Michael screamed and I heard him lashing out once more with the knife.

'Keep still, Michael,' I pleaded. 'Or you'll fall down the stairs.'

I continued raking the carpet frantically.

'Oh, dear God,' Michael sobbed. 'What have I done? What have I done?'

I felt something crack and crumple beneath the weight of my knee. Picking up the flattened matchbox, I slid the lid aside, and took a matchstick out of the tray. Just as I was poised to strike it, I felt a breath of cold air on the back of my neck. A cobwebby caress explored the contours of my face, and then a tuft of my hair was pulled. It was a hard, spiteful tug. I struck the match and turned, expecting to find myself gazing into the hollow eyes of the thing I had half-seen, half-imagined, advancing down the hallway. But there was nothing there. Only the stairs, falling away into obscurity. The match burned out and I struck another. My hands were shaking. Thankfully, I had not lost the candle and re-lit the wick.

Chapman was standing with his back against the landing wall, grimacing, his head twisted to the side, his cheek pressed against the wallpaper. His eyes were shut and he was holding the knife out at arm's length. The gesture was not aggressive, but defensive, a totemic warding off.

I climbed to the top of the stairs and said, 'It's only me, Michael.'

With great care, I peeled his fingers away from the handle – one by one. Then I took the knife from him and put it into my jacket pocket. It was too big to be comfortably accommodated, and the handle hung out at an angle. I inspected the cut beneath my thumb. It was still bleeding profusely and badly in need of dressing. I coaxed

Chapman away from the wall and guided him down the stairs. He seemed to be in a state of shock, so I took his arm and offered him gentle reassurances. As we passed beneath the stag's head, he leaned against me, seemingly anxious to give the animal a wide berth. A dribble of hot wax scolded my fingers.

When we reached the bottom of the stairs I saw that the door to the men's ward was wide open. I immediately checked the door to the women's ward and the hospital entrance. These were both locked.

We entered the men's ward, and as we did so the lamp on the nurses' desk flickered and came to life. I tested the nearest wall switch and found the ceiling lights were in working order. Electricity had been restored; however, the fact that the power cut and the poltergeist activity had coincided suggested to me that the two were in some way related. I blew out the candle, poured the excess wax into a bin, and put the stub down on the desktop.

'Come on, Michael,' I said. 'Let's get you to bed.'

When we arrived at Chapman's room, I couldn't open the door. My first thought was that it had been inexplicably locked – just as the ward door had been inexplicably *unlocked*. Even so, I tried to force it open, and found that it gave slightly. There was something heavy on the other side. Renewing my efforts, I created a wide enough gap to squeeze through, and immediately saw that it was Chapman's bed that had caused the obstruction. Clearly, he could not have put it there himself. Gripping the metal frame, I pushed the bed across the floor and back into its usual position.

Chapman was waiting outside, staring blankly at his slippers. I got him into bed and gave him an injection of sodium amytal.

'I'm sorry, Dr Richardson,' he said, exhaling as his eyelids began to droop. 'I'm sorry about the knife. I didn't mean to . . .' He looked down at my hand.

'I know, Michael. It was just an accident. Rest now.'

'Is it her? Do you think? The girl. Come back to punish me?'

'I don't know, Michael.'

He closed his eyes and two minutes later he was snoring.

I looked in on the other patients and thankfully they were all asleep. Then I dressed my cut and went to see the women. One of them had been sick again and I had to get her cleaned up. In the basement, everything was very still. None of the sleepers were dreaming. After completing another, more leisurely circuit of the wards and the sleep room, I was satisfied that nothing untoward had happened in my absence.

Once again, I found myself in the vestibule, and I sat on the lower steps of the staircase, trying to collect my thoughts. A circle of dark-green needles had collected around the base of the Christmas tree and the air was fragrant with spruce. My mind was curiously vacant and I felt numb inside. All of the earlier excitement and terror seemed to have drained me of emotion. I allowed my head to rest against the banisters and immediately the world began to swim in and out of focus. There was nothing I wanted more than to close my eyes and sleep.

I did not recognize the sound at first. It arrived as nothing more than a subtle incursion, something seeping between the accumulated layers of silence. But it was enough to make me sit up and listen. The sound became louder, and acquired a mechanical, throaty depth. It was a motor car. The pitch changed as the driver negotiated uneven ground. I stood up, crossed to the entrance and unlocked the door.

Outside, the stars had vanished and a light snow was falling. Two powerful headlamps illuminated the scrub and heather as the vehicle rounded the oblique curvature of the drive. It occurred to me that Maitland might have had second thoughts, and that he had decided to travel down from Norfolk to help. Knowing what a stickler he was for proper dress, I straightened my tie and buttoned my jacket. The brilliant beams were dazzling, and I couldn't really see the car – even less the driver inside. I squinted and tried to shade my eyes but this made little or no difference.

The vehicle came to a halt directly in front of me. I could feel its heat from where I was standing and smell the pungency of its exhaust fumes. The engine juddered loudly and then fell silent; the headlamps dimmed and went out. A door opened and I saw a man in an overcoat emerging.

'Hello, Richardson.' It was Osborne. He lurched towards me and his gait was unsteady. A white silk scarf was hanging around his neck and in one of his hands was a bottle. 'Seasons greetings!'

'Bloody hell, Osborne, what are you doing here?'

'Steady on. l don't want to be overwhelmed with gratitude.'

'I'm sorry, I didn't mean to sound . . .' My sentence trailed off in embarrassment. 'I wasn't expecting you, that's all. I wasn't expecting anyone.'

He staggered forward: 'I heard that you'd been dropped in the *merde* and thought that I'd better come out and see how you were getting along.'

'But how did you get to hear? I was told that . . .'

He waved away my question with big, uncontrolled

gestures, and talked over my incomplete sentence: 'Look, Richardson, I don't mean to be a bore, but can we go inside? It's getting pretty nippy out here.'

'Yes. Yes, of course.'

I never thought that I would be glad to see Osborne, but glad I was, and in no small measure.

We stepped into the vestibule and I locked the door. Osborne eyed the Christmas tree for a moment and then laughed. 'Good heavens. Is Mr Dickens at home?' He then turned to look at me. His stance changed slightly as he tensed and cocked his head to one side. 'What happened to you?'

I raised my hand. The dressing was soaked through with blood. 'There was a power cut. I had an accident.'

'A power cut?'

'Yes, the lights went off for a few minutes.'

'What were you doing? Slicing sprouts?'

'As it happens I did have to help out in the kitchen earlier.' Osborne smirked and walked to the foot of the stairs. I noticed that under his coat he was wearing a dinner suit. He leaned on the banisters and said, 'I've come straight from the golf club. The Christmas party.'

'Oh?'

'Yes.' The syllable was protracted. He leaned forward and beckoned for me to come closer. 'What a night.'

233

'I'm sorry?'

'Women, eh?' My puzzled expression encouraged him to go on. 'The chairman's wife. We were getting along nicely enough – all very cosy, in the cloakroom – when, quite suddenly, she seemed to go right off the idea. Talk about blowing hot and cold! One minute she was all over me and the next . . .' Osborne shook his head and belched into his fist. 'Pardon me, the pâté was rather rich.' He seemed momentarily distracted by darker thoughts. 'Anyway,' he continued, 'I was asked yesterday – or was it the day before? – if I could come over here to give you some assistance. The situation was explained but frankly I didn't regard it as my problem. To be honest, I put it out of my mind. Then, just after my less than satisfactory imbroglio with the chairman's wife, I was smoking a cigar in the car park, trying to make sense of it all, when I suddenly remembered you and your . . . predicament.'

He searched his pockets and produced a shot glass which he filled with whisky. After handing it to me, he said, 'Cheers,' and took a swig from the bottle. I threw my head back and poured the single malt down my gullet. It tasted remarkably good: like warm caramel and wood smoke.

'Looks like you needed that,' said Osborne. 'Here, have another.' He topped me up and I disposed of my second shot as quickly as the first. 'You know, Richardson, I have to say, *entre nous*, you're not looking your best. And is that a carving knife I see in your pocket?'

'I haven't been to bed for a couple of days. It hasn't been easy.'

'All those sprouts. I can imagine.' He screwed the top back on the whisky bottle and handed it to me. 'You're whacked. Why don't you run off to bed?'

'You're very drunk, Osborne.'

'Oh, I can cope.' He registered my doubtful expression. 'Really I can.'

'Are you sure?'

'Yes.'

I looked at my watch. It was four thirty. 'There's no one else here. The nurses have flu.'

'A nasty one, isn't it? We're pretty stretched at Saxmundham too.'

'Some of the patients are being sick. Make sure you keep an eye on *all* of them. They're quite heavily sedated.'

'Yes, yes. Don't fret, Richardson. I'm perfectly capable.'

'I'm hoping some of the nurses will be recovered tomorrow. I couldn't manage the sleep-room routine on my own, so I used the ECT restraints to stop the patients from moving around – and I put them on drips.'

'That sounds sensible.' Osborne took off his coat and said, 'I'll go downstairs first. Do you have the keys?'

I detached a jangling bunch from my belt and threw them in Osborne's direction. He interrupted their trajectory with a lightning snatch and his face creased with smug amusement. Words were unnecessary: *You thought I was going to miss them, didn't you?* He slung his coat carelessly over his shoulder.

'Osborne?'

'Yes.'

'It was very decent of you, coming out like this.' He smirked and turned to walk away. 'No, really, Osborne. I won't forget it.'

'Steady on, Richardson, have you been at the sherry?'

'You know, sometimes you can be extremely irritating, Osborne.'

'Ah, that's better! You were beginning to worry me.'

As I climbed the stairs, I heard him whistling the tune of 'I'll See You in My Dreams'.

When I reached the top floor, the door to my apartment was still open and a wedge of yellow light divided the hallway. It was coming from my bedroom. Earlier, when I had tested the switch, I must have left it in the 'on' position. I stripped, finished the last of the whisky, and got ready to get into bed. Gripping the blanket, I pulled it aside, and as it came away I jumped backwards. Something was lying on the exposed sheet. It was a doll. One of the dolls from the Christmas tree.

I only slept for five hours. Perhaps it was the cold that woke me up. Even though the radiators were on, the windowpanes were purled with ice on the inside. I attended to my ablutions, dressed and made myself a cup of tea. The view from my kitchen was extraordinarily beautiful. Beneath a cloudless sky, the heath was carpeted with snow and a violet haze lingered just above the horizon. Osborne's sports car had been transformed into a sculpted object of gentle contours and smoothed, rounded edges. At regular intervals, the wind rolled long streamers of powdered ice in a southerly direction. This unsullied prospect refuted everything that had transpired during the night: the leaping shadows, slamming doors and ghostly apparitions. All of these things seemed to belong to another world, a world of fevered dreams and lunacy. Yet when I placed my hand on the window frame, and the bloodied bandage attracted my attention, I was reminded of their undeniable and horrible reality.

What was I to do?

I didn't *have* to stay. I could always resign. But then I would forfeit the opportunity to be joint-author of Maitland's textbook. I thought of the mansion flat in Hampstead that I had imagined, and Jane, sitting by an open fire, her legs curled beneath her; a suitably stylish conveyance parked on the road outside and holidays spent in the south of France. I wasn't about to throw it all away because of a poltergeist.

With these considerations in mind, I decided that when Jane returned I would tell her everything. We knew each other well enough now. Just the idea of having someone to talk to was enough to get things into perspective. Mary Williams had died because of her psychological vulnerabilities. She was a young woman whose family were members of a religious sect, and from birth her brain had probably been crammed with all kinds of nonsense about devils and demons. It was *fear* that had killed Mary Williams. Although living in a haunted house was disturbing, it was not dangerous. If Mary Williams hadn't been so frightened, she would still be alive. I finished my tea, put the cup in the sink and went downstairs.

On the men's ward, I discovered Osborne slumped forward over the desktop, his head resting in the crook of his arm. I placed a hand on his shoulder and rocked him until he woke up with a start.

'Oh, it's you,' he said, wiping some dribble from the corner of his mouth. 'I must have dropped off.' Then he looked around more anxiously. 'Sister Jenkins isn't here, is she?'

'No.'

'She's up and about, you know. A little unsteady on her feet, but as spirited as ever.' He rubbed his forehead and grunted. 'I think I may have overdone it last night.'

'Just a moment.' I got him a glass of water and two aspirin.

'Ah, thank you, Richardson. Much appreciated.'

I learned that Osborne had had a busy morning – perhaps a little too busy for a man with a hangover. With Mrs Hartley's assistance, he and Sister Jenkins had already given all of the patients their breakfast, even those in the sleep room. The drips had been removed and Sister Jenkins was apparently eager to reinstate the usual routine. 'I had to give two enemas,' said Osborne, shaking his head. 'I hope to God the nurses make a swift recovery, or I'm off.' His expression was uncharacteristically grave. Leaving him to formulate an escape plan, I went down to the sleep room, where Sister Jenkins was restocking the trolleys with medication. She looked pale and gaunt. Even so, she was a determined woman and I knew that she would be offended if I questioned her ability to function. 'I've spoken to Nurse Fraser,' said Sister Jenkins. 'She will be back at work later this morning, and I'm expecting Nurse Hunt to join us by two o'clock.' She covered her mouth and coughed. 'If Mrs Hartley continues to enjoy good health, we may weather this crisis yet.'

I joined Osborne for a late lunch, and afterwards we sat in the empty dining room smoking. Through the French windows I saw bands of dark cloud accumulating. Osborne was a little distracted. I thought this was because of his hangover, but as we spoke I realized that there was more to it. He was ruminating about his failed assignation. 'I mean, it wasn't as if she didn't lead me on. She was the one who took the initiative. I suppose I did take a few liberties, but what's a man supposed to do in that situation?' He was clearly concerned about his conduct and the possibility of repercussions; however, this did not prevent him from contemplating future amorous adventures. He was soon rambling on about the nightingales. 'Nurse Brewer is pretty enough, but she can't take a joke. Likewise, Nurse McAllister. A woman of singularly impressive endowments.' His grin twisted in leery amusement. Ordinarily, I would have ignored his silly innuendoes or cut him short, but on this particular occasion I felt obliged to indulge him. It seemed churlish not to, given that he had come to my aid in the middle of the night – albeit because of a drunken afterthought. In due course, he arrived at a not very surprising conclusion: 'If I'm not mistaken, there are only two nurses worth making a play for: Gray and Turner. Now, the thing is, Richardson, I don't want this to become a bone of contention between us. I've given you ample time to declare an interest, and you have chosen to hold your peace, as it were.' Satisfied with his homophonic *double entendre*, he lit another cigarette and raised his eyebrows.

'Do as you please, Osborne.'

'Gray and Turner.' He imitated the seesawing movements of a scale, one hand going up as the other came down. 'Turner and Gray. A difficult decision, don't you think?'

'They're both very attractive women.'

'When all's said and done, though, I think it's got to be the lovely Jane.' He stopped and waited for me to react. When I didn't, he added, 'Yes, I definitely fancy my chances with Nurse Turner.'

There was something ridiculous, indeed, almost sad, about his complete lack of insight. I no longer saw him as conceited and arrogant, but utterly deluded. A buffoon, a cloakroom Lothario, misjudging the women he meant to seduce, and blaming them for being fickle after his maladroit fumblings had earned him a hard slap across the face.

'What makes you feel so confident?' I asked with weary disinterest.

'Oh, she's a game girl all right.' He tapped the side of his nose.

'How would you know?' Contempt had leaked into my voice.

He leaned closer. 'Not long after this place opened,' he looked back over his shoulder, 'we had a patient here, a depressed woman who also suffered from asthma. She was prone to very bad nocturnal attacks. I was already fast asleep when the duty nurse called; the patient was wheezing and turning blue. I got up, rushed over and got the situation under control. It wasn't half as bad as the nurse thought, but to be on the safe side I went upstairs to get some cortisone. At that time, the medications were still stored in a cupboard on the first floor, where the out-patient rooms are now. It must have been about two thirty. I'd just switched the light off and was about to go back downstairs, when the door to Maitland's office opened. Of course, I was expecting the old boy to come out. He didn't – but someone else *did*.' Once again he tapped the side of his nose.

A finger of ice seemed to stroke the nape of my neck.

'How do you know that Maitland was in the room?'
I asked.

'His car was outside.'

'The transfer of staff and resources from London was a
major operation. Perhaps there was an emergency meeting and they were working late. Perhaps Sister Jenkins
was in there too.'

'Come off it, Richardson. There was no light coming
out from under the door. They couldn't have been doing
admin in the dark!'

'Did Nurse Turner see you?'

'Yes. I must have given her a nasty surprise.'

'What did she say?'

'Nothing. She just glared at me and walked straight
past. I must say, I was quite impressed. Another girl
might have gone to pieces. She knew that I *knew* and
that's all there was to it. She didn't make things worse by
trying to persuade me otherwise.' He flicked some ash
into a teacup and added: 'Now, if she can find a soft
spot in her heart for old Maitland – a married man, let's
not forget, and in his fifties – then I'm sure she'll do the
same for me.' I suddenly felt very sick. 'Bloody hell,
Richardson! You're not coming down with this flu are
you? You look terrible.'

'I think I might be. I'm sorry. Excuse me.' I got up so

fast the chair almost toppled over. Osborne had to reach out to steady it. I left him in the dining room and let myself into the men's ward. As soon as I reached the toilet, I fell on my knees and threw up into the bowl.

14

For the next few days I functioned like an automaton. Outwardly I appeared normal: I dispensed drugs, administered ECT, and wrote up notes. But inside I was seething with anger and could not stop myself from thinking about Jane and Maitland. An endless stream of questions flowed through my mind. How did the affair come about? Did it last for very long? Had she really found Maitland, a man over twice her age, attractive? I reconstructed the stages of their relationship and found that my heated imagination was eager to create a coherent narrative. Glances, touches, smiles and small favours. Meetings in Maitland's office. A dinner, perhaps, at a discreet location near the Braxton Club. It was as though I had been handed a stack of photographs by a private investigator. Each scene showed them in increasingly compromised positions and progressed inexorably to the same end: Jane sprawled naked on Maitland's Chesterfield, her pale skin silvered with moonlight. Very occasionally, a small, dissenting voice urged me to give

Jane the benefit of the doubt, but it was difficult to nourish hope. What Osborne had observed seemed to merit only a single, rather seedy interpretation.

Gradually, the routines of Wyldehope were restored. Osborne went back to Saxmundham and the nightingales who had been away over Christmas started to reappear. There were two new cases of flu on the men's ward, but thankfully no more patients were affected. Throughout this period, Maitland called the hospital every day. He appeared in person on the 2nd of January, and immediately sought me out. 'Well done, James,' he said, slapping me on the back. 'I'm indebted.' We went up to his office and he thanked me again for managing the 'crisis'. I was aware of certain clichés being aired – 'darkest hour', 'call of duty' – but I was unable to give his praise my full and undivided attention. The Chesterfield and the unorthodox uses to which it had no doubt been put were a permanent source of distraction. Even so, I kept a tight rein on my emotions and gave Maitland no reason to suspect that anything was wrong.

I became acutely conscious of his age, the sagging flesh around his neck, the uneven pigmentation of his skin, the paunch that even expensive tailoring could not quite disguise; the grey streaks in his hair and the shine, betokening intemperance, that emphasized the size of his nose. My gaze lingered on his big, bucolic hands: hands that had touched the most intimate parts of the woman I had, until only a week before, intended to marry. Eventually it all got too much for me. I presented Maitland with a thin excuse for my departure and hastened to the door.

As I was leaving, he asked, 'Did you read any of those offprints?'

'No,' I said. 'There wasn't the time.'

'Of course,' he smiled. 'How stupid of me.'

Jane returned the following day. I entered the women's ward in a state of trepidation, knowing that she would be there. She was standing in the corridor, receiving instructions from Sister Jenkins. It is almost impossible to express how I felt at that precise moment, but confused would be a fair description. Anger competed with desire, but in the end anger won. Jane turned, registered my presence with feigned indifference, and carried on nodding her head. I busied myself with the patients until Sister Jenkins had left, then I walked back to the nurses' station.

Jane grinned as I approached.

'Happy New Year.'

The muscles in my face felt tight but I managed to reciprocate. 'Happy New Year.'

'What have you done to your hand?'

'It's nothing. I was careless in the kitchen.'

She stood up, swept her gaze around the ward, and kissed me quickly on the lips. 'I've missed you.' Assuming a sulky pout, she added, 'You didn't call me.'

'I was rather busy.'

The pout became a smile again: 'I know. I heard all about it from Sister Jenkins. She said you saved the day.'

'With a little help from Osborne.'

'Well, there's a surprise.'

We exchanged accounts of our respective Christmases, but as I spoke my delivery was becoming flat and increasingly stilted. Once or twice, Jane looked at me quizzically and asked, 'Are you all right?' I shrugged off her enquiry and said that I was still feeling tired, having lost so much sleep and having worked so hard over the past week. We both heard the sound of jangling keys and stepped apart.

'Tomorrow night?' Jane was bright-eyed, eager.

'Yes. Of course.'

When Sister Jenkins appeared again we were both walking in opposite directions.

That night, I lay on the bed, smoking and thinking. My brief encounter with Jane had reminded me of how much I wanted her. I tried to be rational. *All right*, I said to myself, *let's assume that she did have an affair with Maitland. Is that such a bad thing? She hasn't cheated on me, as such.*

And she's had other lovers, surely? I had always approved of her rejection of conventional morality, the outmoded standards of 'good behaviour' espoused by her parents' generation. Indeed, it was exactly *that* which made her exciting and our relationship possible. I wouldn't have been attracted to a narrow-minded prig. To be the beneficiary of her modernity and to condemn it at the same time was rank hypocrisy on my part. Why couldn't I just accept that Maitland was a former lover, in the same way that I accepted those other nameless individuals from her past?

The first sticking point seemed to be the fact that Jane had kept the affair a secret. True, I hadn't been cheated, but I still felt betrayed. Lovers are not obliged to confess their histories, but given the circumstances I felt that in this particular instance I had had a right to know. Secondly, there was something about their age discrepancy, thirty years at least, that made me feel deeply uncomfortable. A young woman making herself available to a considerably older man suggests the operation of ulterior motives. What was in it for her, really? Jane suddenly seemed much less like a modern woman and more like a common tart. She had cheapened herself irredeemably.

I stubbed out my cigarette in an ashtray overflowing with filters. Swinging my legs off the side of the bed, I got up, coughed, and went to make myself a cup of tea. In the dark rectangle of the window I saw my reflection: a transparent man floating in space. He looked drawn and exhausted. Before pouring the milk, I waved it under my nose. It had gone off and I had to have my tea black. As I was leaving the kitchen, I noticed a mark on the door: a circular patch of discoloration. Moving closer, I saw that the paint had blistered. I ran my fingers over the uneven surface and the brittle bubbles shattered. Flakes came away and fell to the floor. It was as though the door had been exposed to heat, but there was no scorch mark, no sooty residue. I remembered the flame in the darkness, advancing down the corridor. If I had been in a different state of mind, I might have given this new phenomenon the consideration it deserved. But I didn't. I had too many other things to think about.

The following night, Jane knocked on the landing door. As soon as she had slipped through the gap, she hauled me close and pressed her lips against mine. I almost forgot all of my tortured deliberations in that first, heady moment. Yet the desire that her greedy kiss awakened in me was short-lived. Passion was swiftly replaced by objectivity and I suddenly felt disengaged. I pulled away and said, 'Let's go to the bedroom.' Ill-chosen words, because Jane thought that I was impatient to make love and she threw me a look of lascivious intent.

When we reached the bedroom, she took off her cap and primped her hair. Before she could remove any more items of clothing, I offered her a cigarette. It was a crude manoeuvre, but it worked. She sat on the edge of the bed, crossed her legs, and spoke airily about her mother, Christmas and London. I don't know how long this went on for. All that I can recall is becoming increasingly restless and tense. In the end, I couldn't hold back any longer.

'Jane,' I said, 'there's something I want to ask you.' Her expression was so childlike, so trusting, that my resolve almost faltered. 'This is very difficult,' I sighed.

'James? What's the matter?'

'When Osborne was here last he said something that's been troubling me. He was being indiscreet. It concerns you,' I paused before adding, 'and Maitland.'

'Me and Maitland? What on earth are you talking about?'

'He said that shortly after this place opened, he saw you coming out of Maitland's office in the early hours of the morning. He said that it was pretty obvious what had been going on.'

'Going on?'

'Don't make me spell it out, Jane, please. This is difficult enough as it is.'

A number of emotions seemed to pass across her face
in quick succession before she adopted an attitude of
guarded neutrality.

'I *was* in Maitland's office that night. But that doesn't
mean . . .' Her hands moved up and down as if she were
juggling. 'That doesn't mean what Osborne thinks.'

She could not maintain eye contact and her gaze slid
away to the side.

'What were you doing in Maitland's office at that
time?'

'We were . . .' She stopped abruptly and I detected
the outward signs of calculation. 'We were discussing the
nursing arrangements.'

'At two thirty?'

'I was doing a night shift. He called me up and asked
me to give him my opinion of a trainee. She's gone now.
She wasn't very good.'

'Why didn't he ask Sister Jenkins?'

'I'm sure he did. He was in a bit of a quandary. You
see, the girl was the daughter of a colleague.'

Jane snatched the cigarette packet and struck a match.

'Osborne said that there was no light coming out from
under the door.'

'What?'

'He said that you and Maitland were together in the dark.'

She drew on the cigarette and expelled a large cloud of smoke. Her eyes began to brim with tears. I asked her a few more questions, but she simply looked down and shook her head.

'It's true then,' I said, 'you and Maitland?'

There was a long pause. I could hear the sea, the interminable advance and retreat of the waves. Jane was not sobbing, but her face was now lined with tracks of mascara. Eventually she answered: 'What if it is?'

I had known all along that my interrogation would inevitably lead to an admission. Even so, when it came, I was still mentally unprepared. My breath caught and I produced a pathetic little gasp.

Jane looked up. Her eyes had sunk into beds of swollen skin. 'So what are you saying?' she cried. 'That it's all over now? Because I slept with another man?'

But it wasn't just any man. It was Maitland. And that made all the difference.

'You didn't tell me,' I said, my voice quivering slightly.

'There was no need to, was there? I knew it would upset you. I didn't want you to get hurt.' She grimaced. 'Is that a crime?'

'And what about honesty? Doesn't that come into it?'

'I didn't want you to get hurt,' she repeated in a beseeching tone. She drew on the cigarette a few more times and then discarded the filter in the ashtray. 'It was a stupid thing to do. I know that now. It didn't mean anything and we both regretted it after.'

'It happened just the once?' I wanted to hear that there had been only a single transgression. Somehow, that seemed more excusable, easier to come to terms with.

Jane blushed and said, 'Well, no.'

'How long were you . . .?' I halted in order to moderate my language. 'Together?'

'It was a fling,' Jane said. 'That's all. I don't know why I did it and I don't think he knows why he did it either. He's been married for years and he's devoted to his wife.'

'Obviously.'

'Oh, don't be like that, James. Everyone makes mistakes. We can get over this, I know we can. I'm sorry I didn't tell you.'

She clasped me in a clumsy embrace. I felt her breath on my neck, kisses, her hand on my thigh. Lovers often believe that they can resolve their differences in bed. But I have never subscribed to this view. A spasm in the loins is not redemptive. It does not confer absolution or erase memories.

Jane realized that her efforts were having little effect and withdrew. We sat side by side, staring at the wall, listening to the sea and our own uneven respiration. Eventually, she stood up and said, 'I think I'd better go.' I didn't stop her. Her heels sounded a slow, faltering step down the hallway and when the door to the landing closed behind her, it filled the hospital with a sonorous boom. Only then did I allow the grief and misery that had been accumulating in my tight chest to find expression. Something ruptured and I began to weep.

When, after an hour or so, I went to bed, my sleep was fitful and disturbed by bad dreams.

The worst of these woke me at about four o'clock. I was in a subterranean cave, which I recognized as one of the healing temples of ancient Greece. In front of me the sleep-room patients were laid out on beds, just as they were in reality, in two rows of three. Jane, naked but for her nurse's cap, was walking between them. Her body looked particularly statuesque and the proud swell of her breasts parted a thick blue smoke like the prow of a ship. She was approaching an elevated, rocky platform, on top of which stood a high priest. He was wearing a long robe, embroidered with gold symbols, but his face was concealed behind an enormous ram's head. Massive horns projected from the skull and spiralled backwards. I sensed that the high priest was, in fact, Maitland, or at least a version of him supplied by my unconscious. Jane fell to her knees and bowed. Her pale body was illuminated by flaming torches and the air was thick with a sickly sweet incense. I could see the divided perfection of her buttocks, the soles of her feet, and the unbroken smoothness of her back. There was no doubt in my mind that I was witnessing the prelude to some initiation ceremony. The priest stepped down, opened his robes, and as he did so I was abruptly returned to consciousness. I switched on the lamp. The dream had seemed so real that my bedroom appeared insubstantial by comparison. I expected the flimsy walls to topple backwards at any moment like a poorly constructed stage set.

A period of time elapsed, during which I seemed paralysed, unable to feel emotion and unable to make decisions. Headaches rendered me insensible. I spent hours alone in my room. I should have been thinking things through, but my mental apparatus seemed to have seized up. The dusty atmosphere irritated my sinuses and I found it difficult to breathe. I decided that I needed to get out, to interpose distance between myself and Wyldehope's oppressive interior. As luck would have it, I reached this decision just before Kenneth Price arrived from Saxmundham to relieve me for the weekend. I

immediately set off for Hartley's cottage and asked him
if I could have one of the bicycles. All of them were
available.

When I reached the Dunwich road I did not follow it
down to the village. Instead, I veered off in a north-
westerly direction, through some woodland, over a
stream, and then out across a bleak landscape of undulating muddy fields.

On a nearby rise, I saw a shanty town of ramshackle
enclosures constructed from sheets of timber and corru-
gated metal. Pigs busied themselves in the open spaces,
wandering around with their snouts pressed to the
ground. Some collected in groups, while others basked
alone in pools of filth. There was something about their
gatherings and dispersals that evoked human society, a
resonance that quickly acquired more sinister overtones:
watchtowers, barbed wire and smoking chimneys. The
war had changed everything. Even pig farms had become
emotionally complex.

Although I had consulted a map before leaving
Wyldehope, I had no fixed plan, no itinerary, just a vague
notion of following a circular route that would eventually
take me back to Dunwich. It was more or less by chance
that I came to Wenhaston, a pretty enough village, but
very small and quiet. As I walked up and down its main

thoroughfare, I didn't encounter a single inhabitant. I would have moved on, but I was deterred by the appearance of dark splotches on the pavement. Looking up at the sky, I saw that a mass of low black cloud was floating overhead and I thought it would be sensible to wait for it to pass before resuming my journey. I made for the church intending to shelter for a short while.

Beyond the gates was a very typical example of an English country church, the most prominent feature of which was a high, square tower. The rain began to fall more heavily and I felt cold droplets landing on my skin. I quickened my pace and, after passing through a white-washed porch, entered the nave. To my left was a velvet curtain that partially obscured a circle of hanging bell-ropes, and to my right an aisle leading to a raised altar. An excessive amount of devotional clutter made the interior look disordered.

I found myself facing what I at first thought to be a mural of some considerable age, but as I drew closer I realized that the images had not been painted on a wall, but an arch-shaped screen made of horizontal planks. The artist seemed to have chosen a hierarchical arrangement of figures, the King of Heaven hovering near the apex and the denizens of Hell gathered lower down. Attached to the bottom of the screen was a board covered in Gothic script. A typed information sheet mounted in a frame informed me that I was standing in front of *The Wenhaston Doom*, a fifteenth-century depiction of the Last Judgement.

My eye was drawn to a horde of demons, corralling naked sinners into the mouth of a giant fish with teeth the size of elephant tusks. A red devil, with an elongated nose and chin, had a naked woman slung over his back. He gripped her ankles, a foot held either side of his head, with sharp claws. The woman was hanging upside down, flailing helplessly, the seam of her hairless sex exposed between parted thighs.

Adjacent to this hideous spectacle was an Archangel armed with a mighty broadsword. He was being challenged by the largest of the demons, so large he might have been Satan himself – a black giant with piercing eyes and scalloped wings. His most grotesque feature was a malevolent second face extruding from his abdomen.

My gaze dropped to the Gothic script. I could decipher some words – 'God', 'Rulers', 'Evyll' – but it was mostly illegible.

As I looked at this curious world of pain and suffering, I marvelled at the extraordinary capacity of the human mind to summon up scenes of horror. I had no belief in psychoanalysis, but in one respect I was prepared to concede that Freud might be right: there are horrible things lurking in the unconscious, things released in dreams, or given illusory substance by the imbalanced chemistry of a sick brain. I shivered and left the church.

The remainder of the morning was spent cycling from village to village. Around midday, I stopped next to a reed bed where I ate a cheese and tomato sandwich and drank tea from a Thermos flask. It was there that I did my most profitable thinking. The flat expanse was peaceful and the prospect therapeutic. Afterwards, I followed signposts that directed me back towards the coast. The low cloud had settled into charcoal-grey layers, and when the hospital finally came into view it was already getting dark. I rolled the bicycle into Hartley's shed and went straight to my rooms.

I had more or less resolved to leave Wyldehope; however, my day out (the fresh air, the landscape, and the wholesome pleasure of doing something physical for a change) had altered my perspective. I was still angry at Jane, but I wasn't about to let her sordid behaviour ruin my career. The textbook was too important. It had to be finished before I could consider moving on. Then that mansion flat in Hampstead could still be mine. As before, the interior was easily envisaged: tall windows, the city in the distance, chintz settee. A woman, standing by the

fire – not Jane, of course, but someone else – attractive, sophisticated, uninterested in mundane chatter; the
daughter of a professor, perhaps, well-read and witty,
able to appreciate my accomplishments; her copies of
Jean-Paul Sartre and Simone de Beauvoir would pave
the floor. It was just a question of biding my time. In the
interim, work would keep me occupied and I might even
play some golf. According to Osborne, female compan-
ionship was always to be had in the clubhouse bar.

Dr Ian Todd
Highgate Hospital
Southwood Lane
London N6

1st July 1955

Dr Hugh Maitland
Department of Psychological Medicine
St Thomas's Hospital
London SE1

Dear Dr Maitland,

Re: Miss Sarah Blake (d.o.b. 3. 1. 1933)
        No present address.

Thank you for your letter. I believe we have three
patients currently in our care who meet your referral
criteria; however, I would like to begin with Sarah
Blake, who is perhaps the most problematic. She
suffers from hebephrenia and her condition has been

worsening steadily for eight months (logorrhoea with marked clang associations, inappropriate affect, impaired self-care, loss of appetite).

Her history is rather curious: Sarah's mother, Dolores Blake, suffered from post-natal depression and her father, Mr Graham Blake, abandoned his wife and child when Sarah was only eighteen months old. Subsequently, Sarah and her mother received considerable financial help from Mrs Blake's sister, Mrs Louise Clarke (the wife of a successful vintage car dealer).

Mrs Blake and Sarah moved from their tenement in Holloway to a comfortable mansion block on the Highgate–Dartmouth Park border, where Sarah attended a private school and was judged to be very able. During the war, Sarah and her mother moved to Hertfordshire for two years. At eleven, she developed a fascination with fire and got into trouble with the local police. She would empty out bins in public parks, douse the rubbish with paraffin, and set it alight with matches; however, the simple deterrent of the removal of all her privileges was enough to eradicate the problem.

When Sarah was fifteen, Mrs Blake became romantically involved with a younger man to whom

she loaned a significant sum of money. The
relationship ended and the ungrateful absconder
made no attempt to repay his debt. A year or so later,
Mrs Blake became attached to another ne'er do well,
causing her sister to voice objections in no uncertain
terms. An ensuing family row resulted in Mrs Clarke
deciding to withdraw her financial support, and
Sarah and her mother were forced to move back to
Holloway. Sarah attended a new school which was
very inferior and she was deeply unhappy. Once
residual funds had been exhausted, Mrs Blake's
relationship was predictably short-lived and a second
episode of depression followed.

Sarah left school and found employment in a shoe
shop in the Nag's Head area, and shortly after moved
into a bedsit on the top floor. She became obsessed
with occult subjects (astrology, Tarot cards, etc., etc)
and sought the company of others who shared this
interest. Apparently, there is a bookshop situated near
the British Museum where enthusiasts congregate,
and as soon as Sarah learned of this meeting place,
she began to attend talks there.

At twenty, Sarah started to hear voices, which she
attributed to discarnate entities, a view endorsed by
those with whom she was associating. Her behaviour

and choice of clothes became eccentric (her mother described it as 'fancy dress') and she lost her job; however, she continued to pay her rent. She was helped, so she says, by a wealthy gentleman with whom she had become acquainted at the occult bookshop. I have been unable to establish the precise nature of their relationship, but I am inclined to believe that his generosity was not unconditional. Sarah mentioned having acute 'stomach pains' and heavy menses, which I suspect were miscarriages. She did not consult a doctor.

Sarah continued to live in this fashion until last year, when, on the 15th of September, she almost succeeded in burning down the building in which she lived. She was seen sprinkling paraffin on the stairs by another tenant, who immediately ran to get help. The fire station is very close and the blaze was quickly brought under control. Nobody was injured. When asked why she did this, she replied, 'I like to watch fires. The flames are exciting.'

When I first saw Sarah, she was very ill, but still able to give an account of herself. Mrs Blake (now severely depressed and an in-patient at the Royal Northern) gave a corroborative interview shortly after Sarah came to Highgate. Sarah's mental state deteriorated rapidly soon after her admission. She is now rarely lucid, speaks gibberish and spends much of her time drawing concentric circles which she calls 'horoscopes'. Last month she cut her wrist and daubed arcane symbols on a wall with her own blood. It was most distressing for the nurses.

I feel that we have now done all that we can for Sarah and she needs to be transferred to a facility offering a more radical approach. If you would like to arrange an assessment, then please contact me through my secretary, Mrs Hampden (telephone: HIG 3562).

It is regrettable that a child who showed much early promise has been brought so low by her condition. If you were to achieve only modest treatment gains, I would consider that an impressive accomplishment.

Yours sincerely,

Ian Todd

Dr Ian Todd
MB BS, DPM

15

Michael Chapman and I had not discussed the extraordinary occurrences of Christmas night. From the moment Osborne had divulged their secret, I had become entirely preoccupied with Jane and Maitland's affair and had thought of little else; however, after confronting Jane and making my decision to stay at Wyldehope, I found myself thinking more and more about those strange events: the power cut, the slamming doors and the half-seen face behind the advancing flame. I wanted to sit down with Chapman and compare my own recollections with his, but he was becoming increasingly paranoid, and I did not want to aggravate his condition by interrogating him. When he was at his worst, I would find him hiding behind an armchair in the recreation room or trying to decipher scratch marks on the table. If his mood improved, he could still manage a game of chess, although he was listless and frequently complained of headaches. A problem not helped, I am sure, by the development of a curious obsession.

I discovered Chapman sitting on his bed, writing furiously in a notebook and surrounded by discarded pages. He was so absorbed he failed to notice my arrival. I looked over his shoulder and saw what appeared to be a complex algebraic problem, but when I looked closer I realized that he was, in fact, repeating a single proposition:

$$\text{Let } R = \{\, x \mid x \notin x \,\}, \text{ then } R \in R \Longleftrightarrow R \notin R$$

'What's that?' I asked.

Chapman covered the page with his hand. 'Nothing,' he replied. I saw no profit in pursuing the matter and left him alone.

A few hours later he was more amenable. He didn't appear tense and he was writing at a more leisurely rate. I sat beside him, ran my finger beneath a single instance of several iterations, and said, in a tone suggesting casual interest, 'Some kind of logical problem, is it?'

Chapman did not look up. 'Russell's paradox,' he replied.

'Would that be Bertrand Russell?'

He nodded.

Like Maitland, the famous philosopher was always on the wireless. They had both featured on the same programme only a few months earlier.

'Did you ever run into him when you were at Trinity?' I asked.

'His voice annoyed me,' said Chapman.

I pointed at the symbols again. 'Russell's paradox. Would you care to explain?'

'It demonstrates that Cantor's naive set theory leads to a contradiction.'

'I'm sorry, Michael. That doesn't mean very much to me.'

'You must have heard of the barber paradox, surely?'

'No. I can't say I have.'

Chapman chewed the end of his pencil and said, 'A barber's job is to shave all the men in a village who do not shave themselves. But this means that he can't shave himself, because he can only shave people who don't shave themselves. Do you see?' I thought about it for a moment and shook my head. 'All right,' Chapman continued, 'it's a little like saying, "This sentence is false." If the sentence is true, then the sentence is false – which means that what it states is true. A sentence can't be true and false at the same time. But in this case . . .' His expression suddenly changed and he looked worried.

'Why are you troubling yourself with all this, Michael? It doesn't seem to be doing you any good.'

'It's important to know what is true. What one can trust.'

'The evidence of your senses might be a reasonable place to start?'

'But a straight stick looks crooked in water.' He employed his tongue to make a knocking noise on the roof of his mouth. *'Cogito Ergo Sum.'*

'I think, therefore I am?'

'The only certainty. As for the rest . . .' He struck the page with his pencil. 'Full of contradictions. Paradoxes are like fault-lines: they show where the weaknesses are, the shoddy workmanship, the dodgy joins that can so easily fall apart.'

I did not know how to respond.

This conversation turned out to be one of the last I would ever have with Chapman. Soon after, he became agitated and impossible to talk to. 'What have I done?' and 'Will I be punished?' These were the only things he said, and he would stand for hours by the window, gripping the bars and whimpering.

Chapman's deteriorating health might have been due, at least in part, to his new medication. I raised the subject with Maitland, but he was insistent that Chapman should stay on the same drug and even suggested that the dosage should be increased. 'With these compounds,' said Maitland, 'a period of apparent decline often precedes full recovery. The Boston trials show this. Mr Chapman must stick to his treatment plan. It is in his best interests to do so.'

I didn't share Maitland's confidence in the studies he referred to. The results, as I remembered them, were not straightforward. I wondered how ill Chapman would have to get before Maitland took my concerns seriously. Very ill indeed, I suspected.

In spite of my efforts to be rational, to think only of my long-term goals, being in Maitland's company continued to make me uneasy. Especially so when we had meetings in his office. That Chesterfield of his was a constant provocation. Unwanted sexual images would flood into my mind and I was powerless to stop them. Curiously, I found it much easier to be with Jane. When we encountered each other, we adopted the spare, economical speech of professionals, and we only communicated when it was absolutely necessary. Once or twice Jane threw me a hurt, resentful look, but she quickly recovered her poise. She had obviously taken Lillian Gray into her confidence. Her dutiful friend had become aloof and subtly contemptuous whenever I was in her presence. It was not an ideal situation. I found myself eating in my rooms more often than I used to and writing more. Although I had toyed with the idea of joining Osborne at his golf club, I knew, deep down, that this wasn't for me.

I imagined a tawdry provincial bar, bored, tipsy house-wives, the dubious promise of assignations in anonymous hotels. The idea had initially appealed to me only because I wanted to get back at Jane.

I finally finished writing up my third Edinburgh experiment, which I promptly sent to the editor of the *British Medical Journal*. The two papers I had submitted in the summer had already been accepted for publication and I was confident that the third would meet with his approval. Although co-writing Maitland's textbook would be very time-consuming, I did not want to discontinue conducting original research, as the ongoing production of scientific papers would *also* greatly benefit my career. I had been thinking about how the sleep-room patients tended to dream at the same time, and it occurred to me that this was a phenomenon worthy of systematic study.

When I broached the subject with Maitland, he was as sceptical as I had expected him to be. 'You're sure of this?'

'Yes. And it's happening with increasing frequency. One of them starts and the others follow. Then one will stop, and shortly after they've all stopped.'

'I've never seen that happen.'

'With respect, Hugh, I spend a great deal of time in the sleep room.'

Maitland considered the point and judged it to be a fair one. 'Have you seen anything like it before?'

'No. But I've never worked in an environment where patients are kept asleep for so long.'

'Walter Rosenberg's team are a little ahead of us. He hasn't mentioned anything like this.'

'Perhaps they haven't noticed. Or perhaps the phenomenon is unique to our group.'

Maitland shook his head. 'I don't know, James. There isn't a mechanism that could account for what you are describing.' His features gradually contracted into a scowl. 'What are you suggesting? That some form of telepathy is taking place?' Maitland raised his eyebrows.

'Brains *do* generate electric fields. If they didn't, nothing would appear on an EEG. Electrodes are placed outside the skull, not inside. As such, an EEG machine picks up brainwaves at a distance.'

'Come now, James, that's a specious argument.'

'There are similar precedents,' I persevered.

'Such as?'

'Menstrual synchrony. When women live together in groups their periods tend to coincide.'

'That has never been demonstrated.'

'There's considerable anecdotal evidence.'

'As I said,' Maitland's smile was cold, 'it has never been demonstrated.'

I eschewed further argument in favour of a simple, direct request. 'Is there any harm in asking the nurses to make regular observations?'

Maitland squeezed his lower lip and after a long, contemplative pause said, 'No. I suppose not. Providing Sister Jenkins doesn't object. And if there is something happening here, something that you can prove, well,' he finally conceded, 'that *would* be interesting.'

We went on to discuss the textbook. After thirty minutes or so, our conversation had become quite intense. Maitland was in full spate when the telephone rang. He looked at it angrily, as if the caller were trying, on purpose, to interrupt his train of thought. Maitland went on talking, but eventually he accepted defeat and lifted the receiver. After an initial, irascible exchange, he fell silent, and I watched his expression become increasingly anxious. I listened to him asking a series of questions: 'Where did it happen? At what time? Is she all right? How serious? Can I speak to her?' His eyes fixed on one of the framed photographs on his desk. 'Yes, of course. I'll come at once. Thank you.' He replaced the receiver.

'What is it?' I asked.

'My wife,' he replied. 'She's had an accident. I'm afraid I've got to go.'

He stood up and marched to the door. He didn't even stop to collect his hat and coat. I caught up with him on the stairs. 'Hugh? What's happened?'

'She was driving in town . . .' His speech was disjointed, breathless. 'Leicester Square – a collision. Sounds as if she's in quite a bad way.'

'I'm so sorry. If there's anything . . .'

He wasn't listening to me. When we got to the bottom of the stairs he was too distracted even to say goodbye. I watched him leave and waited until the silence was broken by the Bentley's powerful engine. The tyres spun and pieces of gravel sprayed against the porch as he pulled away. I had left my papers in Maitland's office and set off to collect them at once. But, as I made my way up the stairs, I was thinking: *he forgot to lock the door.* This had never happened before and I experienced a vague sense of expanding possibilities, a quickening in my chest.

Standing by Maitland's desk, I could still hear the drone of the Bentley, although it quickly dwindled to nothing as it crossed the heath. I scanned the room, registering familiar objects, now made unfamiliar by the novelty of solitude: glass dome with stuffed birds, globe, drinks cabinet – Chesterfield. The atmosphere was still hazy with cigarette smoke and retained a faint trace of Maitland's cologne. My gaze settled on the photograph that he had been looking at. Maitland had never told me that the subject of this old-fashioned portrait was his wife, but I knew that it must be her. The skin of her face appeared unnaturally smooth and her thin lips had been improved by the reflective gloss of a well-placed studio light. She looked beautiful but synthetic. Even so, something in her eyes, a spark of humanity, survived the brittle glamour of her pose. It was odd, I thought, how she and I were both obscurely connected by the same falsehoods. Her hands were clasped together, but her wedding ring was still clearly visible.

I did not deliberate. I walked straight over to Maitland's grey filing cabinet and tried the bottom drawer. It was locked. I glanced at the door and began a frantic search. Minutes were wasted before the glint of silver in an empty glass ashtray captured my attention. I grabbed the key, returned to the cabinet and slid it into the lock.

The drawer rolled out, revealing six folders. Each one had the name of a sleep-room patient written on the spine. I took out the nearest and turned to the referral letter at the back. It was dated 26th February 1955 and addressed to Maitland at St Thomas's. The correspondent was a consultant based at the Maida Vale Hospital, a Dr

Angus McWhirter. *Dear Hugh, I would be most grateful if you would see Miss Webb: a young woman with a history of schizophrenia and severe mood disturbance.*

I read on.

Kathy Webb's life had been blighted by misadventure and a succession of breakdowns. She had been advised to have an abortion, but after the operation she began asking for the return of her 'baby'. In due course, she became suicidal and haunted by 'devils'. Isobelle Stevens's history was not dissimilar. Her referral letter, written by Dr Joseph Grayson at the London Hospital, detailed a corresponding pattern of events – mental disintegration, misfortune, pregnancy; although, in Isobelle's case, a baby was actually born and removed for fostering. The third referral letter was a personal communication from Dr Peter Bevington, whose name I recognized. He was the colleague Maitland had stayed with over Christmas. The patient who we called Celia Jones, I was surprised (perhaps even shocked) to discover was not the *real* Celia Jones, but an unknown person who had been in a depressive stupor for over a decade.

Out of the corner of my eye I saw something move. The curtains on the opposite side of the room were gently undulating. Yet the cigarette smoke still hung on the air in a state of static suspension.

'Not now,' I whispered. I had waited a long time for this opportunity to learn more about the sleep-room patients, and in all likelihood there would not be another.

I picked up the fourth folder: Marian Powell had lived in a number of children's homes since the death of her guardians – an aunt and the aunt's husband. One of these institutions was the infamous Nazareth House, where she had very probably suffered horrible deprivations and abuse. She was diagnosed with schizophrenia at the age of thirteen. A queer aside stated that one of her teachers believed that she possessed psychic powers, and consequently arranged for her to be tested by members of a learned society.

Perhaps the mere suggestion of the supernatural was enough to aggravate my nerves. I checked the curtains, but thankfully they were no longer moving.

The fifth referral letter was not written by a professional. It was addressed to Maitland at the BBC and was from Elizabeth Mason's mother, Matilda, who had apparently heard Maitland speaking on the wireless about madness. The poor woman was clearly quite desperate and finding it difficult to cope. Elizabeth had been jilted on her wedding day, a trauma so great (at least for her) that she subsequently became delusional. She refused to take off her dress and became a kind of Miss Havisham figure. The clinical picture was later complicated by agoraphobia. Sarah Blake – the last of the six – had been referred to Maitland by Dr Ian Todd at the Highgate Hospital on the 1st of July. She had been caught attempting to burn down the building in which she and another tenant rented rooms. Her pyromania had been foreshadowed in childhood by a morbid fascination with fire, and this had returned, more malignantly, in the context of much wider psychopathology: unusual interests, auditory hallucinations and unorthodox behaviour – namely, the acceptance of financial patronage in exchange for sexual favours.

Apart from Celia Jones's folder, which had very little inside it, the others were quite thick and bulky. Flicking through them, I saw in-patient records from other hospitals, occupational therapy reports, typed letters and treatment summaries. Sarah Blake's folder also contained an astrological chart, drawn by her, and a rather good self-portrait. I dearly wanted to take the folders away with me, but didn't have the courage to do so.

All of the sleep-room patients were of a similar type – orphaned, disowned, forgotten, lost. As I turned the pages, I wondered why Maitland had been so reluctant to discuss these sad histories. I remembered my meeting with Palmer and how I had raised this issue, but he had been dismissive, saying only that he had long since given up trying to fathom Maitland's motives. After reading the referral letters and leafing through the folders, I was prepared to accept that Palmer's conclusion may have been justified; however, as these thoughts were still passing through my mind, I came across a startling memorandum in Marian Powell's notes. It bore the inky impressions of numerous rubber stamps and had been copiously annotated. At the top of the page, printed in black letters, were the words 'Central Intelligence Agency, Washington DC'. I was just about to start reading the memorandum when I was disturbed by sounds coming from the corridor: a heavy, unhurried tread accompanied by a metallic jingle. With great haste I replaced the folders, closed the bottom drawer, locked the filing cabinet and tossed the keys into the ashtray. My papers were piled together on Maitland's desk, so I gathered them up and held them against my chest. The door, which I had left slightly ajar, creaked open and Hartley stepped into the room. He said nothing, but his silence and slit eyes demanded that I explain myself.

'Dr Maitland's wife has had an accident,' I said without preamble. 'He left in a hurry. I was just collecting my things.'

'A serious accident?' Hartley enquired.

'Yes. I think so.'

The caretaker nodded. 'Did Dr Maitland say when he'd be coming back?'

'No, he didn't.'

I passed out into the corridor and Hartley produced a bunch of keys. He selected one and locked the door. Picking up his toolbox, he indicated the room opposite. 'A faulty sash.'

'I see,' I answered. He made a casual, mock salute, and left me standing there, clutching my papers.

16

I wanted to be alone, to consider what I had learned about the sleep-room patients. But when I reached the landing, Nurse Fraser was coming up the stairs. She stopped and said, 'Ah, there you are, Dr Richardson. I've been looking for you.'

'Why? What's the matter?'

'It's Mr Chapman. He's getting very agitated and . . .' She hesitated before adding, 'There's blood on his pyjamas.'

'Blood?'

'He must have hurt himself. He wouldn't let me take a look.'

I deposited my papers at the nurses' station and went directly to Chapman's room. There, I found him pacing and muttering to himself.

'Michael,' I said, 'can you stand still for a moment.'

He took no notice, so I stepped in front of him and grabbed his shoulders. A few seconds passed before his lined, anxious face showed signs of recognition. 'Dr Richardson?' His voice was quavery and uncertain.

'Yes. It's me, Michael.'

'You must let me leave.'

'I'm afraid I can't. You know that.' I released his shoulders and pointed at the left sleeve of his pyjama jacket. The stripy material was mottled with irregular red stains. 'What have you done to yourself?'

'Nothing.'

I reached out to examine his arm but he stepped backwards.

'Come now, Michael, let me see.'

'No!' he snapped. But then his lower lip started to tremble and his mouth twisted. 'I didn't mean to harm her. I just wanted to watch. I just wanted to look.' He produced a great, heaving sob, and tears filled the sagging pockets of flesh beneath his eyes.

'Never mind,' I said, taking his hand. 'Let's not worry about the past.' I guided him to the bed and gave him a gentle push so that he fell backwards and had no choice but to sit on the mattress. Then I rolled up the stained sleeve. It was an ugly sight and I did my best not to recoil. The skin of Chapman's forearm was livid and broken in several places. He might have been suffering from some rare, ulcerating disease. I noticed that there was a black crust of dried blood under the thumbnail of his right hand. 'Michael, have you been pinching yourself again?'

He didn't answer.

I called Nurse Fraser and, together, we dressed Chapman's arm. Subsequently, we helped him into a fresh, clean pyjama jacket and I gave him a sedative.

It didn't work.

An hour or so later he was up again, pacing the room. Worse still, he had removed the bandages so that he could continue pinching himself. I gave him another sedative, which was effective for no more than twenty minutes, after which Chapman was shouting down the corridor at Nurse Fraser, demanding that he be allowed to go home.

I wasn't sure how safe it would be to attempt further sedation. Particularly so, given that Chapman had been taking a new drug that I had little experience of. It was possible that antagonistic substances were interacting and making him worse, rather than better. I tried to contact Maitland, but his secretary at St Thomas's had no idea where he was. Indeed, she didn't even know that his wife had been in a car accident.

Chapman's behaviour was becoming more and more erratic, and when he started banging his head against the iron bars I knew that the time had come for drastic action. I called Hartley and we both manhandled Chapman into a straitjacket. We then took him to the padded cell, which was located in the tower and to my knowledge had never been used before. It felt horrible, forcing Chapman up the stairs like a prisoner, and I had to keep telling myself that it was for his own good. Hartley unlocked the door and we dragged Chapman inside. It was a claustrophobic space, the floor being no more than an eight-foot square. The walls and the back of the door were upholstered with stuffed leather pouches, which made self-injury impossible. There was a naked bulb suspended from the high ceiling, and a small window, set well out of reach, which admitted insufficient light. Chapman had exhausted himself and became limp. He sank down in a corner and groaned. 'Just rest, Michael,' I said, affecting a carefree lightness of tone. 'As soon as you stop hurting yourself, you can come downstairs again. I promise.' Mucus bubbled out of his nostrils and I wiped his nose with my handkerchief. It is hard to explain, but I felt like a traitor. Hartley locked the door and gave me the key. 'I'll leave another one with Sister Jenkins,' he said gravely.

When Hartley had gone I looked through the peephole in the door and saw Chapman, just where we had left him, in the corner, hunched, broken. The spectacle of his lonely seclusion was almost too much to bear. I discussed Chapman with Sister Jenkins and we decided to watch him closely. Every thirty minutes, a nurse would climb the stairs and check that he was all right.

At ten o'clock in the evening there was a knock on my door and when I opened it I saw Jane standing on the landing. It was just my luck that Sister Jenkins had given her the job of monitoring Chapman. The situation of her late arrival reminded me of all those other nocturnal visits in the past – her falling into my arms, hot kisses and the feel of her undergarments through her uniform. I was irritated by a frisson of desire.

'Mr Chapman has soiled himself.' Jane's lips barely moved as she spoke. 'What do you want me to do?'

'He might suddenly become violent again. I think I'd better help you.'

She did not thank me. We went to the padded cell, in silence, and washed Chapman. After we had changed his pyjamas, Jane mopped the floor with carbolic. I tried to engage Chapman, but he had retreated so far into himself that he seemed completely unaware of my presence.

Jane and I parted, stiffly.

I don't know why I tried, at that late juncture, to make conversation, or why I chose a topic which was so obviously freighted with emotion. 'Did you hear that Maitland's wife has been injured in a serious car accident?'

Jane spun round and her expression communicated both anger and exasperation. She showed me her palms and replied, 'I don't know what you expect me to say.' Then, snatching up the mop and bucket, she strode off in high dudgeon.

I went back to bed and slept fitfully. In the early hours of the morning I awoke and was alarmed to hear screams. It didn't take me long to work out that it was Chapman. I jumped out of bed, put on my dressing gown, and rushed up the tower steps. Looking through the peephole, I could see nothing. Jane must have turned the light off earlier, having found Chapman asleep. I flicked the switch and saw Chapman running around the cell. The space was so small he kept colliding with the walls and falling over. He didn't appear to be trying to hurt himself, but rather desperately trying to evade something that was chasing him. 'Go away!' he shouted. 'Go away! Leave me alone!'

'Michael,' I commanded. 'Sit down, for heaven's sake. You'll sprain your ankle if you carry on like that.'

He stopped dead and came right up to the door. 'Let me out, Dr Richardson. Please let me out. I won't pinch myself, I won't. I'll be good. I give you my word. Please, please let me out.'

'Sit down, Michael. I don't want to have to bind your legs as well as your arms.'

I offered him reassurances and told him that I would return if he called. Eventually, he became less agitated and retreated to his corner, where he crouched down and wrapped his arms around his knees. I asked him who it was that he had been telling to go away, but he only twitched and shook his head. His eyes began to revolve in slow, suspicious circles and he pressed his lips together in mute, childish defiance.

When I was confident that the crisis had passed, I said, 'Michael, I'm going now. Try to relax.'

'Please,' he whined. 'Leave the light on.'

'But you won't sleep,' I protested.

'For the love of God, Dr Richardson.' His voice cracked as he made his plea. 'Please. Leave the light on.'

I did as he asked and went back to bed.

The first thing I did the following morning was attempt, once again, to contact Maitland. He wasn't at home, or at his club, but he had telephoned his secretary at St Thomas's. She was able to inform me that Mrs Maitland had had a successful neck operation and that Maitland was still at her bedside. He had promised to call again as soon as his wife's condition was stable.

When I went to see Chapman, he was still restless, but not as febrile as the day before. With Nurse Brewer's assistance, I managed to feed him and he swallowed his pills without complaint.

'You seem a little better, Michael,' I ventured. He

assented with a minuscule movement of his head. 'I'd like to transfer you back to the men's ward as soon as possible, but you must stop all this head-banging and pinching. Do you understand?' He nodded, this time demonstrating more interest in what I was saying. 'Let's see how you're feeling this afternoon. We'll make a decision then.' I had been sitting next to him on the floor and I pressed down on the cork tiles to get back on my feet. When I reached the door, I looked back at Chapman and our eyes locked.

'Goodbye, Dr Richardson.' His croaky farewell was touching.

'I'll see you later,' I replied.

'Goodbye,' he repeated, somehow imbuing the word with ominous finality. It made me feel uneasy. I have many regrets – more than most, I suspect; however, I dearly wish – at that moment – I had listened more intently to the quiet but insistent voice of intuition issuing its mysterious warning. If I had, then things might have turned out very differently.

At eleven thirty I was in the sleep room. All of the patients were dreaming, and had been dreaming for an hour or so. I found myself hovering at the head of each bed, studying the face of each occupant, and thinking about each individual life – hitherto, completely unknown to me. They were such tragic cases: orphaned, disowned, forgotten, lost. I brushed a lock of hair from Marian Powell's forehead, and pitied the child that had suffered so much ill-use. Covering Elizabeth Mason's hand with my own, I imagined her, broken-hearted, refusing to surrender her wedding dress. These were women who had slipped through all of the safety nets that society had to offer – family, charitable organization, asylum. They had ended up at Wyldehope as a last resort. If Maitland failed them, they would be shunted from institution to institution for the rest of their lives. But were they getting any better? I had no idea. Maitland seemed more concerned about how long they could be kept asleep, rather than whether or not they were showing any signs of improvement. Palmer had questioned the efficacy of deep-sleep therapy. I thought of Rosenberg, the athletic Stratton, and the CIA memorandum in Marian Powell's medical notes; the American colonel who Jane had seen visiting the sleep room at St Thomas's, and the rumours that Maitland was connected in some way with British intelligence.

I was pondering these issues when the door burst open and Nurse McAllister almost fell into the sleep room. She had obviously been running down the stairs. Her cap had fallen off and she looked very frightened.

'Quick!' she cried. Almost inarticulate with shock, she only managed to add, 'Mr Chapman. Something dreadful.'

I rushed up to the tower, taking the steps two at time, and when I came to the padded cell I saw Lillian Gray looking through the open door, a hand clasped over her mouth. Something made me slow down as I made the final ascent, an unwillingness to confront the boundless horror prefigured by the nurse's contorted features. I forced myself forward and, by degrees, the interior came into view. What I saw made me halt at the threshold and reach out on either side for the support of the wooden frame.

Chapman was sitting on the floor, back against the wall, his legs stretched out in front of him. His straitjacket was on the other side of the room, a crumpled heap of leather straps and canvas. Blood trickled down his cheeks, issuing from the two dark, empty orbits formerly occupied by his eyes. One eyeball was close to my right foot. It had been hurled with some force, causing the sclera to split and exude a transparent mass of gelatinous humour. I scanned the floor but could not find the other one.

'Dear God,' I said. 'Michael. What have you done to yourself?'

He raised his head and directed his empty black sockets towards me. There was something about the shape of his face that was wrong. It seemed weirdly elongated. A strange presentiment made me call out to Lillian, 'Don't look. Turn away.'

Chapman opened his mouth and allowed the second eyeball to tumble down his chest and roll across the cork tiles. A fine flagellum of nerve tissue whipped the floor with each rotation.

Then, he began to sing: 'Row, row, row your boat, gently down the stream. Merrily, merrily, merrily, merrily, life is but a dream.'

'Go downstairs – call an ambulance.' I addressed Lillian Gray without looking at her. 'And ask Nurse McAllister to bring me some morphine, antiseptic and bandages.'

As Lillian's footsteps receded, Chapman began to sing again: 'Row, row, row your boat, gently down the stream . . .' And he continued repeating the same refrain, until the morphine took effect and sent him to sleep.

I never saw Chapman again. He was taken to Ipswich. The following day I received a telephone call from an orthopaedic surgeon, who informed me that, in addition to gouging out his own eyes, Chapman had also managed to sustain several other injuries. He had broken his leg and numerous hairline fractures had been detected all over his body. 'The poor man must have really thrown himself about,' said the surgeon. A different image suggested itself to me: books with broken spines.

17

The following day, Maitland telephoned. I asked him about his wife's condition and he explained that she was much improved. When she had been admitted to University College Hospital, it was thought that she might have suffered a brain haemorrhage, but this now seemed unlikely. She did, however, require the surgical removal of a damaged intervertebral disc in order to relieve pressure on the spinal cord. Maitland was still obviously very concerned about his wife's health, but he was sounding much more himself, not at all like the distracted individual I had last seen leaving Wyldehope. I took a deep breath and said, 'Hugh, something's happened.'

'Oh?' he responded, failing to register the trepidation that caused my voice to crack. 'What's that?'

'One of the patients had to be transferred to Ipswich.'

'Not one of the sleepers, I hope.'

'No. Not one of the sleepers,' I repeated.

Maitland listened to my account of Chapman's mental disintegration without a single interruption. When I had finished, I braced myself for a broadside of curses and remonstrations. But there was only a thoughtful pause. 'I did try to contact you,' I began again, nervously attempting to essay a defence. 'You were unavailable.' I may have pressed on ineffectually for a while before my excuses petered out.

'Why didn't you give Mr Chapman more sedation?' Maitland asked.

'I wasn't sure how much more I could risk, what with him being on a new drug. I had already given him over four hundred milligrams of sodium amytal and it simply wasn't having any effect.'

With tactful deference, I politely reminded Maitland of my prior reservations. I had always been doubtful about the new antidepressants from America. Maitland was, as a rule, intolerant of contradiction and I was expecting some kind of angry refutation; however, perhaps he was still so preoccupied with his wife that he was disinclined to argue. Instead of reprimanding me, he agreed – albeit with some reluctance – that a 'bad reaction' was a possibility that could not, at this stage, be excluded. He then asked the question that I was, of course, dreading: 'Tell me, James, how did Chapman get out of the straitjacket?'

'I really don't know.'

'Who put him in it?'

'I did.'

'Are you sure that you put it on properly?'

'Yes. Quite sure.'

'Then how . . . ?' Incomprehension prevented his sentence from reaching its conclusion.

What could I say? That I believed a poltergeist was responsible? 'There must be something wrong with the fastenings,' I said firmly.

'Have you checked them?'

'Yes. To be honest, I can't find anything amiss, but that's the only explanation.'

'Unless . . .' He invited me to consider the less palatable alternative.

'Unless I am mistaken and I wasn't paying sufficient attention when I secured the straps.'

'It happens, you know. I assume Mr Chapman was struggling.'

'Yes, he was.'

His next comment was preceded by an ambiguous beat of silence. 'I'm sure you did your best.'

Maitland then asked me if any of the nightingales had been significantly affected.

'Nurse McAllister and Nurse Gray saw the worst of it. But I think they'll be all right.'

'Good,' he responded. It never ceased to amaze me

how Maitland was always so considerate with respect to *his* nightingales. 'Please make a point of thanking them for me – for their dedication and courage.'

We spoke for a few more minutes and Maitland informed me that he intended to visit Wyldehope in a few days. I wasn't expecting his garbled, sympathetic farewell. 'Look, James. I wanted to say: it can't have been easy for you lately. I realize that. What with Christmas – and now this business with Chapman. You've had a lot to deal with. Let's hope things calm down a bit now, eh?'

It was a sentiment I shared. But things didn't calm down. And worse was yet to come.

I dreamt of the lighthouse, once again. I saw its penumbral outline against the starless sky, its yellow beam sweeping across the slowly moving waves, and heard the harsh noise that accompanied each revolution of the lamp. There was something about this image that now filled me with a terrible, unspeakable dread. The fear was formless, overwhelming, and found expression in a cry of terror that woke me up. The gloomy seascape persisted for a moment and then shattered as if it had been painted onto broken glass.

Darkness and preternatural cold: that is what I remember. The curtains were drawn and must have been overlapping, because I could see absolutely nothing. There was no strip of sky, made faintly luminous by a hidden moon or a scattering of stars. The fear that had accompanied the lighthouse dream had survived the dream's dissolution, and it became, if anything, more intense. I did not move, because of a strong sense of expectation that made me hold my breath and listen intently. When I blinked, I could hear my eyelashes on the pillow. I had no idea what I was waiting for but the presumption was so strong I was all but paralysed. My frozen state revived memories of childhood: the indisputable reality of monsters beneath the bed, inhabiting their shadowy realm of dust and silence – always ready to pounce. I was lying on my side, my knees raised and my back rounded. As I might have done when I was a small boy, I gripped the blanket and attempted to cover my head with it, but my efforts met with resistance. I assumed that the edges had been tucked tightly beneath the mattress and pulled somewhat harder. To my utter astonishment, I felt a response. It was as though a rival had taken hold of the other end and was now pulling in the opposite direction.

The terror that I experienced was wholly physical and

confirmed the descriptive cliché of flesh 'crawling'. A tingling sensation rippled over my body and my scalp prickled as each hair began to rise.

I clutched the blanket tightly, but it began to slip from my fingers. There was a sudden wrench and my protective cover was whipped away. The top sheet, blanket and eiderdown flew across the room and landed heavily near the window. I was naked and my sudden exposure reminded me of how cold it was. The fear that had had its origin in the lighthouse dream continued to compromise my ability to take action, and I remained in a state of petrified immobility. If human beings possess a sixth sense, then it must have been through this channel that I received impressions of movement: something travelling from the far corner of the room, past the foot of the bed, and then coming to a standstill beside me.

It is frequently written that the greatest threat posed by the supernatural is to the mind. There is nothing to fear, so they say, except fear itself. But I was in the presence of a power that could raise a man up and cast him down again, a power that could break a leg and fracture bones, a power that might levitate my bed and send it sailing through the window.

I imagined myself hopelessly flailing in the updraught of rushing air, plummeting to my death. What would they say about me? He was odd, like his predecessor, Palmer. He went crazy after an unhappy love affair. He spent too much time in his rooms, alone.

It was coming closer. My eyes were wide open, I could see nothing, but I knew that it was coming closer. This perception was confirmed when I heard a sigh next to my exposed ear. There was a faint sibilance, two syllables of equal length, but lacking in articulation. These words, if they were words, were unintelligible. I began to tremble and, irrationally, closed my eyes. I kept them tightly shut, pressing the lids together, attempting to interpose at least something between my conscious self and the poltergeist. The passage of time was no longer marked out in minutes and seconds but aeons and eternities. I felt the mattress sag, as it might if someone had just sat down on the edge of the bed. The springs groaned and the sheet tilted downwards. I wanted to scream. I wanted to open my mouth and scream so loudly that Hartley, someone, anyone, would come to my rescue; however, when I tried, I experienced the disconnection between intention and action so typical of nightmares. I produced a tremulous, asthmatic wheeze and my mouth was so dry, when I swallowed, it felt like I was choking.

If the poltergeist meant to harm me, there would be no escape. There had been no escape for Mary Williams or

Michael Chapman – and there would be no escape for me. I pressed my eyelids even more tightly together and braced myself for violence, the sudden release of impossible forces. What actually happened shocked me far more than anything I had expected.

I felt spidery fingers repositioning my hair with exquisite gentleness, a touch that was as light and insubstantial as a puff of air. Then a hand landed on my own. For a few moments, it stayed there, the fleshy palm pressing against my knuckles; however, an instant later, the contact was terminated. The mattress springs produced an ascending scale of indeterminate pitches and the sheet beneath me became level again. I could still sense the poltergeist's progress, as it drifted to the door, where it stopped, to turn the handle. The hinges complained and a draught caressed my cheeks. I heard a curious metallic impact followed by a high-pitched chime that quickly faded. After this, there was nothing but the soft conspiracies of the sea, wind and shingle. I don't know how long I lay there for. When I finally opened my eyes, I was confronted by the same unyielding darkness, but the atmosphere in the room had changed. There was no imminence, no sense of something about to happen.

Even after such an experience, habitual rationalism made me reconsider, once again, the tired explanations I had rejected months earlier: hypnopompic hallucination and so on. But it was a sterile exercise, empty intellectualism. In reality I was certain that something very remarkable had happened, particularly so with respect to the 'touching', which seemed to have been imitative of my small ministrations in the sleep room.

I switched on the lamp. When my eyes had adjusted to the light I looked around the room. Apart from the conspicuous and untidy pile of bed coverings under the window, it looked much the same as it always did. The face of my alarm clock showed four thirty. There was little chance of me going back to sleep again, so I put on my dressing gown, picked up the dirty teacup from the night before, and crossed the hallway to the kitchen. I filled the kettle with water, put it on the stove, and lit a cigarette.

My limbs felt heavy. I was exhausted. Not in some trivial way, but profoundly so, the result of a cumulative, ongoing process that would, if left unchecked, bring about my mental and physical collapse.

It was impossible to go on. I realized that now. Palmer had understood the situation and I should have listened more carefully to his advice. A sane man couldn't live under these conditions – at least, not without unburdening himself now and again. And this was the nub of it. A psychiatrist cannot admit to seeing things that cannot be explained. As soon as he does so, he crosses the line that separates himself from his patients.

I would have to resign. Maitland would be furious and my prospects might be damaged, but there really wasn't any alternative.

The kettle boiled and steam billowed out of the spout. Condensation appeared on the window and I turned off the gas. I picked up my used teacup and was about to rinse it under the tap when I noticed something at the bottom, partly submerged beneath the brown residue and dregs. It was a wedding ring.

I fished out the plain band and dried it on my dressing gown. It was darker and larger than the one I had found before, the one that had belonged to Palmer's young wife. I turned the gold beneath the light bulb and watched a yellow spark chase around its circumference. For some reason, I had a strong urge to put it on. I held it close to the end of my ring finger, but could not bring myself to penetrate the inviting circularity. Moreover, I was overcome by a dreadful feeling of despair. A paroxysm of grief that made my breath catch. I had come close to proposing to Jane, and the ring represented a loss that, in truth, I had barely come to terms with. In fact, as I stood there gazing at the ring, I found the courage to be honest with myself.

I had underestimated the emotional impact of everything: not only the poltergeist (or whatever that capricious spirit might be), but the wearing intensity of my relationship with Maitland, Jane's betrayal, Mary Williams, Chapman and the sleep room. I had fooled myself into believing that a combination of hard work and bloody-mindedness would be enough to see me through, but I was less robust than I had imagined.

At six thirty I went down to the wards where I found Sister Jenkins.

'Where did you find it?' she asked, tilting her hand beneath the desk lamp. The fit was snug.

'In my bedroom.' I no longer cared what she thought.

'But how could it have got up there?' Her features acquired the fixity that comes with burgeoning suspicion.

'I have no idea,' I replied, already walking away.

In my diary, I noticed that Edward Burgess was due for his final appointment. I had seen him a few times since Maitland had treated him with excitatory abreaction, and since then Mr Burgess had been getting steadily better. He was less anxious, his nightmares had subsided, and he no longer suffered from transient paralysis. Although he looked much the same – sloping brow, deep-set eyes – his features had filled out and the tightness of his jacket suggested that his appetite had returned.

'Well,' I said, at the conclusion of our interview. 'I don't think you need to come here again. Do you?'

'No,' he agreed. 'I'm feeling very well indeed. Thank you.'

As he stood to leave, he looked at me rather too closely. 'Are you all right, doctor?'

'What do you mean by that?' I asked.

'You look tired.'

'I am. I didn't get much sleep last night and I have a headache.' We walked down the corridor and out onto the landing. 'Is your driver waiting outside?' I asked.

'Yes. He is. Don't come any further, Dr Richardson. There's no need. I can see myself out.' Burgess stopped and looked around at the staircase and vestibule. His expression was not admiring. 'Not sure I'd like to work here. Strange old place, isn't it?' Our eyes locked and he seemed about to say something else, but instead he shook his head and smiled.

'Goodbye,' I said. 'Keep well.' He nodded, buttoned up his coat and descended the stairs. When he got to the door, he turned round and shouted up at me. 'If you feel like a change of scenery, come to Lowestoft. There's a fancy restaurant. Just opened. I'd be happy to buy you lunch.'

I leaned over the stair rail and called down, 'That's very kind of you.'

He raised his hand. 'I hope your headache gets better.' He then opened the door and stepped outside. Sunlight was streaming through the windows and the air was saturated with a heady smell, like tar or paraffin. As I pushed myself away from the banisters I noticed that one of the carved animals had a blackened face. I crouched down and examined the woodwork more closely. It had been scorched. The varnish had bubbled up and when I stroked my finger over the damaged area a sooty residue came off on my fingers. I wiped my hands clean with my handkerchief and returned to the outpatient suite where I began writing Mr Burgess's discharge summary.

It must have been about one fifteen when I heard one of the nurses approaching. I was already looking up, expectantly, when Nurse Fraser appeared. She stood in the doorway looking somewhat flustered.

'Yes?' I prompted her.

'Dr Richardson . . .' she began. 'We have a problem. The sleep-room patients . . .'

'What about them?'

'We can't wake them up.'

'I'm sorry?'

She lifted her arms and let them fall by her side. 'We

can't wake them up.' The repetition of the same phrase did not make it any more believable.

I put my pen down. 'Which patients?' I asked. 'Who can't you wake?'

'All of them,' she replied.

18

In the sleep room, I found Sister Jenkins anxiously pacing between the beds. Nurse Page was standing next to a trolley on which six covered meals had been stacked.

'Dr Richardson,' said Sister Jenkins, beckoning me to her side. 'This is most peculiar.'

'You can't wake them up?'

'No.' She reached out and shook Sarah Blake's shoulders. Then, positioning her mouth next to the sleeping patient's ear, she said loudly, 'Sarah. Wake up. It's time for lunch.' Another vigorous shake was equally ineffective. Sarah Blake's head lolled from side to side but her eyes remained closed. 'They're all the same,' Sister Jenkins went on, 'completely unresponsive. I don't understand it.'

'Might one of the nurses have made a mistake? Too much chlorpromazine, perhaps?'

'I very much doubt it,' Sister Jenkins replied. 'Nurse Fraser has been on duty this morning. All of my nightingales are scrupulous, but she is *painstaking*. She would never have made such a bad miscalculation.'

Notwithstanding Sister Jenkins's confidence in Nurse Fraser, I decided to check the charts, but found everything in order. There was nothing to suggest oversight or error. The patients had received varying amounts of medication depending on how peacefully they had slept in the preceding observation period. If anything, they had been given slightly lower doses than usual.

Sister Jenkins moderated her voice. 'Have they drifted off into some form of . . .' She hesitated before whispering, 'Coma?'

'I don't think so,' I replied. 'Look at their eyes. Rapid oscillations – see? They're dreaming. As far as I know, dreaming isn't observed very often in coma patients.'

'What are we to do, Dr Richardson? They must be fed, washed, voided.'

'Well, you can't do any of that now. Clearly.'

'Shall I telephone Dr Maitland?'

'No. I'll call him after I've conducted some tests.'

I lifted one of Kathy Webb's eyelids and studied the trembling grey iris beneath. Her pupillary reflexes were normal. 'Kathy?' I said. 'Can you hear me?' I clapped my hands together loudly. 'Kathy?' There was no response, not even a twitch. I patted her cheeks, softly at first, on one side of her face, then the other. Eventually, I was giving her hard slaps that made the skin darken. She remained quite still, her expression impassive, the only movement being that of her eyes. I then attached electrodes to her scalp and ran an EEG. There was no generalized slowing in the delta range. Nor was there any evidence of epilepsy. What I saw was the low amplitude waves associated with normal dreaming.

The other sleepers were just the same. No amount of rocking, slapping or shouting could rouse them, and they all produced identical EEGs.

When I was satisfied that I could do no more, I telephoned Maitland's secretary and asked her to get him to call me back. He did so after twenty minutes. I did my best to explain the situation in a calm, clear-headed way, but a panicky excitement kept on threatening to ruin my measured delivery. When I had finished there was a long pause. I thought the line had gone dead. 'Hugh?' I called into the mouthpiece. 'Are you there?'

'Yes,' he replied. 'I'm still here. Just thinking, that's all. I need to see this for myself. I'll be up later this afternoon.'

'But what about your wife?' I asked.

'She's being well looked after,' he replied. 'She'll be fine.'

Just after five o'clock, I was attending to a patient on the men's ward when I looked out of the window and saw two bright headlights travelling across the heath. I quickly concluded my business and went out into the vestibule. When Maitland entered, he dispensed with any civilities and asked abruptly, 'Any change?'

'No,' I replied. 'They're just the same.'

We went directly down to the sleep room, where I demonstrated how the patients could not be woken up. Afterwards, I showed Maitland the EEG recordings. He said very little and his expression was so severe I became quite nervous. Irrationally, I began to think that he held me responsible for what had happened. When I had finished he went to the beds and tried to wake the patients himself. He then ordered Nurse Page to prepare some syringes. 'Benzedrine,' he said to me. 'That should do it. A double dose of Benzedrine. The effect will be similar to that of adrenalin. We'll see increases in heart rate and a steep rise in blood pressure, with fluctuations of 10 to 30 millimetres. Restlessness, tremor – palpitations, perhaps. It'll create a level of physical arousal completely antagonistic to sleep.'

We injected all of the patients. I listened to Marian Powell's heart through a stethoscope and heard the beat accelerating, but she remained stubbornly unconscious. Celia Jones and Elizabeth Mason also failed to stir. I watched Maitland taking Sarah Blake's pulse, before leaning over the bed and lifting her eyelids with his thumb and forefinger. He looked not merely puzzled, but frustrated. Only ten minutes later I saw him preparing more syringes. When all of the patients had received yet another dose of Benzedrine, Maitland drew me aside and said, 'Well, James, I owe you an apology. I was rather sceptical when you suggested that the sleep-room patients had started dreaming at the same time. One can only assume that your prior observations were indicative of an incremental, ongoing process that has now reached its rather dramatic conclusion.'

'What do you think is going on?'

'It's impossible to say. But if you're asking me to speculate . . .' I gestured for him to continue. 'There must be something about the conditions that prevail here, in the sleep room, that have opened channels of mutual influence: prolonged sleep, proximity, altered brain chemistry, or a combination of all three. As to the basis of the phenomenon, I suppose the interplay of electromagnetic fields is a reasonable preliminary hypothesis. That's what you believe, isn't it? You've said as much.'

'There isn't – as far as I know – another *scientific* alternative.'

Maitland grumbled his assent. 'They appear to have entered a collective dream state from which they cannot be roused. Why should that be? Why should they become stuck, as it were, in a rapid-eye-movement phase of sleep?'

'Perhaps,' I replied, 'brains are, in some sense, more porous when dreaming, and thus more likely to influence each other. In due course, this entanglement might reach a critical threshold beyond which the process becomes irreversible.'

'If we had another EEG machine, it would be interesting to compare the traces, would it not?'

'There might be correspondences, similar patterns . . .'

'Which would be a truly astounding result.'

'I wonder,' I mused, all too conscious of the controversial position I was about to articulate. 'If we asked these patients what they were dreaming about, and they were able to answer, would they report dreams with common elements?'

Maitland considered my provocative suggestion for a moment and then said, 'Let's not get carried away, James. Something very interesting is occurring, certainly. But we must remain sceptical. Think of all those medical men in the past, who were professionally embarrassed by patients who purported to have special powers: mind over matter, prescience, telepathy. They were tricked into believing all sorts of nonsense.'

'This isn't the nineteenth century, Hugh.'

'All the more reason why our peers will be unforgiving if we make the same mistakes.'

'Do you really think that *this*' – I swept a hand over the beds – 'has a simple explanation.'

'Probably not. But we have to eliminate all the alternatives before we start making any outlandish claims.'

'Such as?'

'Hysteria. What if these patients are exhibiting a hitherto undocumented form of group hysteria?'

'That doesn't seem very plausible. They are asleep.'

'We must proceed with caution,' Maitland sighed and adopted the manner of a world-weary grandee. 'Believe me, James, I've seen all manner of strange phenomena on my travels – everything from poisonous snake handling by Christian evangelists in Tennessee, to cases of possession by monkey spirits in Bali. Congregations, tribes – all kinds of group or gathering – are exquisitely susceptible to the power of suggestion.'

'I don't believe that these women are in a state of self-hypnosis.'

'Nor do I. Not really. But if we are going to convince the scientific community that human brains can influence each other during sleep, then we had better be confident of our findings.'

Our discussion had been somewhat technical and Maitland had repeatedly betrayed his concerns about how the situation could be best negotiated to ensure the survival of his academic reputation. When I looked at the sleeping patients, however, I was reminded of the fact that the problem with which we were faced had both an intellectual and a human dimension.

'What are we going to do if they don't wake up?' I asked.

'We don't have to worry about *that*,' Maitland replied, sounding a little irritated. 'Well, not yet, at any rate. We'll stop all sedatives and ECT and introduce regular intravenous stimulants. I would also suggest that we keep the lights on. You never know, it might help.' He paused and appeared to be ticking off the items on some mental check list. 'We'll ensure that they are properly hydrated with drips, but if they continue sleeping, we'll also feed them through nose tubes. Voiding will have to be achieved by enema, with digital removal in those cases where faeces have become impacted.'

'This situation will be very difficult to manage.'

'Don't worry. I don't expect you to handle things on your own, James. This is an emergency. I'm staying.' He offered me a tight smile. I sensed that he was expecting me to respond with an expression of gratitude, but all I could do was return an economic nod. He registered my reticence, and became magnanimous. 'You look tired, James. Take a break. I'll see you after supper.'

Outside, the air was fresh and cool. I smoked a cigarette and watched a thin crescent moon becoming periodically dim, and then bright, as a train of small clouds passed in front of it. The sea was calm. A bat flew past, sensed more than observed.

After I had eaten a light meal in the dining room, I went down to the sleep room again. Maitland had switched all the lights on: nine hanging bulbs, hidden within conical shades and projecting interlocking circles of luminescence onto the tiles. I could see the ceiling properly for the first time. It consisted of unvarnished planks, supported by massive, transverse beams. Deprived of its dark recesses and shadowy boundary, the sleep room looked smaller than usual. The alignment and orientation of the six beds no longer evoked sympathetic images of underground temples or standing stones. The atmosphere of enchantment had been dispelled and something more mundane had taken its place.

Maitland was on his own. I could only assume he had dismissed the nurses. He was walking from bed to bed, taking blood pressures, pulses, temperatures, and making notes on the charts. Celia Jones was connected to the EEG machine, and Maitland would occasionally return to her bedside in order to scrutinize the traces on the scrolling paper.

Eventually, he saw me standing by the door and said, 'Ah, James. Come over here. Celia Jones is producing some interesting spindles. My guess is that they are connected with the inhibitory processes that are preserving sleep.' I went over and examined the patterns, which were indeed interesting. Maitland continued to busy himself. He did not seem in the least bit anxious, and his eyes shone with a kind of fevered excitement. His absorption was total and I very much doubted that he had spared a single thought for his wife since his arrival.

It occurred to me that only hours before I had decided to resign; however, that decision now seemed to have lost much of its emotional urgency. I couldn't raise the difficult subject of my departure in the middle of a crisis. Maitland would be furious, and rightly so. I hadn't changed my mind. I still accepted that I would have to leave – and as soon as realistically possible – but it wasn't the right time to hand in my notice. Furthermore, I have to admit (with no small amount of attendant shame) that I was curious to see what would happen next.

When I retired for the evening, Maitland was still freely associating ideas, and making notes with purposeful energy. 'This is fascinating, isn't it?' he said. Then more softly, 'Quite fascinating.'

I ascended the stairs and passed Hartley, who was working an oily substance into the banisters. It was an activity that I had seen him engage in many times before. He looked up from his work and nodded. I almost stopped to ask him if he had seen the blackened carving. What did he make of it, I wondered? But I had too much on my mind, and Hartley had never been very talkative.

On entering my apartment, I went straight to the study. Sitting at the bureau, I toyed with a pen and thought about the sleep-room patients. I remembered their sad histories of abuse and abandonment. They were not merely brains, collections of cells, suspended in communal oblivion, but people.

What if they didn't wake up? I asked myself. Tomorrow. Or the day after – or the day after that. What if they couldn't be roused after weeks, months, or years? What would happen to them? Heart failure? Infections? Stroke? The appropriate course of action would be to transfer them all to Ipswich, a general hospital, somewhere properly equipped to deal with life-threatening medical emergencies. But Maitland wouldn't agree to such a suggestion. He wanted to observe, test and monitor outcomes. He was conducting an experiment now. In fact, he always had been. I should have realized that as soon as I saw the letters 'CIA' on the memorandum in Marian Powell's notes.

I wanted to work through my thoughts on paper, and searched through the bottom drawer of the bureau for a writing pad. The drawer had become quite cluttered and I had to remove several objects, including Palmer's Reserpine. As soon as I picked up the container, I knew that something had changed. It didn't rattle. I prised the lid off and looked inside. There was nothing there. The three white tablets, with their distinctive scored surfaces, had disappeared.

19

The following morning I was summoned to Maitland's office. He was seated behind his desk, the surface of which was completely covered with EEG read-outs, statistical manuals, and sheets of paper covered in his distinctive hand. The folders that I had surreptitiously examined – the ones from the grey cabinet containing the referral letters and documentation for the sleep-room patients – were piled on top of each other next to the telephone.

'Have you been working all night?' I asked.

'More or less. Although I think I managed to get some sleep at about three. Thirty minutes, perhaps.' He pointed to the Chesterfield and then tidied up some of his papers. I would have expected him to show more signs of fatigue, but he was well groomed and looked positively cheerful. He had recently shaved – the smell of his cologne was strong – and his hair glistened with a fresh application of pomade. 'Please,' he boomed hospitably, 'do sit down.'

'How are they?' I asked.

'No change,' he replied.

'Extraordinary.'

'Indeed.' Maitland drew my attention to some unusual wave patterns that he had circled in black ink. He asked me for an opinion, and then informed me that he had already arranged for another EEG machine to be transported from London. 'We can expect it to arrive by mid-afternoon. I have a suspicion,' he continued, tapping the red traces with his finger, 'that these will prove to be significant. If identical spindles are produced by different patients, at the exact same time, then we will have taken the first step towards establishing the physiological basis of this curious phenomenon.'

He continued to speculate, talking at speed, and stopping only occasionally to check that I was keeping up with his arguments. At one point, he suggested (rather wildly, I thought) that synchronous dreaming might be therapeutic. 'What if they woke up and all of them were cured?' Even in the middle of a crisis, Maitland was willing to entertain the possibility that a medical breakthrough could be snatched from the jaws of an impending disaster.

After listening to him enlarging upon his themes for an hour or so, I found the courage to remind him of the question that he had been assiduously avoiding. 'What if they don't wake up?' I asked.

Maitland pushed his expensive fountain pen forward on the desk, and it came to rest parallel with the edge of my chair. The manoeuvre appeared oddly defensive, as if his intention had been to create a physical divide that would clarify our respective positions on opposite sides of a territorial boundary.

'It's early days. And they aren't in any immediate danger.'

'Aren't they?'

He smiled. A smile that carried a subtext of disbelief and mild disappointment. 'Whatever do you mean by that?'

'Well . . .' I paused, my resolve faltered and I almost chose to say something less contentious. But instead, I looked at the files, remembered what I had read, the sorry tales of abuse and loss, and decided that there was a substantial matter of principle at issue. 'Are we really set up to deal with this contingency? I mean . . . do we have the facilities?'

'Facilities?'

'This *condition* that the patients are in. We don't know what it is, or the risks that might be associated with its continuation.'

'The patients are dreaming. That's all. There are no risks associated with dreaming.'

'With respect, Hugh, they aren't just dreaming. They have entered a state that, even accepting the anomalous EEG, appears to closely resemble a coma.'

Maitland shook his head. 'I do not believe that these patients are in any danger.'

The silence that settled around us was tense and layered with unease.

'If they were transferred to Ipswich—'

'That is out of the question,' Maitland cut in. 'They don't have experience of running a sleep room at Ipswich. What on earth are you thinking? We have Sister Jenkins here, the nightingales. How could such a transfer possibly best serve the interests of *my* patients.' His use of the emphatic possessive was ominous.

'I'm not sure, Hugh. If something untoward were to happen, the sleepers would be more likely to get good emergency support in a general hospital setting.'

Maitland's face was like alabaster. 'Nothing untoward will happen,' he said softly.

I was not going to be cowed. 'What are our objectives, Hugh?'

'To keep the patients alive, and comfortable, until such time as they spontaneously wake, or are chemically stimulated into wakefulness.'

'Those objectives could be achieved just as easily at Ipswich.'

'Indeed, but there are certain privileges we enjoy at Wyldehope that I am keen to protect.' He raised his eyebrows, encouraging me to consider the appeal of absolute power. Then he added, with insincere cordiality, 'I have never been persuaded that clinical responsibility is something that can be practicably shared out. Representatives from different branches of medicine have competing priorities. We don't want to find ourselves in a situation where we have to argue with a cardiologist every time we want to modify the medication regimen.'

'I'm sorry, Hugh, but I disagree. I think the patients should be transferred, and if we don't make prompt arrangements, and something goes wrong . . .' I stopped abruptly.

'What? What do you think will happen?'

I took a deep breath, and said, 'I'm not questioning your judgement.'

'Aren't you?'

'I'm just concerned, that's all.'

'About the patients?' he said drily. 'Or the General Medical Council?' He saw me start and continued. 'Well, there was that business with Hilda Wright. The possible arsenic poisoning that you failed to report.'

'What?'

'We discussed the matter as I recall.'

'Yes, and you told me it wasn't worth pursuing.'

'My dear fellow, I said nothing of the sort. I merely urged you to consider the broader picture. The decision to contact the coroner, or not, was entirely your responsibility. How could it have been otherwise? I never even saw the patient.' I was flabbergasted. Even more so when he continued, 'And then there was Chapman. Fortunately, no questions were asked about the straitjacket.'

I felt a flare of anger and Maitland's fountain pen rolled forward. He lunged to stop it but it accelerated out of his reach. I watched as it dropped to the floor. For a few moments I stared at the pen, before lowering my upper body, picking the pen up, and returning it to its former position.

'Thank you,' said Maitland. His eyes fastened on mine. Under any other circumstance, one of us might have commented on this strange occurrence. But Maitland had just issued a threat and my mind was fully occupied with the task of trying to formulate an appropriate response. This concentrated expenditure of mental energy, however, proved unnecessary, because Maitland sighed, made an appeasing gesture with his hands, and said, 'Look, James, you have a very promising career ahead of you. I think we've established a good working relationship and I would like that to continue. Don't be headstrong. I don't want it to be like this.' He was modulating his voice to exploit its attractive tonal qualities, just like he did when he was on the wireless. The sound he produced was melodious, friendly, and above all persuasive. 'I want you to do something for me. Go upstairs, go for a walk – I don't care what you do, but find somewhere quiet, a place where you won't be disturbed and consider, at length, what we've been discussing. Try to take a long view. I understand that you have reservations. You've made that clear enough. Even so, I hope that, given sufficient opportunity to reflect, you will come round to my way of thinking.'

He stood up and offered me his hand. I took it warily and matched the determined pressure of his muscular grip. It was one of numerous communications that had not necessitated the crude medium of speech. As I left Maitland's office I knew full well that the terms of engagement on which my future as a doctor depended had been comprehensively renegotiated. The dilemma that faced me now, as I saw it, was not whether I was prepared to accept those terms, but whether I possessed the courage to reject them.

I remembered what Palmer had said about his relationship with Maitland, how Maitland had taken a 'fatherly' interest in him, and how this had complicated his feelings at the time of his resignation. Perhaps I too had come to see Maitland as a kind of father figure. Because even though he had been manipulative and dishonest, the idea of opposing him churned up a plethora of conflicting Oedipal emotions: principally fear and guilt. I felt that the plan of action that was taking shape in my mind militated against the natural order. Maitland had always mocked 'couch merchants' and I had been a willing confederate. Yet as I ascended the stairs to my apartment, the unpalatable precepts of psychoanalysis seemed to have become unassailable truths.

In my study, I smoked a cigarette and then picked up the telephone. It took me several attempts to find the right official. He was polite but somewhat reserved. After taking down my details he invited me to proceed. On hearing Maitland's name, he said, 'I beg your pardon?'

'Dr Hugh Maitland,' I repeated.

'The psychiatrist?'

'Yes.'

'The famous psychiatrist.'

'Yes.'

I described the situation I found myself in and shared my concerns. 'The patients must be transferred,' I concluded. 'Their lives are at risk.'

'You do realize,' said the official, 'that you are making a very serious allegation.'

'Yes,' I replied, 'I do.'

The medical profession is notoriously hierarchical and conservative. When I put the telephone down, I did so accepting that I had probably done something very foolish. What could I expect to achieve? In all likelihood the sleepers would remain at Wyldehope, Maitland would be left to his own devices, and I would never work again.

I spent the rest of the morning on the wards. There was plenty to do, because Maitland had ensconced himself in the sleep room and seemed completely uninterested in the welfare of the other patients. When I went down to consult him about Alan Foster, whose delusions of control were getting much worse, Maitland barely made eye contact. He was standing next to the EEG machine, stroking his chin, bewitched by the movement of the pens. 'Do what you think is best,' he said distractedly. Having told me to go off and reflect on our prior altercation, I had supposed that he would show at least some interest in discovering the outcome; however, I was quite wrong. He was simply too engrossed to care.

The sleepers had not been fed yet; nevertheless, the drips had been attached to their arms. Perhaps it was because I was unaccustomed to the overhead lights but

already the supine bodies seemed emaciated. Their interior parts were too visible: bones and shadowy vessels
showed beneath transparent skin. When I left the sleep
room, I glanced back and felt a preternatural chill. It
seemed to pass through my ribcage and freeze my heart.
The sensation was profoundly uncomfortable and persisted, albeit less intensely, for some time after.

It was difficult to work, because I kept on wondering
whether or not someone from the Health Board or the
General Medical Council would arrive to undertake an
inspection; although, in actuality, I knew that such a swift
response was unlikely. Maitland would be courteously
forewarned by telephone, and I would then have to go to
his office and justify myself. I imagined having to stand in
front of him, while he expressed incredulity at the magni-
tude of my betrayal. The prospect of what I would have
to face made me feel slightly sick. Indeed, it occurred to
me that it might be for the best if I simply packed my
bags and got Hartley to drive me to the train station. But
this felt too cowardly to countenance. I was reminded of
men like Burgess: men who belonged to a generation not
so very far removed in years from my own, who had
had to fight and win a war. Surely I could stand up to
Maitland? Surely I had that much courage? The sleep-
room patients were in danger and I was the only person

in a position to do anything about it. A quote popped into my mind, one that was frequently repeated by my history master at school: 'All that is necessary for the triumph of evil is that good men do nothing.' The sentiment was bracing. It revived my spirits and toughened my resolve.

On returning to the men's ward I went to see Alan Foster who was still in an anxious state. 'They're putting thoughts into my head,' he said. 'I don't know which ones are mine any more.' I sedated him, tried to make him comfortable, and then went to see some of the other patients: Mr Cook, Mr Murray and Mr Drake. When I had finished, I found myself thinking about Michael Chapman and of our many chess games and conversations. Under the influence of these maudlin recollections, I wandered, without clear purpose, down the corridor and into the recreation room. Jane was sitting on one of the battered armchairs, a handkerchief clutched in her hand.

'Oh, I'm sorry,' I said, embarrassed. 'I didn't realize . . .'

I was about to leave when she looked up at me. She had obviously been crying and I didn't know what to do. My indecision caused me to vacillate on the threshold; however, there was something about her expression that stopped my confused movements. Her eyes made an arresting appeal that caused an emotion to snag in my chest.

'Must we be like this?' she said.

'What do you mean?' I said, rather disingenuously. Then, becoming self-conscious, I turned and looked back down the corridor at the nurses' station.

'It's all right,' Jane said. 'There's only me here. Have you got a cigarette?' I walked across the room and offered her one, which she took and lit herself. 'Thank you.' After taking a few puffs she said, 'What's going on in the sleep room?'

'I don't know. But it isn't very good.'

'Do you think Maitland will be able to wake them up?'

'They should have been transferred to Ipswich. We're not equipped to deal with this kind of thing – whatever it is – at Wyldehope.'

'Have you told Maitland what you think?'

'Yes.'

'And what did he say?'

'He doesn't agree.'

She shivered and brought her knees together. 'I've been thinking.' She paused and I had to wait a long time before she spoke again. 'What I did. I understand why you're angry. Really I do. And I'm sorry I didn't tell you everything before . . . before we got close. But the

opportunity never presented itself. And I was happy –
with you – and didn't want to spoil things.'

The hem of her uniform had risen and I had to avert
my gaze. A tactile memory of body heat rising through
silk produced a throb of arousal in my loins.

'I'm not sure that we should be having this conversation here,' I said.

'Why not? We won't get disturbed. I've looked at the
rota.'

'All right, I'm not sure that we should be having this
conversation at all.' It was a gratuitous rebuff.

Jane turned her head, and the movement emphasized
the length of her neck and the classical regularity of her
profile. Her eyes shone more brightly as they collected
light in a new film of tears. 'I just wanted to say that I
understand why you were so upset,' she said in a slightly
strangulated voice. 'That's all. I was hoping . . .' She
brought the cigarette to her mouth again before adding,
'I was hoping we could be a little more grown-up about
all this.'

I went over to the window. Maitland's Bentley was
parked outside and, due to an unfortunate chain of associations, I found myself thinking of the Chesterfield once
again: the rhythmic creak of leather accompanied by
moans of satisfaction in the dark. Maitland, panting over

Jane's back, searching out the full, ripe weight of her breasts with his big hands. My head began to ache.

'What's the point?' I said, exhausted and bitter.

'We were happy together.'

'Yes, we were.'

'Well, then.'

'I'm afraid I don't see what you're getting at.'

I heard her stand up and watched her image in the window, expanding as she came closer, until she halted behind me. Through her ghostly reflection I could see the heath, distant woodland and the sky. I felt rigid with expectation. She wanted to reach out, I could feel it – her desire to touch building steadily.

'People make mistakes,' she said. 'I made a mistake – and I'm sorry. Really I am.'

I felt her hand on my shoulder and observed its appearance in the glass. My attention was immediately drawn to a glint of gold. She was wearing a wedding ring. Or at least I thought she was. Because, when I looked more carefully, it seemed to fade away. Was my willingness to give this particular interpretation to a glimmer of reflected light significant? Did it reveal the survival of my fantasy of an idyllic life with Jane, now relegated to the murky underworld of forbidden wishes, something only expressible through the Freudian trickery of faulty perception and slips of the tongue? I felt her grip on my shoulder tighten and she took a step forward. Her breath warmed the back of my neck.

'No,' I said. 'It's over. We can't pick up the pieces. It's too late.'

She did not have time to respond. Because it was at that point that the screaming started.

20

The door at the end of the ward opened and Nurse Page rushed down the corridor. 'Jane?' she hollered. 'Where are you?' Then, seeing us standing at the entrance to the recreation room, she shouted, 'Fire! Fire! Get the patients out!' I looked beyond the nurses' station into the distant extremity of the vestibule and noticed signs of activity. Sister Jenkins was directing a procession of women in hospital gowns, making frantic gesticulations to encourage speed. The scene was bathed in a sinister lambency and I could hear a continuous wailing. Nurse Page turned on her heels and ran back out again.

Jane and I were so stunned for a few long seconds we remained in fixed attitudes of horror and surprise. 'Come on,' I said. 'We'd better hurry.'

Some of the patients were already coming out of their rooms, bleary-eyed and blinking. 'Nurse?' said Mr Murray. 'What's all that shouting?'

'There's a fire,' Jane replied. 'We're evacuating the building. Move along now. This way.'

I grabbed Jane's arm and indicated the doors which faced each other across the corridor. 'You do this side, I'll do the other.'

We worked systematically, getting patients out of bed and corralling them towards the vestibule. Although heavily sedated, many became distressed.

'Are we going to die?' asked Alan Foster.

'Not if you're quick,' I replied, pressing my palm against his lower back and encouraging him to move faster.

Smoke had begun to billow onto the ward and several of the patients had started to cough and splutter. When we entered the vestibule, I felt a blast of heat on my face. The entire wooden staircase was ablaze and the loud crackling it produced sounded like an enormous bonfire. Individual reports, sharp and clear, could be discerned against a swelling, background roar. Sister Jenkins was, necessarily, holding the front door open, but this was fuelling the conflagration with a fresh supply of air and causing the flames to burn more fiercely. The smoke was stinging her eyes and her cheeks were damp with tears.

I positioned myself at her side. 'Sister Jenkins, where is Dr Maitland?'

She coughed into her hand and croaked a reply: 'In the sleep room.'

'Why in God's name isn't he coming out?'

'Nurse Page said something about the door being stuck. Perhaps you could . . .' The remaining syllables of her sentence were rendered incomprehensible by more coughing. She waved me away and followed the last of the fleeing patients onto the drive.

Shielding my face with my forearm, I peered through the thickening smoke. Breathing was painful: it scorched my lips and left a foul taste at the back of my throat. 'Hugh?' I called down to the basement. 'Hugh? Get out of there!' Before going to his aid, I hesitated, because at any moment I guessed the staircase might collapse. The entrance to the sleep room was situated directly beneath it. Maitland did not respond, so I made a swift, stumbling descent, and when I reached the bottom I grabbed the door handle. It turned easily but when I pushed nothing happened. I banged my clenched fist against the door and shouted, 'Hugh? Hugh? Are you all right?'

There was an explosion followed by the sound of shattering glass. One of the windows had blown out. Something large fell onto the stairs behind me and I was showered with sparks and cinders. When I turned round, I saw a hefty piece of charred timber angled between the walls. Undeterred, I threw my weight against the door, but still it did not yield.

'Dr Richardson?'

Hartley was standing at the top of the stairs. He glanced upwards, at something only he could see from his position, and his expression became anxious. Even so, he began to make his way down, only stopping when he came to the fallen timber.

'The door's locked,' I said. 'Do you have the key?'

'There is no key. I was never given one.'

That made perfect sense. The customary security measures did not apply to the sleep room. 'Then the door's stuck. Dr Maitland and the patients are still inside. I'm going to need your help.' I slapped my hand against a sunken panel. 'The two of us might be able to break it down.'

Hartley looked up once again, but whatever hazard he was monitoring did not prevent him from jumping over the timber and joining me. 'After three,' I said, and counted. We slammed our shoulders against the door, but to no effect. 'And again,' I said. 'One, two, three.' The force of our impact caused us to rebound and Hartley fell over. 'It's no good,' he said, shaking his head.

'What are we going to do?' I asked. 'We can't just leave them there.'

Pieces of burning wood rained down on us and I had to pull my jacket over my head for protection. At my feet

I saw part of a blackened banister. A delicately carved owl was still visible, its claws wrapped around a branch.

'Let's go,' said Hartley, straightening his glasses. 'The whole damn staircase is going to come down.'

'But we can't leave them. The patients. Maitland.'

'Don't be a fool. If you stay any longer, you'll get yourself killed.' He clutched my sleeve and gave it a firm tug.

'No,' I protested, twisting myself free.

Hartley gave me a searching look. I could see his eyes through the reflected flames that danced on his lenses. Suddenly he swore, turned his back on me and scrambled up the stairs.

I tried to force the door open again, but its stubborn intransigence made me feel that I was engaged in a hopeless endeavour. There were no promising indications of future success: no splitting or splintering to encourage further violence. The door felt as if it was bolstered with iron, unnaturally solid and secure.

'Hugh,' I called out in desperation, pounding the door with both my fists at once. 'Can you hear me?'

Retreating a step, I noticed the keyhole, and I crouched down so that my eye was level with it. The lights were on in the sleep room, and what I saw was so strange that I thought that I must have breathed in too much smoke and be suffering from some form of hallucinatory intoxication. The six patients were sitting up in their beds. Their backs were very straight. I couldn't see if their eyes were open or closed, but their heads were turned at different angles, as if they were all studying the same thing. The object of their common interest was Maitland, who occupied a central position, and appeared to be deep in thought. He looked much the same as he did when I last saw him. With his hand poised in readiness to stroke his chin, there was something about his appearance that suggested that the action had been arrested in mid-movement. I pummelled the door again, but Maitland did not react. He stood, perfectly still, like a wax model.

There was a sense of opening up and expansion, as my mind became elastic and stretched to accommodate the significance of what I was seeing. The human animal thinks along pathways prescribed by habit, and I had exhibited predictable conformity in this respect, by attributing all of the supernatural phenomena I had experienced to a spirit agency. But, at that moment, it was quite clear to me that I had encountered something more subtle, and more frightening, and that it – the poltergeist – had arisen from the deepest regions of the minds of the slumbering women.

Maitland had violated their brains, with drugs and electric shocks, and now they were violating his.

'Dear God,' I groaned.

What must it feel like, I wondered, to have the very fabric of one's being, one's identity, one's very soul, torn asunder? And in what place, what impossible landscape of the imagination, was this appalling horror being enacted? I remembered something Maitland had said shortly after my arrival at Wyldehope. He had observed that physical pain, no matter how bad, was never the equal of mental pain. And then I remembered standing in front of *The Wenhaston Doom*, and marvelling at humanity's genius for imagining worlds of suffering, grotesque forms of torment. Where was Maitland now? And what were they doing to him? His body was in the sleep room, but I had no doubt that his consciousness had been removed to another reality.

A massive beam dropped like a guillotine from the ceiling and crushed the nurses' desk. I saw masonry skittering across the floor, the lights went out, and there was only darkness.

The heat was now intolerable and I felt like I was suffocating.

I could not delay my escape any longer. I leapt up the stairs, dodging burning debris. The atmosphere was so opaque I could hardly see. I tripped over the suit of armour, which had toppled over and broken into separate pieces. High above me, another window shattered, and the delicate tinkling that followed was soon followed by a punishing shower of broken glass. I got to my feet and launched myself at the front door, which was still open and admitting a dim luminescence into the benighted vestibule.

Quite suddenly, I was brought to a jarring halt. The sensation of restraint was not unfamiliar, and one that I associated with two very particular situations, both remote in memory: the school playground and the rugby field. It was the feeling of someone holding on to one's clothing to prevent progress. I did not turn. But instead narrowed my shoulders and lowered my arms. My jacket slipped off and I managed to get to the entrance in two energetic bounds.

From beneath the porch, I glanced back and saw the entire wooden staircase collapse: a concertina effect that produced a searing gust of hot air. My hair and eyebrows sizzled unpleasantly and a new, acrid odour infiltrated the existing, incendiary reek. I staggered out, onto the drive, and let my lungs expand: the pure pleasure of the experience made me feel vaguely delirious. Bending over, with my hands clasping my thighs, I coughed so much that I thought I was going to be sick. My knuckles were covered in blood and my trousers were smouldering.

Sister Jenkins, assisted by a small number of nightingales, was leading the male and female patients to safety
along the drive. Another, much larger group of nurses,
who had obviously just left the accommodation block,
were trudging across the heath and following a diagonal
that would eventually intercept their colleagues. Mr and
Mrs Hartley and the kitchen girl had positioned themselves outside the Hartleys' cottage, where they could
view the destruction of Wyldehope at a respectable distance, while – it appeared – enjoying the panacea of Mrs
Hartley's tea.

I limped past Maitland's Bentley, registering the image
of a haunted-looking man in the semi-transparent depths
of the windscreen. His face was filthy and his hair was
standing on end. Clouds with fleecy edges raced over the
tower, and another window exploded.

21

The following day I received a telephone call from a journalist who had thought that he might build a story around my failed attempt to rescue Maitland.

'I've spoken to Sister Jenkins.'

'Yes.'

'She speaks very highly of you, Dr Richardson. Indeed, she says you're something of a hero.'

'I wouldn't say that.'

'Weren't you the last one to leave the building? Didn't you try to save Dr Maitland and his patients?'

'The door to the sleep room was stuck. Perhaps the wood had been warped by the heat. I tried to force it open a few times, but without success, so I ran for my life. No, I wouldn't say that I was a hero.'

When the journalist realized I wasn't going to cooperate he brought our conversation to an abrupt end.

The investigation into the causes of the fire proved inconclusive; however, the general opinion of all those involved was that an electrical fault was to blame – a plausible hypothesis and reassuringly predictable. Mr Hartley had been in the habit of treating the staircase with an improvised wood preserver, and this dubious concoction most probably contained flammable ingredients.

I didn't stay in East Anglia. There was no reason to. When the police had finished questioning me, I travelled down to Bournemouth to stay with my parents, and from there I began making arrangements for my return to London.

The tragedy was widely reported and Maitland's obituary appeared in several newspapers. Opinion was unanimous. He was 'a gifted communicator', 'a modern visionary', and 'the most significant British psychiatrist since Henry Maudsley'. Sir Paul Mallinson, who I had worked with at St George's, wrote that Maitland was 'a personable colleague' and 'a man of singular purpose'. He was 'the enemy of unreason, a formidable critic of psychoanalysis, and a shining example for generations to come'.

Maitland was even the subject of a programme on the wireless, broadcast very late, in which a panel of distinguished guests discussed his life and work. All of the speakers were very positive, except a philosopher, who was critical of Maitland's 'crude' reductionism. 'There is more to a human being,' said the philosopher in a querulous voice which suggested considerable age, 'than chemicals.' Nothing was said about Wyldehope, although Maitland's advocacy of deep-sleep therapy was periodically mentioned and applauded.

My association with Maitland was extremely advantageous. I enjoyed a kind of vicarious celebrity. The obituaries were still fresh in people's minds and when I went for job interviews I was treated with an inordinate amount of respect. Within days I was offered a locum position back at the Royal Free Hospital, which I accepted. I then found a room to rent in Dartmouth Park. Fortunately, my new landlady was very different from my old one in Kentish Town. She mixed with local artists and wandered around the house in a silk kimono smoking black cheroots. Her greatest virtue was complete indifference to my comings and goings.

Just after Easter, I received a letter from Jane. She had made some enquiries and had discovered my whereabouts. It was a relatively brief communication. She had been thinking of me and wanted to talk. 'Could we go for a drink, I wonder? I'm working at UCH now. Perhaps we could meet in town?' I didn't reply. In fact, I crushed the letter into a tight ball and threw it into the bin.

I had persuaded myself that our relationship was well and truly over and that I no longer cared. Yet on Sunday afternoons, as I walked around Hampstead, I would often look up at the high mansion-block windows and remember the fantasy I had had of our future life together. I would reflect on what might have been.

Clearly, I had a lot of thinking to do – and not just about Jane.

On that terrible Christmas night, when Chapman and I had been standing together on the second-floor landing at Wyldehope, he had stiffened, stared into the darkness at the far end of the hallway and said, 'It's coming.'

I can remember how I experienced his use of the word 'it' as particularly chilling, because the word suggested the approach of something impersonal and unknown.

In psychoanalysis, the term 'id' is used to describe the deep unconscious. A classicist would also be familiar with the term as the Latin word for 'it'. Freud described the id as an inaccessible chaos, a cauldron full of seething excitations; a primitive part of the mind, constantly seeking to bring about the satisfaction of its instinctual needs. Thus, when Chapman had said 'It's coming' the language he employed had had a double meaning and at some level I must have registered this.

I had read through the referral letters of the sleep-room patients only once; however, I could remember, quite clearly, every detail of each case, and one didn't need to be so very insightful to identify certain correspondences between the histories of these women and the activities of the poltergeist. For example, the theft of the wedding rings and the fire-setting. Moreover, the women in the sleep room had in common the frustration of that most fundamental of female instinctual needs: the need to have and care for a child. Most of them had lost a baby, one way or another, through removal, termination or miscarriage, and those that hadn't lost a baby demonstrated strong maternal feelings. Marian Powell had cherished her rag doll, 'Little Marian', and for Elizabeth Mason, the prospect of marriage and raising a family was, evidently, everything.

Their minds had come together, in their long, communal sleep, and the 'whole' that resulted from this merging had become something much greater than the sum of its parts. The poltergeist was a vehicle for the fulfilment of wishes, a dream that had escaped from the confines of their collective unconscious.

Had they meant to die with Maitland? Probably not. Nothing that they did was intentional, as such. The unconscious is entirely irrational. It does not plan ahead or consider consequences.

And what of Marian Powell's psychic powers? As a child, she had been investigated by representatives from the Society for Psychical Research. Had her abilities been reawakened and amplified by membership of this unique community of souls? Did she generate energies that could be used to levitate books, slam doors, release the fastenings of a straitjacket, and, in the final instance, prevent my entry into the sleep room? These were fanciful speculations, but I could think of no better way to account for the facts.

I asked myself many questions, but one in particular came back to me, again and again, to disturb my quiet moments. What was Maitland *really* doing at Wyldehope? I had long since abandoned the naive notion that he was simply trying to develop new treatments. Naturally, I had ideas, notions, but nothing that could be substantiated, nothing that I could actually prove. This unsatisfactory state of affairs might have lasted indefinitely had I not, quite literally, bumped into my old girlfriend, Sheila, in a smoky pub in Soho.

'James?' she said, wiping a damp hand on her skirt. We had both spilled our drinks as we collided.

'Sheila?'

'Good God, it is you.' She raised herself up on her toes and kissed me on the lips. A boisterous group of people in the corner cheered. 'Take no notice,' she added, and then asked me what I was doing in London. I gave her a much-abbreviated account of my experiences at Wyldehope (omitting any mention of the poltergeist) and explained how the fire had necessitated my return.

Sheila's face showed signs of recognition. 'I think I read about it in the newspapers. You were *there*. Heavens. Some people died, didn't they?'

'Six patients and the medical director.'

'What caused the fire?'

'An electrical fault.' I did not want to dwell on Wyldehope and was anxious to change the subject. 'How about you? What have you been up to?'

She extended her fingers and showed me a diamond ring that flashed when she tilted it beneath the light. 'I'm engaged.'

'That was quick. Who's the lucky man?'

'His name is Nigel. Nigel Reeves. He produces comedy programmes on the wireless. He did a few episodes of *The Goons* last year.' She seemed bashfully reticent for a moment, before adding: 'He took me to a party on Tuesday and Peter Sellers was there.'

'Was it fun?'

'Fantastic fun.'

'Did you meet Nigel at the BBC?'

'No. In a jazz club, which is mad, considering that our offices are on the same floor. He's always looking for new talent.'

Our lives couldn't have been more different since we had chosen to go our separate ways. I remembered Sheila jumping on a bus and waving through the window. My recollections of saying 'goodbye' to her on the Charing Cross Road seemed as distant as childhood.

'You must be very happy,' I remarked.

'I am.' She smiled and looked at me askance. 'Anybody special in your life?'

'No. Not really. I became very fond of a nurse at Wyldehope but it didn't work out. You know how it is.'

This admission aroused in Sheila a disproportionate volume of pity. She was insistent that I 'absolutely must' meet a friend of hers who was also single and who Sheila was certain I would like. I found myself being cajoled into accepting a dinner invitation. We were to be a foursome: Sheila and Nigel, the friend and myself.

'Are you sure this is wise?' I asked Sheila. 'I mean, do you really want your fiancé and me sitting on opposite sides of the same table?'

Sheila laughed. 'Oh, that won't be a problem. I'll tell him who you are and he won't mind a bit. He isn't the jealous type.' Clearly, they were a good match.

A week later I went to dinner at Nigel's town house in Kensington. He was a good ten years older than Sheila and clearly in receipt of some form of private income. He wore loose, casual clothes, had the yellow fingers of a chain-smoker, and drank large quantities of wine without showing the least sign of inebriation. The slim, red-haired girl who stood to greet me as I entered the sitting room was Sheila's friend, Tosca Summerfield. Her exotic name provided the first topic of conversation. Apparently she had been conceived in Milan after her newly married mother and father had visited the opera house.

It turned out to be a very pleasant evening. Nigel Reeves was a splendid host and Tosca and I got along famously. She was a friendly if somewhat excitable young woman who worked in a publishing house and harboured aspirations to be a writer. We swapped telephone numbers and started seeing each other soon after. Subsequently, I saw quite a lot of Sheila and Nigel, and for a brief period of time I found myself escorting Tosca to parties where most of the people present seemed to either make programmes for the BBC or write for a newspaper.

It was at one of these gatherings that I met a journalist called Leonard Grimwood. He was a Marxist and writing a highly critical book on modern America. When he discovered that I was a psychiatrist, he started talking about the CIA. 'It looks like they're trying to develop a procedure that will enable them to erase human memories and I have good reason to believe that some very senior members of the medical establishment have been helping them. All *hush-hush*, of course, but you'd be surprised at how bad they are at keeping secrets.' He noticed that his pipe had gone out and paused to relight it. 'Have you been to the United States?'

'No,' I replied.

'The whole of American culture is obsessed with mind control and brainwashing. I blame the ad men. They've made everyone paranoid.'

Maitland had believed that narcosis and ECT might work by destroying unpleasant memories. I remembered turning the pages of Marian Powell's file: the CIA memorandum, covered in rubber stamp marks and scrawled annotations.

'Have you ever come across the name of Dr Walter Rosenberg?' I asked.

Grimwood looked startled. 'Yes, I have. He's based in New York. Do you know him?'

'I met him once.'

'A slippery customer if ever there was one. He's been sending patients home with their memories wiped clean for years. And he's a lot wealthier than he should be. I know some lawyers in Queens: young Turks, eager to stir things up a little. They specialize in civil rights and have become increasingly interested in mental health lately.

They've been trying to put together a case against Rosenberg for some time – some kind of negligence claim – but they haven't got very far, as yet.' Grimwood narrowed his eyes in such a way as to suggest that this lack of progress might be attributable to some kind of sinister interference. He produced a vast amount of smoke from his pipe and continued to stare at me from within a thick, brownish cloud.

'What about Maitland?' I asked, 'Dr Hugh Maitland?'

'Well, of course I've heard of him. He died quite recently, didn't he?'

'Yes. I worked with him.'

'I'm sorry.'

'We weren't close. Maitland knew Rosenberg very well. In fact, I met Rosenberg when he was visiting Maitland.'

'Maitland was British.'

'Does that matter?'

'It does to me. My book is about America.'

22

In the autumn, Tosca was offered a job in Paris which she accepted. I had never really expected our affair to last for very long. Even so, I was saddened by her departure. She had been good for me, a welcome distraction. Of course, the fact that I judged the success of our relationship in those terms shows that we had never really progressed beyond a superficial acquaintance. Our lovemaking had been efficient rather than passionate. There had never been any rapt embraces or trembling exhalations that might, at any moment, have carried an admission of love.

When my contract expired at the Royal Free I applied for a position as senior registrar to Professor Aubrey Lewis at the Institute of Psychiatry. He was the inaugural chair and a man of considerable importance. Unlike Maitland, who was leonine and seductively charming, Lewis was bald and pedantic. An unflattering moustache gave him the appearance of a retired sergeant major. The interview was arduous but I managed to impress Lewis and

drub some stiff competition. Once again, my prior association with Maitland proved useful.

On the face of it, one day was much like the next. I
saw patients, undertook research and did a little lectur-
ing; however, the Institute was an interesting place to be.
One felt at the centre of things.

My relationship with Lewis was good, but lacking in
warmth, because he was not given to showing his emotions. Indeed, he was probably the least demonstrative
person I have ever met. Some of my colleagues found this
trait discomfiting, but as far as I was concerned Lewis's
reserve was a refreshing and welcome contrast to Maitland's intensity. Travelling from Dartmouth Park to South
London every day soon became tiresome, so I gave my
bohemian landlady notice of my imminent departure,
packed my bags, and moved to Herne Hill.

One Saturday, I was walking past the forecourt of a
car showroom in Camberwell when I noticed a rather
eye-catching, second-hand Wolseley. It had lustrous black
bodywork and silver appurtenances that reflected radiant
spears of morning sunlight. I opened one of the offside
doors and inspected the leather upholstery, pile carpet,
and walnut trim. *Why not?* I thought. *I can afford it.*

When the spring came, I got into the habit of going for
long drives every weekend. I would usually head for the

coast, stopping for a few hours in Brighton, Margate, or Southend, but occasionally I would travel north, into Hertfordshire and beyond. On one of these jaunts I went as far as Cambridge. I arrived much earlier than I had expected and, while strolling along Silver Street, it occurred to me that I could probably get to Wyldehope by way of Ipswich in just over two hours. The idea took hold and began to acquire a compulsive quality. I experienced what I can only describe as a 'strong urge' to see Dunwich Heath again, to hear the sound of waves breaking on shingle, to stand in front of the ruined hospital and to remember. Perhaps at the root of this impulse was the untrustworthy supposition that returning to Wyldehope would be therapeutic. For over a year, my actual life had felt vaguely unreal and lacking in substance, whereas my memories of the sleep room, Maitland, Sister Jenkins, Chapman and Jane were extremely vivid. A symbolic and final encounter with the past seemed to offer the prospect of release. I would satisfy some obscure and wholly imagined propitiatory requirement and be able to move forward. The flat monochrome of the world would swell into three dimensions and colour would gradually bleed back into its surfaces.

It is difficult to describe what my feelings were as I drove between the old gateposts. Two mutually exclusive states of mind, excitement and a kind of numbness, vied for supremacy. Looking to my left, I saw an expanse of purple heather. The sun was a pale, floating disc; however, from time to time it would discover a small breach in the quilt of clouds and a thin, coppery light would pour through.

I stopped the car and the engine fell silent. Peering through the windscreen, I gazed at what was left of the hospital. The central tower had collapsed, the roof had fallen in, and rectangular portions of the eastern sky were visible through the upper windows. Parts of the brickwork were blackened, debris was scattered in front of the facade and a shaggy moss had started growing on the sills. I pushed the car door open against a sudden blast of wind. After getting out, I cupped my hands around a cigarette and lit it. The reed beds shimmered and I heard, once again, their distinctive sound. Ripples spread across pools of silver water and a flock of birds ascended vertically in the distance.

The outbuildings were clearly uninhabited. Mr and Mrs Hartley's cottage had all of its windows boarded up and the paintwork was peeling badly. The area in front of the bicycle shed was overgrown with weeds. When I had finished the cigarette, I dropped the filter onto the gravel and flattened it beneath the sole of my shoe.

I set off down the drive, all the time keeping my eyes on the hospital. As I advanced I succumbed to a curious illusion. It seemed to me that I was walking on the same spot, not progressing, and that the diminishing distance between myself and the hospital was the result of Wyldehope gliding forwards. Somewhat sooner than I had expected, I found myself facing the porch, deliberating whether or not to enter. I doubted very much that the structure would be safe, but curiosity got the better of me and I stepped inside. There was no floor – only exposed beams covered in rubble and broken slate. The vestibule, with its faded wallpaper, grand staircase and suit of armour, was entirely gone, and in its place was a bombsite enclosed by four high walls. Some seagulls, disturbed by my arrival, fluttered across the big, open space, exchanging a low perch at one end of the building for a high perch at the other.

The stairs leading down to the sleep room had been destroyed and all that remained of the basement was a depression in the debris. I cautiously stepped over the wreckage and, as I moved forward, the bottom of the hollow came into view. Among the rubble and slate I saw a twisted, rusting bedpost. I then noticed something among the scorched bricks and detritus that made my heart jump. The pounding in my ears was loud and furious. I was looking at a miniature doll: one of the Christmas tree decorations that Hartley had found in the tower attic. From my vantage point, the doll looked completely undamaged. *How could that be?* I wondered. *Surely, it should have been reduced to ashes by the fire?* The seagulls flapped their wings and emitted harsh calls. Another bird was wheeling high overhead. I edged down the slope, but the rubble beneath my feet began to shift, and I had to scramble back up to the lip. In doing so, I created an avalanche of broken bricks, and when I looked back down the doll had been completely buried. I knew exactly what I had seen, but even so, the indefatigable voice of reason had already started to suggest that perhaps I had seen nothing at all.

I stood very still, listening to the sound of my breathing. In spite of this reminder of my own physicality, the sensation of my lungs working like bellows in my chest, I felt like a ghost, a fragile assembly of motes, floating in the air and easily dispersed. The close transit of a moth would threaten my integrity. I left the hospital and took the path that led down to the sea. For a long time, I sat among the dunes, watching the dun-coloured waves crashing on the shore. A tear trickled down my cheek, but it did not come with a note attached, explaining the reason for its existence. Was I crying for Chapman? Mary

Williams? The sleep-room patients? Maitland? Was I crying because I had lost Jane, or was I crying because, somewhere along the line, I had lost myself? I wiped the tear off my face and studied the tip of my finger. Moisture on skin. I had no sense of ownership. I had shed a tear, but it seemed to belong to a stranger.

In due course, I walked back to the car. I looked at the hospital for the last time, knowing that I would never return. Clouds glided past the sun, dappling the front elevation with patches of light and shadow. It was then that I noticed the figure, framed by one of the upper windows. A small figure, no bigger than a child, looking out across the heath, in my direction. The light changed and a moment later, she was gone.

That night, I dreamt of the lighthouse: an oil-black sea, a starless sky, and a yellow beam sweeping across the sluggish waves. As usual, each revolution of the lamp was accompanied by a sound that evoked heavy industry. The roar of a furnace, the scrape of metal against metal. But then the scene began to fade, until all that remained was the sweeping beam, which shrank and became a blinking light embedded in a grey metal box. At the same time, the mechanical sound softened and became an electronic pulse, repeating on a single pitch. *Beep. Beep. Beep.*

I was lying in a bed, and when I rolled my head on the pillow to look in the opposite direction I discovered that there were other beds, close to mine, and beyond them a desk, behind which a nurse was sitting. All of the other patients were asleep. The nearest was Celia Jones. My mouth was dry and I felt very hot. Curiously, even though I was dreaming, I seemed to lose consciousness, and only woke again when someone rocked my body. I opened my eyes and saw Maitland and Jane gazing down at me. Although I recognized Jane, she looked very different. Her hair was much longer and parted in the middle. She was wearing a short orange jacket, a frilly blouse and a necklace which seemed to be made from wooden beads. Maitland also looked different. His complexion was tanned and he had grown a peculiar, drooping moustache.

Jane pressed her palms together beneath her chin, as if in prayer, and I noticed that she was wearing a wedding ring. I could smell her perfume. It was Chanel No 5.

'James,' said Maitland. 'Wake up. Wake up. Your wife is here to see you.' But I could not respond. My tongue was stuck to the roof of my mouth.

'What happened to his hand?' Jane asked.

'An accident, I'm afraid,' Maitland replied. 'One of the

trainee nurses was careless and he slipped over. The cut was quite deep. I'll get one of the nightingales to change the dressing this afternoon.'

Their eyes met. Maitland's brow creased and his expression communicated deep concern. But the longer they looked at each other the more I detected other registers of feeling. Tenderness, self-interest, guilt and desire.

'James?' said Jane, rocking me gently again. 'It's me.'

Maitland stepped to the end of the bed and examined a chart. 'I'm sorry. He's only just been medicated.'

'I should have let you know I was coming.' She bent her knees and lowered herself to my level. 'James? Can you hear me?' I wanted to reply, but my eyelids felt heavy and closed over my pupils.

'He'll be like this for some time.'

'I should have called,' Jane repeated.

'It's all right. I wanted to see you anyway.' There was a long pause. 'Have you decided?' Maitland's voice contained a suggestion of eagerness. Hope?

'You're right, of course,' Jane replied, obliquely.

Maitland made a noise, a sudden release of breath that I was sure – if only I could have seen his face – must be accompanied by a smile of satisfaction. 'It's for the best. You can't . . .' He hesitated, and Jane finished his sentence for him: 'Go on. Yes. I can see that now.'

'Shall we go to my office? There are some papers you should sign.' When Maitland spoke again, he sounded less confident. 'Although, you don't have to do the paper-work *right* now. If you want to spend some time with him, on your own I mean—'

'No,' Jane cut in. Then, more firmly: 'No. That won't be necessary. I have many faults, but hypocrisy isn't one of them.'

Maitland lowered his voice to a whisper. 'Jane. Not here.'

'I'm sorry,' she replied. 'It's just, sometimes . . .'

'You don't have to explain. Really. Come on. Let's go to my office.'

I could hear Jane's wooden beads rattling as she moved away. With considerable effort, I was able to raise my eyelids again. Jane was wearing trousers that were very wide at the bottom. Maitland's arm was extended, horizontally, behind her. It would have been an innocent gesture – and one much favoured by paternal physicians – had his fingers not made contact with her waist. Jane did not protest, and the last thing I saw was the nurse's private scowl of disapproval.

When I surfaced from the dream, it was as though I had been drowning. I awoke, gasping for air, and kicking wildly. It was some time before I calmed down.

I sat up in bed and lit a cigarette. Through the net curtains I could see the sulphurous luminescence of a street
light. I remembered Chapman's Chinese conundrum: 'A
man dreams that he is a butterfly, and in the dream he
has no knowledge of his life as a human being. When
he wakes up, he asks himself two questions: am I a
man, who has just dreamed that he was a butterfly?
Or am I really a butterfly, now dreaming that I am a
man?' I pinched myself. And then I pinched myself again.

Dr Hugh Maitland
Department of Psychological Medicine
St Thomas's Hospital
London SE1

12th December 1972

Dr Peter Bevington
Oak Lodge
Nr Biggleswade
Bedfordshire

Dear Peter,

You will forgive, I hope, some lapses of formality in
a communication that for all intents and purposes
must serve as a letter of referral. But it concerns an
individual with whom I have worked closely for two
years: my senior registrar, James Richardson. I believe
you met him on two occasions, once at the club, and
once again when you were visiting our department.

He was, I am sure you will recall, a serious minded
and able fellow. Unfortunately, he is now very ill.
I have always enjoyed close, almost familial
relationships with junior colleagues, and Richardson
is no exception: therefore, I find it incredibly hard to
write with detachment about an impressive young
man who until very recently had everything to live
for and now faces an uncertain and very questionable
future. Nevertheless, I will endeavour, as best I can,
to set out the salient facts.

Richardson comes from a medical family. His father
was the Superintendent of Wyldehope, an asylum on
the Suffolk coast. I don't believe it is there any more,
not even the building, as it was apparently destroyed
by fire. Richardson senior died when James was a boy,
and an uncle – the proprietor of a haulage business
in Lowestoft – was kind enough to provide the
widow and her son with an allowance. Richardson
distinguished himself at Cambridge, first as a Rugby
Blue, and then as an outstanding member of his
college chess team. He went on to conduct some very
interesting sleep research in Edinburgh, and just prior
to his appointment, here, at St Thomas's, he was at
St George's and the Royal Free.

About ten months ago, James started to experience episodes of agitated depression. These episodes became increasingly frequent and, over time, were complicated by attacks of morbid sexual jealousy (which is perhaps best understood, I believe, as an atypical instance of paranoia). Apart from being a little less talkative than usual, I can't say that I noticed anything amiss. He was rather good at concealing his agitation, and, as for his jealousy, there was no reason, one supposes, why this should have surfaced in the workplace. I only learned of his deteriorating health when his wife, Jane Richardson (a nurse at the Royal Free), wrote to me in confidence. She is a very conscientious type and was worried about the welfare of the patients in her husband's care. It must have been extremely difficult for her to compose such a letter – to go against the grain of spousal loyalty, especially for a woman – and I am much indebted to her. We arranged to meet the following week and she explained that Richardson's behaviour was becoming increasingly odd at home. He was restless, irritable, and prone to angry outbursts. He was interrogating her for hours (especially when she returned home late) and rummaging through her possessions. She even caught him inspecting her undergarments and the bed sheets for signs that might confirm her alleged infidelity. I felt sorry for her. She had obviously been coping with an extremely trying situation and had had little or no opportunity to unburden herself. I assured her that she had taken the correct course of action and immediately had a frank talk with Richardson. I insisted that he should take some time off work, which he accepted, rather reluctantly, and he voiced no objection when I said that I was willing to advise with respect to medication.

I put him on the usual phenothiazine derivatives, but he was troubled by a number of side effects: low blood pressure, blurred vision, constipation, and pyrexia – to name but a few (all the regimens are detailed in his records). The fact is, I had a great deal of trouble finding anything that he was able to tolerate, and in the end I had to resort to Reserpine (3 mg by mouth, 5 mg intramuscularly). Even then, he still complained of constant headaches and nasal congestion.

I continued to meet with Jane Richardson on a regular basis. Although the Reserpine had had a beneficial effect, the agitated depression and morbid sexual jealousy returned after only three weeks. Poor Mrs Richardson was, by this time, very distraught. Indeed, I began to have very grave concerns for her own mental health. They (that is, Jane and James) had only recently purchased a mansion house flat in Hampstead and the joint mortgage was substantial. Jane was having to work additional shifts to earn more money, but her extended periods of absence were, predictably, making Richardson even more suspicious.

Things came to a head in September. Richardson became fixed on the idea that he must make his wife pregnant in order to save their marriage. Needless to say, Mrs Richardson did not agree. She resisted her husband's advances but this only seemed to inflame his ardour, and on one occasion, when Jane returned in the early hours of the morning, he attempted to force himself upon her. It was all very unfortunate. I admitted Richardson onto Ward 5 at the Royal Waterloo Hospital a few days later. Narcosis was an attractive treatment option, because I was able to medicate him properly, irrespective of side-effects, and give him a course of 16 ECT. So far, I am sorry to report, there has been no change. His condition remains intractable. When awake, he sometimes refers to the child that he and his wife never had as if it were real.

Mrs Richardson and I have discussed the current situation at length, and she agrees with me that it would now be better for James if he were transferred to Oak Lodge. Your lovely gardens, with their views of the low rolling hills of Bedfordshire, are as good a place as any to convalesce. And if James does not recover, I can rest assured that you and your team of excellent nurses will look after him.

I am convinced that the removal of Richardson to Oak Lodge will also be good for Mrs Richardson. Her husband's presence, here, in London, is a constant reminder of what must have been a very traumatic period in her life. Moreover, a misplaced sense of duty obliges her to make frequent visits to Ward 5 – but these visits only make her upset. I do not think the marriage has any future and if James is taken to Oak Lodge I am sure that Mrs Richardson will be able to think more clearly about making a new start. What has happened to Richardson is bad enough. It would be unconscionable to allow his wife to suffer a similar fate. That really would be a tragedy.

I have taken the liberty of completing some preliminary paperwork that you will find enclosed. Please feel free to give me a call if you have any questions.

Yours Sincerely,

Hugh

Dr Hugh Maitland
M.A., M.B.(Cantab.), F.R.C.P, F.R.C.Psych.
Physician in Charge of the Department of Psychological Medicine and Lecturer in the Medical School, St Thomas's Hospital.

Sources and Acknowledgements

I would like to thank Wayne Brookes, Catherine Richards, Clare Alexander, Dr David Veale, Steve Matthews and Nicola Fox for their comments on the first and subsequent drafts of *The Sleep Room* and Lorraine Green for some impressive proofreading. I would also like to thank: Philip Loring (Science Museum) for answering many questions about electroconvulsive therapy, but particularly about the operation of the model R1135 ECT machine, which was used in a Suffolk asylum between 1945 and 1960; Francis Maunze (Royal College of Psychiatrists) and Professor Malcolm Lader, for answering questions about the qualifications required to practise psychiatry in the 1950s; the Royal College of GPs archivists (and an anonymous veteran GP) for answering questions on the composition and layout of referral letters in the 1950s; Dr Diana Dixon (Southwold Museum) for answering questions on the condition of the Southwold pier in 1955; Peter Homan (Royal Pharmaceutical Society) for providing information about Reserpine and its uses in the late 1960s and early 1970s; Wendy Fox for answering questions on the everyday use of the BNF and the British Pharmacopoeia in the 1950s and 1960s; and Dr Naomi Fersht for sending me an extremely useful academic paper on the characteristics of sleep in disorders of consciousness.

Concerning the plausibility of whether a consultant in psychiatry would take on his or her senior registrar as a patient – and whether or not this would be permitted – I've actually seen this happen. At the time, the propriety of such a peculiar arrangement was never questioned or debated.

The character of Hugh Maitland is based on the psychiatrist William Sargant (1907–1988). It was not my intention to introduce the real William Sargant into my story; however, Sargant provided me with a near perfect model for Maitland and I have made extensive use of Sargant's autobiography, *The Unquiet Mind*, and his book on brainwashing and indoctrination for the general reader, *Battle for the Mind*. The sleep-room procedures and drug regimens are authentic and taken from *An introduction to Physical Methods of Treatment in Psychiatry* (5th edition) by William Sargant and Eliot Slater.

Sargant was a major figure in British psychiatry, who promoted 'somatic' treatments for 'psychological' problems. These included chemical sedation and stimulation, excitatory abreaction, brain surgery, insulin shock, electroconvulsive therapy (ECT) and narcosis (deep-sleep therapy). Sargant's most controversial treatment project was undertaken in Ward 5 of the Royal Waterloo Hospital, otherwise known as 'the sleep room'. Remarkably, given the rise of the anti-psychiatry movement in the 1960s, it was still operating in the early 1970s.

Some sources suggest that Sargant's activities at the Royal Waterloo Hospital were connected with a larger programme of research into brainwashing ultimately sponsored by the CIA (see *Brainwash: The Secret History of Mind Control* by Dominic Streatfeild for an evaluation of the evidence). Although Sargant's links with the CIA are doubtful, he certainly worked for MI5. According to one intelligence historian, Sargant was MI5's 'in-house psychiatrist'. Interestingly, there are no records of the patients treated in Ward 5. Sargant removed and destroyed all the relevant files before his retirement.

Maitland's speech to James Richardson about physical illness, mental illness, and suicide is based on one of Lord Owen's recollections of Sargant. As Dr David Owen, Lord Owen worked with Sargant in the 1960s. The original quotation can be found in *Brainwash*.

Sargant was a larger-than-life character who we can easily demonize. Professor Malcolm Lader, a very distinguished and respectable member of the British medical establishment, is on record as having said, 'There was a whiff of sulphur about him.' Moreover, Sargant's book *Battle for the Mind* is alleged to be a firm favourite at Al Qaeda training camps. In actuality, Sargant was one of many psychiatrists who believed that mental illnesses have a biological basis and should be treated with interventions that affect the brain directly. Today, Sargant's methods appear crude and barbaric; however, psychiatry is a notoriously fickle discipline. Different approaches become fashionable and unfashionable in cycles. Recently, for example, persuasive arguments have been made for the more widespread use of ECT, which has hitherto been in decline for many decades (see *Shock Therapy: A History of Electroconvulsive Treatment in Mental Illness* by Edward Shorter and David Healy). It is quite possible that at some time in the future, Sargant's reputation as a 'brilliant' doctor and scientific visionary will be restored. At present, however, a positive revision of Sargant's contribution to medicine seems a distant prospect.

In the end, it was the 'couch merchants' (or at least those who inherited the psychoanalytic legacy of curing by talking) who won the clinical 'battle for the mind'. There are no longer any sleep rooms.

F. R. TALLIS
London, 2012

A conversation with F. R. Tallis

What inspired you to write *The Sleep Room*?

The point at which I realized narcosis had fictional possibilities was shortly after listening to a BBC Radio 4 documentary called 'Revealing the Mind Bender General', made by the reporter James Maw and originally broadcast in 2009. It was a fascinating programme about controversial psychiatrist Dr William Sargant (1907–1988) and his advocacy of deep sleep therapy. I found the image of a darkened room in which patients were kept asleep for extended periods of time (weeks, sometimes months) both powerful and haunting. Prior to listening to James Maw's programme, I had become interested in William Sargant after discovering a battered 1959 Pan paperback edition of his magnum opus *Battle for the Mind* in a second-hand book shop. My curiosity was aroused by the glowing reviews on the back cover supplied by luminaries such as Aldous Huxley and the philosopher Bertrand Russell. I was also intrigued by the enigmatic and sinister subtitle, '*A Physiology of Conversion and Brainwashing.*'

The Sleep Room **is set in a psychiatric hospital in the 1950s. How much research did you have to undertake as preparation for this novel?**

I am an avid student of the history of psychiatry, so I didn't have to do a great deal of general research; however, I was keen to get the specific details of deep sleep therapy correct. In order to achieve this I had to track down a copy of an old text book authored by William Sargant which contained detailed treatment instructions. I made such a close study of the relevant chapter that, if asked to, I could probably manage a sleep room. Another aspect of the novel that had to be carefully researched was the location of the hospital. When I write, a sense of place is very important to me. I drove around Suffolk looking for a precise position where sea, reed beds and heathland meet. Dunwich Heath was perfect. I am sure that at the back of my mind I was also trying to identify *The Sleep Room* with some august literary predecessors. The Suffolk coast is strongly associated with the classic ghost stories of M. R. James and the name Dunwich comes with its own pleasing Lovecraftian resonances.

Before writing fiction you were a clinical psychologist. How has your work as a psychologist influenced your writing?

Virtually every aspect of my writing has been influenced by psychology. Firstly, I tend to favour clinical settings. For example, I have written a six-volume series of psycho-analytic detective thrillers set in Freud's Vienna. Without an appreciation of Freudian theory and my experience as a practitioner I could never have written them. Secondly, a lot of my work blurs the boundary between imagination and reality. Sometimes I make it clear to the reader what is happening, but not always. For example, my novel *The Forbidden* can be read as a supernatural adventure, or the fantastic imaginings of a nineteenth-century French neurologist. This second reading removes the novel from the horror genre and makes it, instead, a kind of literary case study. There are no obvious clues in the text with respect to the second interpretation. Stanley Kubrick (my favourite director) did much the same in his film *Eyes Wide Shut*. It is an exploration of a marriage in crisis observed through the murky medium of the unconscious; however, Kubrick doesn't employ a single cinematic device to signal departures from reality. In many respects, I don't see myself as a former clinical psychologist but, rather, as a clinical psychologist now working in a different context.

In a previous life you wrote crime fiction under the name Frank Tallis. What made you decide to turn to horror?

I thoroughly enjoyed writing crime novels, but deep down, I've always wanted to write supernatural fiction and horror.

Indeed, I think this desire was so strong, characters and themes associated with supernatural fiction kept on surfacing in my crime writing. For example, my psychoanalytic detective series features séances, occult societies, the golem legend, a secret alchemist's laboratory, and visitations by the angel of death, none of which are staples for most traditional crime novelists. It was more or less inevitable that my fascination with the supernatural would eventually necessitate a genre change.

What normally comes to you first: an idea for the plot or the character(s)?

Neither. What usually comes first is an idea, a theme, or a single image. So, the starting point of *The Sleep Room* was an image of a darkened room full of sleeping patients. I then learned more about deep sleep therapy and thought a great deal about where the action of the novel might take place. It was only at a relatively late stage that I started to construct a plot. Of course, I knew that I wanted to write a 'ghost' story, but I wasn't at all sure how the supernatural element would manifest itself. As for characters, I like my characters to develop as the novel progresses. I like them to surprise me occasionally. This isn't possible if their behaviour is limited by too many preconceptions.

A conversation with F. R. Tallis

What do you feel is the hardest part of writing a convincing horror story?

The hardest thing to achieve when writing horror novels is suspension of disbelief. Fiction is most compelling when the reader is completely immersed in a story. If something seems absurd, or ridiculous, then the reader is quickly delivered back to reality. He or she will become self-conscious and disengage from the book. The problem with supernatural fiction is that its *dramatis personae* (ghosts, vampires, monsters) are – by their very nature – incredible. Therefore, the horror writer is presented with a unique and substantive challenge: to sustain suspension of disbelief while working with 'materials' that test credulity to its absolute limit. Essentially, one must make the unbelievable believable.

Your last book, *The Forbidden*, was set in nineteenth-century Paris. Was it difficult to make the transition from nineteenth-century Paris to England in the 1950s?

I didn't find the transition difficult at all. Indeed, it was very easy, because *The Sleep Room* was less problematic with respect to the choices I had to make about language. I simply wrote it in the 1950s English I am familiar with from watching post-war British films. *The Forbidden*, however, was technically more demanding. I wanted to create an impression of it being written in the style of a nineteenth-century French novel, but without compromising accessibility. In other words, I had to create a literary illusion.

Which authors have had the biggest impact on your writing?

For the purposes of this interview I will consider only those authors who have had an impact on my supernatural fiction. Needless to say, I am indebted to all the genre colossi of the nineteenth and twentieth centuries: Edgar Alan Poe, Charles Dickens, Henry James, Charlotte Perkins Gilman, Bram Stoker, M. R. James, William Hope Hodgson, H. P. Lovecraft and Shirley Jackson. In addition, there are two other writers with whom I feel a more personal connection: Dennis Wheatley and J. Meade Falkner. I discovered the black magic novels of Dennis Wheatley when I was a schoolboy and found them deliriously enjoyable. Although Wheatley is no longer fashionable (he is a complete stranger to political correctness) and his writing style leaves much to be desired, he remains a profound formative influence. *The Devil Rides Out* is a stupendous supernatural adventure. I was still an adolescent when I read *The Lost Stradivarius* by J. Meade Falkner and I was immediately captivated by this strange tale of an English aristocrat who obsessively pursues a vision of absolute evil. It is sometimes described as the novel that M. R. James never wrote. It remains, to this day, my favourite full-length ghost story. Indeed, I am prepared to commit heresy and suggest that it is not merely comparable to the best work of M. R. James but superior.

Do you have any advice for an aspiring horror author?

I was recently asked to contribute a writing tip to a book of writing tips for aspirant authors. My tip was: beware of tips. It was considered such an unorthodox tip that it was given its own special place at the back of the book. Perhaps I should elaborate. I once overheard two writers discussing the role of research. 'The important thing is the story,' said one. 'I always make sure I have a good story first and then I do my research after. Otherwise I end up doing too much research, most of which I never use.' The other writer responded, 'That's a really good tip: so very professional!' And he was right. It is a good tip, except *I don't work like that at all*. In fact, I do the exact opposite. I get an idea, go off and read a large number of books on related topics, and gradually a story emerges. I am not against giving tips and advice; however, I think there is always a danger of implicitly suggesting that some working practices are inherently superior to others and will get better results (and this is clearly not the case). Different writers benefit from different methods.

What scares you?

I have had only one supernatural experience in my life. It was while on holiday in an old French farmhouse in the Loire. I know a lot about the circumstances in which people see ghosts. I also know a lot about psychological and scientific explanations of supernatural occurrences. Yet I am unable to provide a plausible alternative hypothesis to explain what I experienced that night. I wasn't alone. My wife (a barrister with a scientific background) was also present. She still refuses to accept that what occurred was supernatural (although I suspect more as a matter of principle). I, on the other hand, have my doubts. An invisible presence making noises in the bedroom in the early hours of the morning and then running up and down the hallway is not, to my mind, easily explained. Nor are lights having no obvious source. The only alternative hypothesis that has any credibility, as far as I'm concerned, would be some sort of shared hallucination. But that is almost (although not quite) as implausible as a supernatural visitation. Spontaneous, complex, shared hallucinations are extremely rare, particularly among individuals with no prior history of hallucination, psychiatric illness or drug abuse. Besides (for what it's worth) I felt perfectly normal at the time. Was I scared? Yes. As well as bemused, confused, and outraged by the impossible!